*Iona McGregor* was born 'in the year of the first UK General Election when women had exactly the same voting rights as men'. A teacher for most of her working life, she is now a full-time writer. She has written five historical novels for young adults, and a number of educational books. An active campaigner within the Scottish gay liberation movement since the early 1970s, she lives in Edinburgh.

Iona McGregor

# Death Wore a Diadem

 The Women's Press

First published by The Women's Press Limited 1989
A member of the Namara Group
34, Great Sutton Street, London EC1V 0DX

British Library Cataloguing in Publication Data
available

Typeset by Input Typesetting Ltd, London
Printed and bound in Great Britain by Cox & Wyman,
Reading, Berks

# Saturday

The affair of the false Grecian diadem, which occurred during the Empress Eugénie's visit to Edinburgh, is one of the most carefully suppressed scandals of that discreet and respectable city. Those most directly affected were Christabel, her lover, two teachers at the Scottish Institute for the Education of the Daughters of Gentlefolk, and one dead servant maid.

Events began when the York express steamed in at eight o'clock on the evening of Saturday, 17 November 1860. For several hours the platform below Waverley Bridge had been seething with a crowd that stamped frozen feet, pulled out silver flasks from muffs or frock-coat pockets, and surged forward whenever a train pulled in.

Eugénie's flight from Paris had baffled the public journals. She was travelling *incognita*. In London, the manager of Claridge's had panicked when he realised that the Comtesse de Pierrefonds — one of five French aristocrats who had booked into his hotel — was in fact the Empress of France. Eugénie had a special affection for this title: it was at her château of Pierrefonds, during a picnic excursion, that one of the Emperor's mistresses had dislocated her wrist.

The *Scotsman* proudly reminded its readers:

*Since hapless Mary Queen of Scots landed at Leith three hundred years ago, no Royal Lady of France, has, we believe, visited the Scottish capital. The Empress Eugénie seeks the enjoyment of strictest privacy as aiding attainment of the main object of her visit – the renewal of her impaired health. The visit recalls ancient days of firm alliance between France and Scotland; and between the two peoples a hereditary liking yet continues, which might well, were occasion suitable, find especially frank and warm expression towards the Empress Eugénie, seeing that she herself is of Scotch descent, and so adds to those of royalty the yet more potent and kindlier claims of kindred.*

South of the Tweed the world was unimpressed by the Empress's Caledonian ancestry. It marvelled that someone prostrated by the death of a beloved sister should seek recovery at the wintry knuckle-end of Europe, instead of joining other invalids in fashionable Nice.

At seven o'clock on Saturday night, James McLevy, ex-detective officer, leaned forward to give his fire a poke. No more night duty; no more waiting in closes for a door to open; no more hardening himself against the grey, bruised faces of children spawned in the slums of the Royal Mile. He'd asked for retirement in May. Officially, he was still on half-call; but they didn't need him. These days he went to Head Office only on Wednesdays, to collect his pension.

As McLevy rose for his pipe the black-and-tan bitch lying on the hearth lifted her head eagerly.

'Not tonight, lass.' After thirty years in Scotland his Irish vowels were still strong. Groping in his tobacco pouch, he found only a few shreds. 'You're in luck after all.' He put on his boots, his coat, and his topper, and tied a length of washing line to the dog's collar.

'Easy now,' he warned as he let her go. She rushed downstairs to the cobbled alley and waited for him, wagging her tail.

McLevy plodded up the narrow, angled passage of Old Fishmarket Close to the High Street. In the old days it had been handy to be so near Head Office. Now the steep rise was hard on his lungs. He'd once thought of returning to Armagh when he retired; but his people there were all strangers. Home was here, among his old colleagues and the villains he'd called his bairns.

He walked to his usual tobacco-shop and stood in the doorway to fill and light his pipe. Above the gas-light the gaunt tenements lost themselves in blankness. Seven or eight storeys above, the chimney-pots breathed out showers of sparks through the mist.

The Royal Mile – a gey queer name! Between castle and palace the whole street had been crumbling in on itself for a hundred years. Everyone who could afford it had moved out to the New Town or the expanding suburbs.

McLevy decided to walk down to the railway station. The dog needed a walk, and maybe he'd be in time for the Empress's arrival. He gave the washing line a shake.

'On your road, Jeanie.' He'd named her after Jeanie Brash, his most audacious thief.

The mongrel collie trotted on joyfully, sniffing at the appetising muck in the gutter. Her master kept an even pace behind her, but one step aside. He still walked on the outside of the pavement, as police regulations demanded.

As McLevy reached the station, the crags of Arthur's Seat echoed back the shriek of the York express. McLevy picked up his dog to go down the passenger steps. Lieutenant McLellan was standing on the platform with a knot of station officials. He looked anxious: probably thinking about that bomb attack on Louis Napoleon and Eugénie in Paris last April. Yet it was unlikely the Empress would encounter any trouble in Edinburgh.

The train steamed into the platform and clanked to a halt, hissing gently. Passengers emerged, fussing over children and luggage and pet animals. Several horse-drawn cabs and carriages edged along the platform towards the first class saloon cars. The crowd moved forward. Attention centred on the one car that remained closed.

At last its doors swung open. Two men in plain frock coats stepped out. They handed down three women deeply veiled in black. A dozen servants came out of the other compartments and handed out luggage to the porters.

There was a murmur of disappointment. It was not even clear which of the three women was the Empress. Then someone let off a cheer; the sound spread erratically and men's hats came off.

The visitors stepped up into the waiting carriages. One of the women lifted her veil, leaned out, and bowed to the crowd. There were ecstatic sighs as Eugénie's famous beauty was revealed. Those at the back had to be satisfied with counting the carpet bags, bandboxes and trunks that were being piled into the other carriages. The Empress was staying overnight in Edinburgh. Those disappointed today might catch a glimpse of her tomorrow.

McLevy walked over to the lieutenant.

'That went off pretty quietly, sir. Just a few pocket-books gone missing, I suppose.' McLellan nodded.

As the Empress's carriage pulled away two figures rushed out of the crowd. A bearded man in spectacles waving a thick black book shouted, 'No Popery! No Bishop of Rome! Here is God's true word!'

He raised an arm to hurl his bible through the carriage window; and the second figure untwisted a banner striped in green, white and red – the colours chosen for the future Kingdom of Italy. He ran towards the carriage crying, 'Viva l'Italia, viva Garibaldi!'

The two demonstrators collided and fell flat on their faces. There was a derisive hoot from some sections of the crowd, overtaken by cheering as the carriage drove off. The Empress withdrew her head, still smiling.

The man who had shouted the second slogan rolled over, sprang to his feet, and disappeared into the crowd. The last carriage drove over his banner. The spectacled man, not so agile, was hustled into a corner by two constables. McLellan went over to question the demonstrator. He was recognised as the Reverend J. Begbie, a fierce anti-Papist.

McLevy chuckled as the embarrassed officers moved away with their catch. He took a zig-zag route through the dispersing crowd, and under a gas-lamp caught up with the second man, a slim, bareheaded figure in a dark blue cape.

'That's a dangerous toy you have in your pocket, sir.'

The figure turned round more in surprise than alarm.

'That's none of your business, is it?'

He was a youth of about fifteen, with an oval, sensitive face, and dark curls far too tight to be natural. Very tall for his age. McLevy wondered if he'd made a mistake.

The young man looked down at the dog. 'Are you a police officer?' McLevy was reassured by his unceraiun tone.

'Still on half-call, laddie. Show me what you pointed at the carriage when you fell down.'

The youth put his hand into a pocket and handed over a pistol. 'A Smith and Wesson Number One. Takes rimfire cartridges. It isn't loaded.'

McLevy grunted to hide his ignorance. The cold was jarring his bones, and his little collie was shivering beside him. He'd send the laddie away with a warning. 'You could be taken up for waving this about! Put it away!'

'I aimed with perfect accuracy,' came the hot reply. 'The assassination was only theoretical, of course.'

'Who are you?' asked McLevy severely.

'From the Military.' The young man flapped his cape open to show a blue jacket and white duck trousers. He put on a glengarry cap with a bronze crest. The uniform of the Royal Scottish Military Academy at the north end of Lothian Road. McLevy decided he must have a word with Captain Orr. Tell him one of his cadets was being a bit too enthusiastic about his small arms training.

'Loaded or not, don't carry that pop of yours in the street again, Mr – what's your name, anyway?'

The boy fidgeted. 'Same as the chap who threw the bomb. Orsini. There's no connection, honestly.'

'Right, you cut along home, Mr Orsini.'

'It isn't *mister*, constable. It's *Count* Orsini.'

McLevy's brogue thickened. 'And it isn't *constable, signor* your excellency! It's ex-Detective Officer and Principal Criminal Officer James McLevy of the Edinburgh Police Establishment.' He strode off, pulling Jeanie behind him.

In St Andrew Square the Empress and her suite were having dinner. Upstairs the twelve servants were unpacking. Douglas's Hotel was one of the best in the city. But a hotel is a hotel: it is not the Tuileries.

Madame Pepa Pollet, the Empress's head maid, was taking it out on her two underlings as they laid out the dress boxes in the extra bedroom that was to hold the Empress's clothes.

'Only three wardrobes and two chests of drawers!' she lamented. In the palace a whole room was set aside merely to hang Eugénie's gowns. The *ensembles* for each day were made up on dressmakers' models and sent up by private lift to the Empress's apartments. Not for nothing was Pepa a general's daughter.

'What a tragedy!' cried the younger maid, as Pepa shook out the crinolines of sober lilac, grey, black, and dark blue. 'If only *Sa Majesté* were not in mourning!'

Sadly the two under maids spread out the hinged steel hoops that would support these dull-toned creations.

Out of the last trunk Pepa lifted an embossed pasteboard box. Her eyes glittered as she untied the silk cords. She lifted out a shimmer of sky-blue gauze beaded with pearls. The maids cried out in astonishment.

'*Sa Majesté* does not know I have packed it. Monsieur Worth created it while she was in Algiers. It is for the ball at Hamilton Palace.'

The older maid sniffed. '*Sa Majesté* will not attend.'

'Fools, how should you know what the Empress will do?' said Pepa scornfully. Much as she grieved for Eugénie in her loss, she thought it most inconsiderate of the Duchess of Alba to have died in the prime of life, and thus strip Pepa of her rôle in making Eugénie the most fashionably dressed woman in Europe.

She unlocked a tooled leather casket stamped with Eugénie's monogram. 'I have brought this to wear with the gown. See!' Inside lay the crown jewel known as the Grecian diadem. The maids gasped with horror.

'Oh, madame, how did you persuade Monsieur Thélin to let you bring it?'

'Monsieur Thélin my backside,' retorted Pepa. It was a standing grievance that the Keeper of the Privy Purse, and not herself, was in charge of the state jewels. She held the diadem up to one of the gas chandeliers; there its six hundred brilliants flashed and coruscated liquidly.

Pepa glowered; in her heart she knew that the Empress would never go to the ball. And now she would have to admit the truth, in case one of those stupid little Frenchwomen betrayed her.

'It is paste. I use it when we prepare for state occasions. No one would know the difference. Even the weight is correct. And if *Sa Majesté* would wear it in the carriage, as she drives to the ball . . .'

She let the two maids handle the diadem. One of them tried to put it on.

'That is enough,' said Pepa sternly, snatching back the jewel. 'We must finish here before the Empress retires.'

Moray Place lay on the western side of Edinburgh's New Town. Its circular façade was massively porticoed and pillared, and four short streets broke the circumference, like the icing on a hot-cross bun.

It was mainly occupied by judges, university professors and fashionable physicians. There was also an Episcopalian sisterhood whose doleful chanting was much disliked by the other residents. For the past twenty-five years Numbers Nine and Ten had been taken up by the Scottish Institute for the Education of the Daughters of Gentlefolk (shortened by its pupils to SINDOG).

Six hours before Eugénie's arrival in Edinburgh, the front door of the Institute opened and let out one of the senior pupils Christabel MacKenzie, and the under housemaid, Peggy. From the upper windows they were watched with envy by other pupils who were sucking lumps of toffee bought in Leith Walk that morning, on the only permitted outing of the day.

Christabel and Peggy took the exit road that led into Church Lane. This was a narrow mews street running

7

between coach-houses down towards Stockbridge, an area on the fringe of the New Town. Once out of sight of the Institute they stopped, and Christabel flipped up her petticoats to extract three letters which she handed over to Peggy.

'I'll see you at four o'clock.'

Peggy darted off to deliver the letters and enjoy two hours of illicit freedom. She was supposed to stay with Christabel all afternoon, but they had come to an arrangement.

Christabel strode down the lane with a release of stifled energy. Under a carelessly perched hat her dark red hair swung to and fro across her back. Today was her seventeenth birthday, and she was going to meet her beloved. But her face was sullen with discontent.

That morning she had received a letter from her aunt telling her that her extra botany lessons were to cease at the end of term. This afternoon's would be one of the last.

Mrs Napier, the Lady Superintendent of the Institute, had been obliged to complain to Christabel's aunt shortly after the new pupil had entered her school in the autumn of 1859. Lady Elizabeth was Christabel's guardian. Mrs Napier acknowledged that Christabel could read and translate French with ease, but her accent was atrocious. She had only a smattering of German, and her Mathematics and Botany would have disgraced a child of three. Her knowledge of Natural Science appeared to pre-date Galileo. In History and English she had a disagreeable tendency to demonstrate that she knew more than her instructors.

Moreover, [wrote Mrs Napier] between Miss MacKenzie's leaving of India and your ladyship's assumption of responsibility for her, she appears to have been allowed reading of a most unsuitable nature . . .

May I venture to hope that you will allow your niece to be instructed in the pianoforte by our renowned Logier method? I must respectfully remind your ladyship that it is time she became accustomed to the wearing of stays under her gown. I shall arrange that Miss MacKenzie be given extra tuition where it seems needed.

But Christabel was tone deaf, and her widowed aunt lived in Paris, and was in a weak position to rule her strong-willed charge. Sixteen years previously Elizabeth had eloped from the Institute with her Italian tutor.

This was Christabel's second year at the school. By now she had been more or less accepted by her fellow-pupils. She was helpful if one got stuck on one's English theme, and co-operative in smuggling out the letters which were exchanged with young gentlemen behind Mrs Napier's back.

That morning Elaine Dewar and Jane Rintoul had given Christabel six lace-edged handkerchiefs from Kennington and Jenner for her birthday, and there was to be a pineapple pudding at the boarders' supper. Nevertheless, Christabel now walked down Church Lane in a gloomy mood. The day had been completely ruined by Aunt Elizabeth's decree that she was to give up her Saturday afternoon lessons.

The improvement of Christabel had been handed over to the student governesses who were training at the Institute. The six male Directors and the full-time governesses who taught the younger classes were all much too busy to coach one pupil on her own.

By the end of summer 1860 Christabel had overcome her deficiencies in other subjects; but in botany she remained stupidly muddled as to details of leaf, flower and seed-case. So, for the fourth term running, Christabel still walked down to Claremont Street every Saturday afternoon for a two-hour lesson with Eleanor Stewart, a student governess who lived with her aunt and uncle in Stockbridge. By 17 November 1860 these lessons had been going on for more than a year.

Much earlier than this – by January, in fact – Christabel had made considerable progress. On one occasion she managed to get through the questions without a single mistake. The lesson was over in half an hour.

'You might as well go back to the Institute, Chrissie,' said Eleanor, beginning to clear the books and pressed flowers off the dining-room table. She was anxious to get on with her own studies.

9

'What if I don't choose to go? Peggy isn't calling for me until four o'clock.'

Eleanor smiled. 'Then I'll have to chase you out like a thrawn sheep that won't go through the dyke.'

'Ha! All five-foot-three of you! Have you ever seen a sheep being handled, Miss Stewart?'

This was insolencce, even to a youthful student governess.

Eleanor retorted, 'I've sheared a whole penful when my father was short-handed. *And* I've been out on the hill lambing. So don't you talk to me about sheep, Chrissie MacKenzie!'

Christabel leaned towards her. 'Have you honestly?'

'Yes – honestly.' With some awkwardness Eleanor mimicked the English slang.

'I'm sorry, Miss Stewart. I didn't mean to be rude. I thought you were like the rest of them.'

After that, Christabel's written work continued to be faultless. But she had a mysterious relapse over the standard oral questions.

At first Eleanor blamed herself. She was only sixteen months older than Christabel, and a great deal of their time had begun to be taken up by their curiosity about each other. She tried harder to keep them firmly attending to botanical matters. However, towards the end of the spring term of 1860, the Director in charge of scientific studies asked her to give outdoor instruction in the Botanic Garden. This was agreeable to both of them; but the informality of walking round the gardens made their lessons even laxer.

Christabel's memory still let her down. Eleanor asked one of the full-time governesses, Miss Merchant, whether she found Miss MacKenzie unable to remember such significant dates as 1066 and 1603. Miss Merchant said she was greatly surprised that Miss MacKenzie's recollection appeared to be at fault.

When Eleanor heard, for the fourth time, that Christabel had a remarkable ability to memorise facts, figures and long passages of verse by Mr Tennyson, she became suspicious.

Their next lesson was almost the last of the spring term.

(Mrs Napier had imposed her own ideas on a school year originally devised by Presbyterians. There were lengthy vacations centred round the festivals of Christmas and Easter.) Eleanor took her pupil into the museum room of the Botanic Garden. She had decided to set a small trap over the cone collection.

'*Araucaria, pinus, cedrus, larix* . . . Translate, please.'

'I am afraid I can't,' said Christabel. Eleanor was annoyed. Christabel was taking up her limited free time.

'You are a sham and a humbug. You know more Latin than I do. Surely you don't want these lessons to be prolonged into the summer?'

'Yes, I do. What beautiful brown eyes you have, Eleanor. Eleanor is too long. I'm going to call you *Lena*. I love you, Lena.'

Eleanor did indeed have beautiful eyes. Their lively, confident expression was rather at odds with her quiet personality. At a first glance she seemed on the plump side; this was the result of her sturdy build. It was also contradictory that she should give the impression of being shorter than she actually was; but there were many aspects of Eleanor that were misleading to a superficial glance.

She was non-plussed at Christabel's remark, although she was used to being pursued by homesick little girls. When they brought her flowers and sweets she gave them a motherly pat on the head (she could not bring herself to take up the English habit of kissing) and distributed the offerings amongst their friends.

But this was very different. It is hard to feel motherly towards a self-possessed young woman taller than yourself who leans across a glass case and smiles at you boldly.

Eleanor said, 'I think we should go outside to look at some trees.'

She kept them walking round the southern collection of conifers, in a state of exhilarated panic. The blood was leaping and falling in her cheeks; she could not look at Christabel, but she knew that Christabel was looking at her.

A burst of rain drove them indoors to the newly completed

11

section of the palm house. They were alone except for a gardener who was doing something around the roots of *Arenga Saccharifera*. He had his back to them. Christabel pulled Eleanor towards her and kissed her passionately on the lips.

Later, Eleanor decided that it was the drugging warmth of the atmosphere which had paralysed her. She found that her arms were round Christabel's waist and their mouths seemed to be fused together.

Pushing Christabel away, she said, 'We ought to go home now.'

When they reached Claremont Street she did not give Christabel the usual invitation to come in for tea and hot buttered scones while waiting for Peggy. Eleanor was very annoyed with herself. She had managed neither to ignore Christabel's silliness, nor crush it.

Next Saturday – the last before the school dispersed for Easter – brought raging gusts of sleet. Eleanor looked out of the dining-room window at the tormented daffodils cowering in the garden of a little villa across the street. Christabel was late.

Perhaps she had decided to stay indoors in such violent weather. Eleanor felt relief. The six months which by now she had spent on Christabel had held back her own studies.

She returned to the set of anatomical plates which she had been working with all morning. They had been borrowed from a medical student she had met at one of the city dispensaries. On Monday and Wednesday mornings Eleanor worked as an unpaid nurse.

When the bell rang Eleanor put on a smile and went to the landing to pull the heavy brass lever connecting with a chain which opened the front door of the building. Christabel mounted the stairs rather more slowly than usual. The slanting light from the cupola made her expression ambiguous.

Eleanor said graciously, 'You poor child. You must be frozen. Come in and let me help you off with your mantle.'

Christabel bounded up the last few steps and held her cheek against Eleanor's. 'Can you feel how frozen?'

12

Eleanor recoiled as a galvanic shock went through her.

'My goodness, yes, you are cold,' she said, convincing herself. They went across the hall into the dining room and sat down opposite each other. Christabel's eyes were shining.

'Shall we begin our lesson?' said Eleanor, forcing herself to look steadily at her pupil. She would have preferred it if Christabel's eyes had not continued to shine so brightly, nor her glance been so intimate.

As she concluded the lesson, Eleanor said, 'You are so much nicer when you are being sensible.'

'Your approval is all I need, Lena,' replied Christabel flirtatiously.

'I shall not be thrown off my pin by mockery, Miss Mac-Kenzie.' Eleanor was horrified to hear the same note in her own voice. 'It's not kind of you to spoil our friendship with nonsense,' she appealed.

Christabel's forefinger bored into the green baize tablecloth. 'I wanted an excuse to go on seeing you.'

'Hmph! To jink out of the Institute on Saturday afternoons, more likely.' They both laughed, but Eleanor's laugh turned into a yawn she could not control.

'Aren't you pleased to see me?' Christabel asked gloomily.

'Of course I am, but I rose very early to make some notes for my own studies.' Eleanor's eyes went to the anatomical plates.

Christabel walked round to look at the plates; her arm slid round Eleanor's shoulders, and as she stooped her hair fell over Eleanor's cheek. She brushed it back unselfconsciously, and once again Eleanor felt that startling pang go through her. She edged away on her seat, realising with dismay that this embarrassment arose from some confusion in her own feelings. She turned over the plates, trying to obliterate the questions that one half of her mind was asking the other half.

Christabel pulled a face. 'Ugh! They're horrid. Like skinned rabbits. I suppose they're for your work at the dispensary. I wish I could go there with you.'

13

'Oh, it's quite dull most of the time. I roll bandages and pour out spoonfuls of Gregory's Mixture.'

'You said you sometimes went with the students to houses in the Royal Mile. Isn't that exciting?'

'It is *distressing*, but it is part of the work.'

Christabel made the same assumption as the medical students whom Eleanor worked with. 'Surely nursing the sick is much harder than teaching little girls. Why do you want to do it?'

Eleanor hesitated, before saying, 'You must promise not to laugh at me. I want to be a doctor, not a nurse. I hope to pass a degree in medicine.'

'Women aren't allowed to join medical classes!'

'Not in this country. It has been done in America.'

'And Paris?'

'Yes, there too, I believe.'

'So you could study in Paris?'

Eleanor said, 'I do not know where it will be. Or even if it *will* be. There are so many obstacles.'

Christabel seized Eleanor's hands. 'Say it will be Paris, Lena! When I leave the Institute at the end of next session. My aunt has an enormous apartment. You could live with us in Paris.'

Eleanor laughed. 'Do not be so absurd!'

'Why is it absurd? Don't you like my company?'

'I dare say I could tolerate it for a year or two longer.' At Christabel's look, she went on quickly, 'Dear Chrissie, of course I should like to live with you and your aunt. I am very fond of you. But I am sure that Lady Elizabeth would prefer someone like Miss Rintoul or Miss Dewar as your companion.'

'That's all they would be, companions. Please say you will come to Paris with me!'

Eleanor shook her head in mock despair. She was glad to hear Mrs Stewart's tap at the door as the clock struck a quarter to four. She took the tea tray, and managed to avoid any more talk of Paris before Peggy arrived to escort Christabel back to the Institute.

14

During the Easter holiday, a letter from France was delivered to her twice a week; and Eleanor did reply once.

Eleanor avoided contact with Christabel up at the Institute unless they met accidentally. One day in June 1860, Christabel entered Eleanor's classroom when she had dismissed one group of pupils and was waiting for the next. Christabel handed her a thin parcel.

'I bought this magazine on my way over from Paris. But I shall hate you if you do go to America!'

She rushed out before Eleanor could reply.

Unwrapping the packet at home that evening, Eleanor found a copy of *The English Woman's Journal*, a publication much concerned with 'the woman question'. Inside it was an article written by Dr Elizabeth Blackwell of the New York Infirmary for Indigent Women and Children, entitled 'Medicine as a Profession for Women'.

When Eleanor thanked her the following Saturday, Christabel said, 'I shouldn't like you to think that my love is entirely selfish. Have you written to Dr Blackwell?'

'I shall wait until the summer holiday. Unfortunately there is no haste. It would take me a long time to put by the steamer fare, even if she were willing to find me a place in a medical school.'

Christabel flushed. 'I could help you with that, and the course fees as well.'

'That is kind, my dear, but I would never allow you.'

'Your pride is so stupid! I *love* you.'

'I love you too, Chrissie, and I hope we remain dear friends after you leave Edinburgh. But I could not put such a burden on anyone. If ever I'm admitted into medical classes, I shall have to attend for a great many years. By that time you might have someone else's wishes to consult.'

Christabel looked outraged. 'I shan't be married, if that's what you mean.'

'Not by then, perhaps, but eventually.'

'I've told you before, I shall not marry. I've known that

15

since I was seven years old. I hate it when you are so missish, Lena! Why do you never take me seriously?'

Eleanor protested, 'I'm merely pointing out that you do not know your own future. Of course I take you seriously! I'm *glad* you don't fill your mind with romantic nonsense.'

'That is not what I meant. Perhaps *you* are not serious? Perhaps *you* will give up your ambitions and marry?'

Eleanor said curtly, 'Unlike you, Chrissie, I have to earn my living, so I cannot afford to give them up.' She tried to restore good humour with a joke. 'As for marrying, I am one of the six hundred thousand surplus women.'

Christabel's reply was sarcastic. 'My commiserations!'

'Your offer is well meant, but you are unlikely to be your own mistress for as long as I shall require to study. Is that blunt enough?'

'Why are you going back to that? We were talking about something entirely different.'

Eleanor pressed on, aware that in trying to win this argument she was hiding from some other issue.

'You are well-looking, you are rich, and once you leave the Institute you will meet a dozen eligible young men. Your aunt will see to that.'

Christabel snapped, 'I shan't want to marry any of them.'

'Now you are being too general. One day you will be struck to the heart by a pair of fine eyes, and you will—'

Eleanor remembered and broke off, appalled at her blunder. She could feel her heart thudding, but it seemed to have displaced itself to somewhere in her throat.

Christabel stood up and uttered a word which Eleanor had heard only once, on a stair in the Canongate.

'Why do you go on treating me like a child? There are things I know which *you* don't understand. When I'm walking here to see you I am so happy I could run over the roof tops. When one Saturday is over I wait for the next. If a dog attacked you in the street, I would *kill* it, and I am very fond of dogs. I shall not marry because I love you and want us to be together. For always. I would not marry even if I didn't love you. But I do.'

16

Eleanor was filled with panic at her own urge to pull Christabel towards her.

'You are talking like a young man, Chrissie, which you are not. This is nonsense. Let us go on with our lesson.'

Christabel sat down beside her. 'Yes, if you will say you do not feel the same as I do. Then I'll promise never to speak nonsense again.'

'That is unfair.'

Christabel took Eleanor's hands. 'There!' she exclaimed triumphantly.

After a few moments' silence, during which they had somehow become entangled, Eleanor said, 'Chrissie, I do feel the same about you. Only I don't understand. How can it happen? But please don't call me *Lena*. It sounds so daft. I am Eleanor or Nelly.'

Christabel leaned over and her lips carefully touched Eleanor's cheek. Eleanor burst into tears. When she stopped crying, they had another long conversation, but none of it was about botany.

At the end of that summer term of 1860 Christabel went to spend a fortnight with her grandfather in Perthshire, taking Eleanor with her.

Mr MacKenzie lived in a broken-down laird's house that had not been much improved since the seventeenth century. The land attached to it had been sold off long before. Mr MacKenzie was an amateur chemist, a collector of books, and a democrat in the old-fashioned French style. He despised the gossip which his eccentricities aroused in the county. An old horse grazed in the thistly paddock that fenced him off from his landed neighbours, keeping company with a couple of pigs, a cow, and a dozen hens. A naval widow of doubtful status looked after Mr MacKenzie and the house.

Here, aged ten, Christabel had arrived, sent home from India, where her father was a military surgeon with the East India Company. Her grandfather kept her with him after both her parents had died in the Great Mutiny.

For five years she had the run of Mr MacKenzie's library,

supplemented by instruction from the local minister, while an odd-job man taught her to fish and shoot. It was recognized that she could not now return to India, as had been planned, to be married off by her family. No alternative arrangements were made.

Mr MacKenzie had another son who was attached to the British embassy in Paris. In the summer before Christabel's sixteenth birthday, in 1859, he also died. Shortly afterwards, his widow arrived on a visit. She was the youngest daughter of the Earl of Glencorrie, one of the aristocracy Mr MacKenzie hated. He was ashamed of a connection which his acquaintances regarded as much too good for his family. He ordered the naval housekeeper to put Lady Elizabeth into the damp north bedroom.

Within a week he was dressing for dinner, shaving regularly, and every night plundering his best claret from the cellar. Elizabeth stayed long enough to sever Christabel from her savage freedom. Whom would the girl meet in such surroundings, she demanded. Did her grandfather intend to condemn her to spinsterhood?

The old man was shocked by his own thoughtlessness. He whined and grumbled, for he was very fond of Christabel's company. Finally he gave in: he would allow his granddaughter to be sent away to a school in Edinburgh.

Christabel wondered what it would be like to eat, work and play with a hundred and thirty duplications of herself. She had met few girls of her own age except in books.

The reality had disappointed her. Nevertheless, she tried to settle down to please Aunt Elizabeth, the centre of her world until she fell in love with Eleanor Stewart.

When she went with Eleanor to Perthshire in that summer vacation of 1860, Christabel had not seen her grandfather for a whole year. He had aged greatly, and now talked to himself rather than to Mrs Kelly, the naval widow. He was pleased to see the two young women, but he left them to entertain themselves.

So when it rained (which it did for most of the first week) they retreated to the former laird's worm-eaten four poster, where they played cards, read aloud to each other from the old newspapers lining a cupboard, and made love. When it became fine again they took prodigious walks into the hills, after which they picked the bracken off each other's hair and clothing.

On 7 August, they rode Mr MacKenzie's horse to the foothills and left it tethered in the shade of a rowan tree, beside a tumultuous burn. They followed the water up the mountainside; from the summit they could make out a hazy silver line that might have been the Firth of Forth; and Christabel said that she could hear cheering from the twenty-two thousand Volunteers whom the Queen was reviewing that day in Holyrood Park. Eleanor said it was only the blood pounding in her ears.

At the end of the fortnight they travelled back to Edinburgh. Christabel was to continue on to Paris with her cousin, Elizabeth's son by her first marriage, who also lived in Edinburgh. Parting at the station, each of them promised to write a journal letter that would be posted once a week. In Paris, to quench the rage of separation, Christabel notched up the days on a leg of her walnut bedside table. The damage was not noticed until she had returned to Edinburgh. Eleanor went to her parents' home in the Borders, and found that Christabel had put tentacles into every crevice of her mind and body. She forced herself to let at least two hours elapse between each reading of the letters from Paris.

And now it was the afternoon of Saturday, 17 November, in the autumn term. Christabel was walking down Church Lane towards Eleanor's house. It was her birthday, and she was in a bad temper because her botany lessons with Eleanor were to cease before Christmas.

New York Infirmary for Indigent Women and Children,
64, Bleecker Street, N.Y.
31 October, 1860.

My dear Miss Stewart,

Forgive me for taking so long to reply to your letter, which I read with the profoundest interest. I am happy to confirm that your studies are suitable for the course you have in mind. My only doubt is whether you are sufficiently well-grounded in chemistry. I have made some suggestions which you will find at the end of my letter.

You assume correctly that after the recent legislation in the British Parliament, you would not be able to register without a medical degree from your own country. Will you allow me to offer a remedy?

This winter we shall raise a subscription fund to establish a medical school for women, which will be attached to our Infirmary. I invite you to apply for a place in it. Your only problem would lie in the advancing of your studies to the point where you would be qualified to enter. Until that time we should be most glad to give you work at the Infirmary of a kind suitable to your experience in the Edinburgh dispensaries.

Will you let me know if this plan is agreeable to you?

I am, my dear Miss Stewart, your sincere well-wisher and friend,

Elizabeth Blackwell.

'So that is why our Saturday lessons are to stop!' exclaimed Christabel, after reading this letter.

She had come with the intention of discussing ways to circumvent her aunt's decision. But Dr Blackwell's invitation made her feel that the whole world was against her. She vented her feelings in a torrent of anger.

'My darling, whatever is the matter? It was your idea that I should write to Dr Blackwell.'

'But you didn't have to tell Miss Erroll that I was doing so well in the botany lessons! It all went into that monthly report they send out – and now Elizabeth writes they are to stop. How are we going to see each other?'

'Chrissie, I can't let your aunt go on paying for the lessons. We haven't opened our botany books once this term. It's so deceitful and undignified.' Eleanor tried to put her arms round Christabel, and was coldly pushed away.

'You didn't mind that in Perthshire, when Mrs Kelly used

20

to ask us if we had enjoyed our picnic. You were quite a brazen little fibber then, weren't you?'

'It's just going on with the lessons, nothing else,' floundered Eleanor. 'I love you, Chrissie, but I couldn't lie when Miss Erroll asked such a direct question.'

'Love!' screamed Christabel. 'If you loved me, you would not be such a squeamish, metaphysical prude! Oh, it is plain what has happened. Now that you have received Dr Blackwell's invitation to go to America, you want to be rid of me. Well, do not think I shall try to keep you!'

Christabel picked up her mantle and pulled it over her shoulders.

'There!' she said, banging her hat on to the back of her head. 'I'll go at once.'

'Darling, please do not be so angry,' wailed Eleanor.

'I am not angry. I am deeply disgusted. What a fool I have been!'

Christabel rushed to the door and then returned, as she thought of a more cutting exit line. She repeated it several times, but finally, she did go, and Eleanor bent her head over the table and wept. She felt as if lightning had vaulted down the chimney to blast her. And she had not even wished Christabel a happy birthday.

A little later Mrs Stewart entered with the tea tray and looked round the room pretending to be surprised.

'Is Miss MacKenzie away? I didna hear the door. Have some tea, hen, it'll do you good.'

Eleanor swallowed the tea noisily and nibbled a scone.

'That's nearly our last lesson,' she said, in the tone of one announcing the end of the world. Mrs Stewart gave her niece a fond look and patted her hand.

'You'll miss her, but it's maybe for the best. You work ower hard, Nelly, what with your singing, and your book-work, and up at the dispensaries forbye. Yon Mr Cargill got a fine bargain when he caught you for the Institute. But the gentry aye think they're doing us the favour.'

A key scraped in the front door. This time Mrs Stewart's

surprise was genuine. 'Is that your uncle back from Leith? I hope he's no expecting his supper this early.'

She went out to meet her husband, and Eleanor stared miserably into her cup, wishing she had never been lured to the Scottish Institute.

Mr Cargill, the singing master, had met her by chance during a fishing holiday in the Borders. He had been delighted by her performance at an amateur concert in the local county town. He thought she had the perfect voice to demonstrate *The Airs of Caledonia*, a work he had composed to use at the Institute. He had other ideas as well, but Eleanor did not know about those.

Mr Cargill said he would use his influence to have Eleanor enrolled as a student governess at the Institute. Eleanor's parents had urged her to accept the offer; and it seemed that perhaps a way had opened to her secret ambition.

When it turned out that she was going to live with her aunt and uncle, Mr Cargill gave up his plans for seduction in unchaperoned lodgings, and concentrated on training Eleanor's pure soprano voice. She had come to the Institute at the same time as Christabel. Now she wished they had never met.

The excited voices in the hall broke into her mournful thoughts. Eleanor forced herself to look cheerful and went to find out why her uncle had returned home so early. Mr Stewart said that he had left his ironmonger's shop in charge of his assistant, and yes, he did want to be fed, and soon. Then they would all wrap up warmly and go out, because they would never see such a sight again. He wanted to take his wife and niece to watch the arrival of the Empress of France.

Walking back to the Institute that Saturday afternoon, Christabel spoke not a word to Peggy. The frustrations of spending many hours in the same building as Eleanor without being able to be alone with her had been building up for weeks. If this particular dispute had not sprung up Christabel would probably have quarrelled about something else. But she was aware only of a burning sense of disappointment and betrayal.

Once inside the front door of the Institute she leapt the stairs two at a time and went into the library, where she helped herself to the writing paper reserved for the senior boarders.

Still thinking hard thoughts about Eleanor, Christabel squeaked her lacquered steel pen across the inkwell until the nib broke. After fitting another she ruled off fourteen lines and filled them with an extempore sonnet which began:

O cruel nymph, when from they beauty's sight—

When she reached the final couplet she sliced the paper into neat tenths and threw them into the wastepaper basket. Feeling better, she drew out another sheet of paper and started writing her English theme for Dr Graham, 'True Beauty'.

Mrs Margaret Napier, the Lady Superintendent of the Institute, was on the short side and rather portly. She had mousy brown hair and undistinguished features. However, like the Queen to whom her admirers compared her, she moved with dignified ease and had a melodious voice. In her ten years at the Scottish Institute she had added even more lustre to its high reputation.

The school claimed to be the originator of serious female education in the British Isles, and 1860 was the year of its Silver Jubilee.

The pupils of SINDOG had to endure a strenuous curriculum in the sciences as well as the arts. Yet as Mrs Napier never tired of pointing out, this was not education for its own sake: her young ladies must be trained as future wives and mothers of Christian men. Having gauged the speed of change exactly, Mrs Napier was careful never to be ahead of her time, and abhorred all talk of 'women's rights'.

The Institute's one hundred day girls were drawn entirely from the middle classes of Edinburgh. Among the boarders some tenuous connections wandered towards the landed gentry or aristocracy. Those from overseas – some from as far away as Australia and the Americas – were divided up among the households of the married masters, where their exotic influence could be neutralised. Only girls of Scottish origin boarded at the Institute itself. An exception was made for 'Indian children', who usually had strong family links with Scotland. This was how Christabel came to be admitted to Moray Place; and Mrs Napier now regretted what she felt had been one of her rare mistakes.

She was highly thought of in Edinburgh society; and in her own world she functioned as smoothly as a shark inside its skin. Officially she was employed by the six Directors who owned the school. In reality she was their lynch pin and controlled all their decisions. She thought three times as fast as any opponent, and her will was inflexible.

On the evening of Saturday, 17 November, Mrs Napier had asked the senior governess to dine with her. Miss Erroll had looked forward to the meal all week. It was not that the food would be any better than the pupils': Mrs Napier was much too clever to take such crude advantage of her position. What Miss Erroll longed for was release fom the communal dining room. Every year, the pressure of that young energy wriggling and bursting around her became more excruciating, and so did her headaches.

The meal was served in Mrs Napier's apartments on the second floor. The senior housemaid waited on them. She was also Mrs Napier's personal maid. Mary brought up a tea tray at the end of the meal, and the two schoolmistresses moved through to the sitting room. Mrs Napier settled down in a rustle of dark grey silk. She waved her guest into another armchair.

As far as she could, Miss Erroll relaxed. She was tall and gaunt, and her dry-skinned face had an androgynous quality, without being forcefully masculine. She had been at the Institute since the day it opened.

In its early years the school had been small and contro-versial. Pupils had frequently been removed by parents who disliked the heady talk about social justice and women's rights which frothed up during lessons.

Inevitably, some of the strong-minded women who helped in the early days – sisters and daughters of the founders – lost their enthusiasm in the daily classroom drudgery. They had given their services for nothing; when the school was well established, they felt they could leave the work to others. The pioneering spirit began to dwindle. Then, in 1850, Mrs Napier was appointed as Lady Superintendent.

Soon she had eased out what remained of those eccentric and independent volunteers. Mrs Napier began looking for another breed: women who would match her ideas of what a school governess should be. Well-educated, of course – the high standards of the Institute demanded no less – and of pleasing manner and appearance. Above all her circumstances should make her pliant to Mrs Napier's will. Whenever possible, Mrs Napier engaged governesses who were distantly related to the pupils at her school. She felt that being under the scrutiny of more fortunate members of the family would spur them to greater efforts.

Miss Erroll's social views and background were very conservative. Until recently she had fitted in admirably with Mrs Napier's plans. Now the ground had begun to shift a little, and they both knew it.

Mrs Napier poured out two cups of tea.

'How pleasant to forget our responsibilities for one evening!'

Miss Erroll smiled stiffly. She had no talent for small talk. Besides, she felt it unseemly to indulge in chit-chat in this room, filled as it was with reminders of Mrs Napier's widowhood.

The Lady Superintendent was inscrutable even to people much more wordly than Miss Erroll, who would have been astounded to learn that Mrs Napier had hated her husband. After one strange month he had shown himself hard-drinking and brutal. Their marriage was only two years old when he was knifed in a Calcutta brothel. The scandal was suppressed for the sake of his regiment (*lost on a scouting mission*).

Mrs Napier's eyes also took in the colonel's gloves and regimental badges under their glass dome. But any connection between sight and memory had long since snapped.

The two women sipped their tea. Miss Erroll waited for a lead. There were many discontentments in her life: she was going deaf, the work exhausted her, and she knew that her position depended on her being useful to Mrs Napier.

The Lady Superintendent said at last, 'I see little change in any of the girls since October. Would you agree?'

Miss Erroll searched for useful titbits. 'I think your fears about Miss MacKenzie can be relieved. She is not so solitary as she used to be. Yet it is hardly what you call a romantic friendship, Margaret.'

'Now, now, you must not tease me. I am convinced that a modest tenderness between two young women is the best preparation for the affections and duties of marriage. Provided it does not become too absorbing.'

Mrs Napier of course referred to that schoolgirl pairing where one partner cannot bear the shortest separation from the other, lest she miss the chance to convey her deepest thoughts about life, or the fact that her boot button has become unstitched. She smiled whimsically at Miss Erroll. 'I must not ride my hobby-horse. Who is this favoured twin soul of Miss MacKenzie's?'

'Miss Eleanor Stewart, the governess in training. I have seen them conversing in the corridors this term. They will have become acquainted through their botany lessons.'

'That young person is not a suitable companion for Miss MacKenzie,' declared Mrs Napier. 'They are almost of an age, so there would be no objection there. But Eleanor Stewart is a farmer's daughter. A *tenant* farmer. Had we not been obliged to replace poor Miss Christison-Findlay so suddenly I should never have agreed to Mr Cargill's request. She is useful in the singing lessons, I admit.'

Eleanor's Borders accent was considered helpful in teaching the correct pronunciation of the old Scots songs. Otherwise the vernacular was strongly discouraged at the Institute.

'Their conversation is about books and public events.'

'Oh, well,' said Mrs Napier genially, 'in that case one can hardly call it even a passing fancy. Their lessons cease at the end of this term and then they will find their different levels . . . Now to more important matters. Is Miss Stirling still communicating with Miss Rintoul's brother at the Military Academy?'

'I am certain the correspondence has ceased.'

'That is good news. The Stirlings of Renzie would not be pleased to have it continue. I know I can rely on you to see that it does not, Madeleine.'

Mrs Napier beamed her most brilliant smile, and Miss Erroll's heart lurched. The neutral tone did not deceive her. It loosed the moorings of her deepest discontent.

Miss Erroll was consumed by an abstract passion totally disembodied from her outward circumstances. Mathematics was the jewel of her life. Yet whenever she kindled the light in some young mind – and how rarely that happened! – her pupil was snatched from her by the Directors.

She said, 'I would be in daily contact with Miss Stirling, if you would let me teach the senior mathematics class.'

Mrs Napier's eyebrows lifted a fraction, and she sighed humorously. 'My dear, we have been through all this before. You know I cannot do what you ask. Unlike the gentlemen, we do not possess University degrees.'

Miss Erroll's pale lips writhed. 'You cannot doubt my ability after all these years. I had the best tuition in Scotland.'

'Of course, Madeleine! It would be impertinent in me even to praise Professor Erroll's *Mathematica*, used as it is by every seat of learning in Europe. We all respect your brilliant intellect. But–' Mrs Napier leaned forward confidentially. 'How I feel for you, my dear! I myself would like to give scriptural instruction to the senior pupils. But we are only women, gently nurtured. Are we fit to bear such responsibilities? How could I approach the Directors with your request?'

Miss Erroll dared not voice the anger that boiled up inside her. Under her dark green woollen gown, her left foot began to tap the floor.

The Lady Superintendent was adroit at exploiting the weak points of her subordinates, but she did not want to antagonise this most useful contact with the hidden life of the school. She spent another fifteen minutes trying to soothe the senior governess. When she felt that ruffled vanity had been appeased, she suggested that they bring the evening to an end. She greatly underestimated the strength of Miss Erroll's resentment.

When she was alone, Mrs Napier sat for a while pressing her fingers together. Then she rose to unlock her writing-desk and took out a heavily bound ledger whose pages had been divided alphabetically. She turned them over until she found one headed Madeleine Dunlop Erroll. Underneath were date of birth, details of family background and service at the Institute, and a summary of incidents in which Miss Erroll had called attention to herself.

Mrs Napier added, '17 November 1860. *Again* asked to conduct the senior Mathematics class.' Then she locked the book away. On it was founded her reputation for uncanny feats of memory, especially for misdemeanours.

On Saturday evenings the girls of fourteen and fifteen were allowed to stay up as late as their seniors and be mildly frivolous in the salon until bedtime. The youngest boarders went to bed early every night. After their tea of bread and hot milk, Miss Stephens, the callisthenics mistress, took them through the partition door connecting Number Nine with Number Ten. Because of these transmigrations she was nick-named Fräulein P.P. (for Pied Piper) and the youngsters were known to their elders and betters as 'the little rats'. The older girls slept in Number Nine, which also contained the dining room and the private rooms set aside for Mrs Napier and the senior governesses. The teaching rooms were divided between the two houses.

There had been a great amount of partitioning and sub-dividing to make these two Georgian houses suitable for use as a school. The only unaltered room was the first-floor salon of Number Nine. This was used as a music studio, dancing room, and place of general assembly. On Saturday nights the four pianos used for Logier teaching were pushed back against the walls, and the salon regained something of its original function as the main drawing room.

Since the Directors and governesses in training all lived at home, the teaching governesses had to supervise the boarders in the evenings. They also had to find the time to prepare the next day's lessons and look over the pupils' essays before they were passed on to the Directors.

On Saturday, 17 November, the evening was proceeding in the usual way under Miss Merchant's supervision. Two earnest students were comparing their notes on the beauties of Shakespeare. The biggest cluster was discussing clothes and the young men with whom they were currently infatuated. A small breakaway group were pooling their knowledge of sex. Two girls were playing a duet on a piano.

One figure sat alone. This was Christabel, who was reading Mr Darwin's recently published *Origin of Species* hidden behind the covers of *The Churchman's Family Magazine*.

Suddenly the sedate evening took a dramatic turn. The doors of the salon were flung open. There, shaking the brass lesson bell, stood a day girl called Amelia Menzies.

'Hark ye, hark ye!' she bawled.

Fifteen faces turned round in astonishment. One of the Shakespeare students ran over and stamped her foot.

'Daydogs aren't allowed here after four o'clock. Scarper, Amelia Menzies, or we'll have the drawers off you!'

'Sally!' quavered Miss Merchant.

Amelia advanced into the middle of the room. 'I've come here with Mama to tell you the news. Her Imperial Majesty, Eugénie, Empress of the French – Christabel isn't listening.'

'Never mind her,' urged another girl. 'Go on, Emmy.'

Christabel put down her book. Amelia flounced down on the rug beside Miss Merchant. 'Listen, everyone. You too, Miss Merchant. You know my cousin is one of the Empress's ladies-in-waiting?'

'Cousin to your aunt's step-sister, you mean!' jeered one of the piano-players.

29

Amelia put out her tongue. 'Flippers! The Empress is coming here.'

Most of the girls gave a loud groan. 'Oh, Emmy! That's been in the journals for *months*.'

'She's coming to visit us, SINDOG.'

There was an immediate hush. Miss Merchant said, 'Are you sure, Amelia? How do you know?'

'We had a letter about it today. The Empress is awfully keen on popping into schools and orphanages.'

Jane Rintoul said superciliously, 'SINDOG is not an orphanage.'

'Why shouldn't she come here, Jane? She used to go to a boarding school in Bristol. The Empress and her sister, the poor Duchess of Alba who's just died.'

'What a mine of information you are, Emmy,' mocked Christabel. 'Can you tell us how many gowns the Empress has ordered from Monsieur Worth for her visit?'

'Of course she can't!' said Jane.

'I can so!' retorted Amelia. Drawing on previous letters she described the jewels and ballgowns which would accompany Eugénie's visit to Edinburgh. She had their attention now. Even Miss Merchant put aside her work to listen. But Amelia's moment of glory was cut short by the arrival of her mother with Mrs Napier.

Mrs Menzies' arrival had annoyed Mrs Napier very greatly. Beneath a thin skin of apology Amelia's mother was throbbing with excitement.

Mrs Napier gave her visitor soft words and a glittering smile. She was vexed that her secret was out. The Duke of Hamilton had written to her at the beginning of the week about the Empress's proposed visit.

'Still, we must not pin our hopes too high, must we?' said Mrs Napier to her visitor. 'There will be many calls on Her Majesty's time.'

So, having deflated Mrs Menzies without giving offence, Mrs Napier steered her downstairs. On their way to the hall she was even more put out to hear that Amelia had accompanied her mother and was now unleashing her secret in the salon.

After the two visitors had left Mrs Napier spent several minutes reducing the frenzied babble to a calmer level. As soon as she departed it began to ferment again. In a moment they were shrieking at each other.

'Ladies, ladies,' pleaded Miss Merchant, 'we do not want Mrs Napier to think us unworthy of this honour, do we? Lower your voices, please!'

The senior girls considered Miss Merchant babyishly innocent. She also looked like a baby grown to adult size and wearing adult clothes. Everything about her was round and chubby. Even her wispy hair, scraped back with pins and combs, escaped into corkscrew curls around her forehead, reminding one of a tousled and well-washed infant.

Christabel had unkindly dubbed Miss Merchant 'The Virgin of Venice'; but her pupils quite liked her, so they responded to her plea by dropping their voices. Now clustered in one large group they began to talk about Eugénie, while Miss Merchant tried to continue checking essays. It was useless: the discussion around her was far too interesting.

She was in her late thirties, the youngest of five daughters of a china-merchant who towards the end of his life was elected to the Town Council of Edinburgh. Miss Merchant had kept house for her widowed father from the age of fifteen. When he died eight years later her family agreed that she should live either with one of her married sisters or her brother, who now took over their father's business.

She was a difficult guest: with unshakeable patience she interfered in every household arrangement, from the best recipe for floor polish to the way the children should be disciplined when they refused their rice pudding. Her sisters found relief in making her a rotating visitor. Finally it was agreed that she should take up residence with her brother; but after a week his wife declared it was either herself or Anna Merchant.

What was to be done with her? Without some paid occupation, an unmarried daughter could not disgrace her relations by living on her own outside the family bosom. Yet what kind of work would not be equally shaming for the daughter of a city baillie, who had owned one of the leading business houses of Edinburgh?

There were scenes of martyrdom and a family council, and a surprisingly happy outcome. While pursuing a shadowy ancestor on her mother's side, Miss Merchant had picked up a respectable smattering of history and geography. So at last she found her niche, as eyes and ears and busybody of the Scottish Institute.

She was a royalist through and through; on hearing of the forthcoming visit by the Empress of France she felt that she could almost forgive those ungrateful sisters who had treated her like a female Lear. She might even be presented to the Empress! The thought of sisterly envy provided Miss Merchant with infallible proof that Providence blessed the meek.

She joined eagerly in the conversation around her; behind her spectacles, her plump face glowed like a young girl's.

After helping her father arrange the salon the under house-maid Peggy had to clear up after the boarders' supper. Mary, the senior maid, was excused evening duties because she waited on Mrs Napier, to Peggy's great resentment.

Eventually Mrs Rogers, the cook, was satisfied, and told Peggy she could go home. Peggy threw a shawl over her shoulders and slipped out of the back door into the garden. She giggled as she ran down the path.

'Old bitch, she'd split her stays if she kent.'

The cook and Mary slept in the attic at Number Ten. Peggy lived with her parents above a coach-house at the back of Moray Place. The whole family worked for the school.

Peggy shivered as the sharp air of the garden hit her. Whipping off her frilled cap and giving her hair a pat, she skipped over the frost-stiffened grass and through the back gate of the empty coach-house. On the other side, a wicket in the double doors let her into Church Lane Square, an area which had been squeezed into the back of Church Lane to serve as a mews for this side of Moray Place. To return home, Peggy had to take this route and then go upstairs from a door in the square. But she was not going home. Not yet.

A figure detached itself from the outside wall.

'I thought you were never coming!'

'Yon cook's an old deil. The pans she made me scour! I'm sorry I kept you waiting, sir.'

The man grasped her arm and hurried her out to Church Lane. 'Don't call me sir. It's so ridiculous.'

'Then you'd best treat me like a lady. You're hurting me.' Peggy shook off his grasp.

In Church Lane a four-wheeled brougham loomed out of the gas-lit mist. There was a ghostly munching from the horse. The man helped Peggy step inside.

The driver bent down from the box. 'Where to, sir?'

'Oh, up Bridge Street, round by the Meadows, and back here again.'

The driver tapped the man's disappearing leg with the end of his whip.

'Hey, my birkie, this is Edinburgh, no Paris. I run a respectable business. I'm no losing my licence for the likes of you.'

The man backed out of the carriage. 'Any more of your impertinence and I'll have your plate revoked myself. My niece wishes us to discuss a legal matter. I am her solicitor as well as her uncle. We cannot talk in front of the family – though what affair it is of yours, I fail to see. Now move on.'

'Right, sir.' The driver flicked his whip. As he heard the blinds drawn down he resolved to jundie the pair of them over the most uneven cobbles he could find. Legal matter, indeed!

Inside the cab Peggy cuddled up to her admirer. 'Coorie in and keep me warm!'

'I'll warm you all right,' came the mock-growl. Peggy gasped, but her half-hearted efforts to push away his hands lasted only a minute. Their clasped figures swayed up and down with the movements of the cab.

Suddenly the man drew away. 'Confound it, it offends

one's sense of decency. In a hired cab, with all our clothes on! I can't even see you.'

'That's an awfy thing to say!' exclaimed Peggy.

The man laughed. 'What a little prude you are! Wouldn't it be better if we had a comfortable bed, with a fire?'

'You'd not dare take me into your house.' There was a taunt in her voice. Peggy had mentally fixed on certain conditions before she would complete this adventure.

The man said, 'We could go down to the coast for a few days. Ask them to let you go.'

Peggy laughed. 'It's well seen you dinna ken how simple folk live. Maybe my sister could help.'

'For heaven's sake don't mention my name!'

'Och, dinna fash yourself. I'm not wanting to lose my place. I'd trust nobody, not even Phemie. But I could ask her where to go.'

In fact, Peggy had already done so. She was waiting for the opportunity to follow up her sister's suggestion.

'Do that soon.' The man's voice became thick. 'My God, Peggy, I do want you so.'

Silence fell again until a violent jolt threw them both against the front of the cab. Peggy shrieked.

'Damn!' cried the man, and rapped angrily on the front window. The vehicle rolled to a halt. The driver got down and opened one of the doors a fraction.

'We're home again. Are you wanting another hurl?'

The man helped Peggy out. He followed her to the wicket in the coach-house doors and after whispering something returned to the brougham.

'Take me to Regent Terrace. I'll alight at the near end.'

The driver grinned sourly and set off again. At the end of the mile-and-a-half journey, out of malice he drew up under a gas-lamp. The man kept his hat pulled well down as he paid the fare and set off along the road at a brisk pace.

The cabbie spat into the gutter.

'Ach, Balaclava,' he addressed his horse, 'it's good for some that me and you dinna ettle to go into the blackmail business.'

It was as easy to count doors at night time as by day. But

he couldn't be bothered to work out the address of the man who was taking out the lassie from the ladies' college.

'Daft wee bitch,' he thought regretfully as he drove off. 'Only one way she'll end up. Poor daft wee bitch.'

Half-way along Regent Terrace the man glanced back to make sure the cab was out of sight. He took out his door key. Robert Cargill, singing master at the Institute, slipped quickly into his house.

Miss Merchant consulted her pocket watch and decided she must end this conversation about the Empress of the French. She told the girls to go quietly to their bedrooms while she stayed behind to extinguish the gas-lamps. For reasons of safety a single light was kept burning all night in the hall.

Then Miss Merchant went upstairs to her room. She and Miss Erroll slept on the same floor as the senior pupils, at the top of the house. Her fire was almost out. She managed to poke it into life, and after using a spill to light the gas-lamp, settled down in the armchair by her bed to finish checking the essays for Dr Graham, the English Director.

Thankfully she found only eight remained, all by the oldest pupils, so they were unlikely to contain any elementary errors. Might it not be safe to hand them over unread? Miss Merchant told Satan to get behind her. Nevertheless she must finish before midnight. She was scrupulous about not toiling on the Sabbath.

'True Beauty, or the Most Memorable Moment of My Life.'

The first two were stuffed with abstractions. True beauty was neither this nor that, although the world's specious values would have us think so. It was very much the other. It was moral beauty, sanctified by religion and improving literature, etc., etc., etc. Miss Merchant's approval was acidified by the lateness of the hour, and she skimmed impatiently.

Miss Raeburn cited *Light of the World* by Mr Holman Hunt, currently on view at a Princes Street art gallery. Miss Rintoul described a childhood visit to the Crystal Palace. She had been struck dumb with wonder not by the costly merchandise wafted from every corner of the earth; not by the skill of brain and hand; no, Miss Rintoul had been flabbergasted by the tender look on Her Majesty's face as she paced the central aisle on the arm of Albert, Prince Consort.

Miss Merchant's eyes softened, although she was doubtful about 'flabbergasted'.

The other essays praised a Highland sunset; a wild swan defending her cygnet (Miss Willowfield had persuaded her barbaric younger brother to drop his gun); a gypsy child singing barefoot in the street to buy soup-bones for her dying mother. After all this Miss Merchant was glad to find that Christabel's essay covered only one page.

'Shakespeare tells us that beauty is in the eye of the beholder. Does this mean that absolute beauty is all a matter of opinion.'

Miss Merchant added a question-mark to the end of the second sentence.

What should be our criterion, asked Christabel, 'that we feel ourselves struck with sudden amazement, as Keats describes the Spaniards who conquered Mexico, standing at their first sight of the Pacific, "silent upon a peak in Darien"?'

Miss Merchant's pen hovered. *Two* literary references in one paragraph? And the pupils were not allowed to read Keats. The management considered him much too luscious for young female palates. However, she would leave Dr Graham to deal with that.

After two more short paragraphs the essay ended abruptly. Miss Merchant shook her head. This was not up to Christabel's usual standard. She was not too upset, for she considered Christabel arrogant and was rather jealous of the girl's facility with words.

Her eyes were cantering happily along the home stretch when the last few words lifted her to her feet. The paper fell as if snatched from her hands. She forced herself to re-read the last sentence, in case fatigue had blurred her eyesight. No, she was not mistaken. Miss Merchant sank into the chair again, her thoughts blown about in a gale of agitation.

She shrank from the idea of disturbing Mrs Napier at such

a late hour. Yet what else could she do? Miss Merchant lit a candle and hurried down to the Lady Superintendent's apartments.

After she had rid herself of Mrs Menzies and Amelia, Mrs Napier read for a little, and then decided to ring for Mary to help her undress. Before she could do so, she heard a nervous tapping at the sitting-room door.

Miss Merchant was breathless with dread. 'Oh, Mrs Napier, the most horrible, unbelievable – how shall I tell you? I have never been so shocked–'

Mrs Napier drew the governess inside and shut the door. 'Do calm yourself, Anna. Whatever has happened?'

'It is Miss MacKenzie's essay. I have been checking the themes for Dr Graham. I hardly dare show it to you.'

Mrs Napier took the wavering sheet of paper from Miss Merchant's hands and turned aside to read it. At the end she said, 'You did right to bring this to me. Leave it here, and I shall deal with it in the morning. Do not mention this to anyone, Anna.'

When the governess had left Mrs Napier re-read the last lines of Christabel's essay.

'I now choose my own example of true beauty, and confine myself to visual beauty. During the past week, I have seen nothing more beautiful than Miss Stephens' breasts.'

In Douglas's Hotel, in the drawing room reserved for the Empress's suite, four people were glumly playing cards. These were her equerries, Colonel Favé and the Marquis de la Grange, and the two ladies-in-waiting, Madame de Saulcy and the Comtesse de Montebello. The last had been a close friend of the Empress's dead sister.

Favé tapped his cards on the table.

'Your hand, madame . . . Madame!'

Madame de Saulcy started. She had been gazing into the fire.

'I beg your pardon, colonel.' She laid down her cards. 'I cannot concentrate on our game. Shall we or shall we not travel to this Hamilton Palace tomorrow?'

De la Grange shrugged. 'Perhaps you can persuade Her Majesty to divulge her plans.'

'Her Majesty has no plans,' said the countess.

Favé muttered below his breath, and the countess burst out laughing.

'Ah, Compiègne, Compiègne,' (for that was where the French court usually went in November) 'when shall we see you again? Those charming balls, those hunts, those masked charades after dinner!'

Favé stood up and began prowling around the room, grumbling to himself.

The marquis said, 'It's no use, my dear Favé. You cannot be excused to chase the *cocottes* of Edinburgh.'

'He would not find any,' said the countess. 'They never show themselves out of doors. How can anyone live in such a climate?'

'Do sit down, colonel,' urged Madame de Saulcy. 'In a moment we shall all feel we have to join you, and that would be so ridiculous.'

'Moreover,' added de la Grange, 'it is a conspiracy. *Madame la comtesse* and I were winning.'

'Nonsense!' cried Colonel Favé. He returned to the table and said in a theatrical whisper, 'Now that the Empress has retired, if the ladies do not object, what about putting a few louis on the game, eh?'

Eugénie had left them at ten o'clock. This was unusual: she seldom went to bed before one in the morning. When the under maids had left the room Pepa began to brush her mistress's hair. It was a light coppery gold, thick and lustrous. At her English school Eugénie had been nicknamed 'Carrots'; but only Pepa knew why the Empress's hair was no longer of the same deep auburn colour as Christabel's.

Having seen the Empress into bed, Pepa extinguished the lights and she left the room with an elaborate sequence of reverences and curtsies. Eugénie was staring at the ceiling.

Once she was alone the Empress got out of bed and knelt on a prie-dieu beside the small table near her pillows. She touched a diamond-set photograph of the Duchess of Alba, taken after she died. Then she lifted a silver crucifix and began to pray with her eyes fixed both on her sister's picture and the little twisted body of Christ.

Eugénie prayed first for her sister's soul, and then for herself, for release from the anger and hatred that still corroded her two months after Paca's death. This was the illness that had driven her out of the Tuileries, and out of France.

All through that summer she and Paca had prepared themselves. The Duchess had an incurable spinal disease.

In September Eugénie had accompanied Louis Napoleon on a state visit to Algiers. The imperial yacht, *l'Aigle*, had broken its voyage at Corsica. There an urgent message awaited the Empress: Paca's illness had taken a serious turn. Eugénie stifled her own wish to sail straight back to France. It was her duty to remain at her husband's side. There was some relief in knowing that she could be contacted swiftly by the underwater cable which had been laid that week between Toulon and Algiers.

They reached North Africa on the morning of 17 September. There was no report on Paca's condition.

As they went through the ceremonies organised for the visit, Eugénie tried to crush her anxiety. She laid the foundation of a sea-front boulevard, and sat through a military display on the Mitidjah Plain. She was told there was still no news about Paca.

She began to panic in this long silence, and did not appear at the ball that evening. Next day she forced herself to attend another review. It was Wednesday, 19 September. Late that night, Louis Napoleon told her that he wanted them to leave for France at once.

*L'Aigle* arrived off Marseilles two days later. Before they disembarked the Emperor took his wife aside and told her that Paca was already dead. She had died almost a week ago, a few hours before they had docked in Algiers. The funeral had already taken place.

'You knew, and you did not tell me!'

'I heard only last night,' Louis Napoleon protested. The

cable had broken forty miles offshore from Toulon and it had taken two days for the news of Paca's death to arrive from Paris. Later he would show her the reports of this in the English *Times*. Yes, he had been weak and cowardly. But he had not intended to mislead her.

None of that counted. He had let her go on thinking that her sister was alive – the person who, with her son, was dearest to her in the world. She would never trust him again. Such deceit was far worse than any infidelity with his mistresses.

The wound festered on, long after she had become resigned to Paca's death. Eugénie was tortured by regret that she had not been at her sister's deathbed. Her agonised thoughts hounded her like demons; and she had broken away from the French court in the hope that this journey to Scotland might exorcise them.

# SUNDAY

On Sunday morning, the young callisthenics teacher Barbara Stephens was waiting in her room at Number Ten for the bell that would summon her downstairs to escort the boarders to church.

Miss Stephens' unusual height and flaxen hair proved her descent from the ancient Viking forbears who had settled around her native town of Harrogate. But the moist, protuberant blue eyes, at that moment full of tenderness, suggested that over the centuries there had been a toning down of such stern ancestry.

She had already put on her mantle, bonnet and gloves, and a bible lay in front of her on the dressing table. In her hands was a much-creased letter which she was reading with a foolish smile. Miss Stephens was in love.

There was a knock at the door. Mary, the senior housemaid, put her head into the room without waiting for an answer. Miss Stephens thrust the letter into a drawer already almost overflowing with similar sheets of paper.

'Mrs Napier wants to see you, miss.'

Miss Stephens stared at the pale face gazing back at her from the mirror. Had Mrs Napier unsealed one of her letters before passing it on? Or worse still, held one back? She tried to pinch some colour into her cheeks, and breathed deeply. 'To breathe is to relax,' she used to say to the pupils exercising in Turkish smocks and trousers, as they waved their dumb-bells in the salon.

Miss Stephens hurried downstairs, through the partition

door connecting Number Nine with Number Ten, and stepped lightly up to Mrs Napier's apartments. She was in the prime of health: the raggedness in her breathing was not brought on by the speed of her ascent.

Since the beginning of October she had been meeting Lieutenant Ross of the Castle garrison in various art galleries, book shops, piano rooms and other more private places. There was nothing *sinful* in their behaviour; she expected a proposal of marriage any day now. Still, their embraces had gone beyond the strict limits of chastity.

By the time she came face to face with Mrs Napier Miss Stephens was finding it hard to conceal her agitation.

'Please be so good as to read this, Miss Stephens. I must warn you that some of the sentiments are indelicate.'

Mrs Napier handed over Christabel's essay.

Miss Stephens gave a tremulous smile and bent her eyes to the paper. Mrs Napier was surprised to see the young woman look relieved. She made a mental note that Miss Stephens had a secret; but for the moment that could wait.

On arriving at the reference to her own breasts the young governess blushed and gave a nervous laugh. This died at once when she saw the expression on Mrs Napier's face.

'I think I can explain what has happened. I always remain with the young ladies when they change their attire at the end of my lesson. That was your request, Mrs Napier.'

The older woman nodded impatiently.

'Last week, they expressed some dissatisfaction that their drawing lessons were confined to flower studies and copies from the antique. One said that she yearned to sketch the human figure.'

'Miss MacKenzie?'

Miss Stephens looked surprised. 'Why, no. It was – I cannot remember. I offered to serve as a model.'

'You did *what*, Miss Stephens?'

The young woman's voice faltered. 'Now I realise that it was hardly proper. Our informal costume and our exercise together impelled me to forget that I – that I should not intrude into another area of the young ladies' studies. I am most – most -'

She stumbled into silence under Mrs Napier's fish-cold stare. Worse still, Miss Stephens began to recall her sensations as she had posed for the pupils. She was a young woman of exuberant vitality. The connection between her stimulating meetings with Lieutenant Ross and that impetuous disrobing became all too clear. She was now aghast at her stupidity. She might lose her position at the Institute, be sent home to Harrogate, and never see dear Ewan again! As Mrs Napier's silence continued, Miss Stephens began to gabble.

'It was all in the strictest privacy, I assure you. There were none present but Miss MacKenzie, Miss Rintoul, Miss Dewar and Miss Sinclair. I sat for the torso only – almost fully draped. I kept the drawings. I felt it not right that they should be taken away and perhaps – er -'

Mrs Napier's face unchilled a little. 'I am glad to hear that your sense of decorum prevailed to that extent at least. Please fetch the drawings to me at once. I must reflect on what I should do about this incident. Meanwhile, I need hardly remind you what should be your occupation for the rest of the day.'

For a few seconds Miss Stephens was bewildered, before she remembered that it was Sunday. 'Oh, yes, yes! I shall pray for guidance.'

She bounded towards the door, straining to be released from this dreadful interview. Another thought occurred to her.

'There are only three sketches. Miss MacKenzie tore hers up at the end of the sitting.'

'Indeed? I have been told that she draws passably well.'

'I allowed them only thirty minutes. Miss KacKenzie had difficulty in commencing. She was – ah' – Miss Stephens blushed once more – 'studying the subject for most of the session, and could not find her stroke.'

Mrs Napier bowed her head without comment. When Miss Stephens had escaped, the Lady Superintendent took out her thick black ledger, opening it at the page headed Barbara Alicia Stephens.

Then she leaned back, tapping her beautiful fingers together. Mrs Napier did not waste time on being angry with the young governess. She expected other people to be stupid and saved her energies for retrieving their mistakes. It would be better to suppress the incident, rather than go through some public ritual of outrage. The four girls all boarded at the Institute. It she spoke to them in time the scandal would be unlikely to reach the parents of the day girls. And if it did come out, thought Mrs Napier, she would dismiss Miss Stephens at the end of term.

*The Empress, with her suite, attended St Mary's Church, Broughton Place, where High Mass was celebrated. A considerable number of people had collected in front of the Church when the Imperial party came up, and we understand that the Empress expressed to her attendants her warm appreciation of the cordial and respectful welcome which she has everywhere met with. The Imperial party walked to and fro from the Chapel, and the Empress (whose health, by the by, would scarcely seem to warrant the application of the term delicate) did not seem the least put about by the journey to the hotel having to be taken through a smart snow shower.*

Precisely as the Empress came out of the cathedral door, the skies flung down a mass of whirling snowflakes. Eugénie laughed and, brushing them from her face, set out at a brisk pace towards St Andrew Square.

Delicate be damned, thought Lieutenant McLellan, remembering the rumours about Eugénie's health. She looked a lot more robust than he felt after three hours' sleep and no more time off until Her confounded Majesty had left Edinburgh.

After seeing Eugénie enter her hotel the weary officer walked up to the High Street to visit James McLevy. McLevy was not a churchgoer, so he was sure to be at home. His 'bairns' had never taken the Sabbath off. In fact, it was their busiest time of the week. All the godly at kirk, and so many empty houses.

McLevy had settled down by the fire and was put out by McLellan's interruption.

'You'll mind you're still on half-call, Jamie,' said the lieutenant with brutal jokiness. 'I want you to keep an eye on the Scottish Institute during the Empress's visit there. They think it's to be tomorrow, at the back of half three.'

'Do you want me to cry in on the place first?'

'Aye, make your face known. But not before tomorrow forenoon. They're hardly the kind of folk to be sociable on the Sabbath. Not like you and me, Jamie,' he added with a cruel grin.

In graduated order of height the boarders of the Institute set out for morning service at a Presbyterian church in the West End. They were escorted by Miss Merchant, Miss Stephens, and two other governesses. Three little girls were taken by the French governess to the Roman Catholic cathedral in Broughton Place. Their smug air of piety was due not to any certainty of belonging to the one true faith but to the fact that they were going to worship with the Empress – a privilege for which most of their fellow pupils would have apostatised on the spot.

Neither Miss Erroll nor Mrs Napier walked with the main crocodile. Mrs Napier was an Episcopalian. She attended St John's with the boarders from England and overseas. Miss Erroll still rented a seat in her parents' church, which belonged to a Free Presbyterian sect with harsh anti-Papist views. This was situated at a considerable distance from the Institute.

Miss Erroll could feel snow in the wind; she was wearing stout boots and carried a large black umbrella. She had passed a wretched night, kept awake by her indignation against Mrs Napier. However, this had veered in direction. It no longer centred on that continuing refusal to let her instruct the senior mathematics classes but rather on the invasion of the Institute by the Catholic Empress of France.

45

For the Errolls, Catholicism was linked with everything sensuous, self-indulgent and corrupt in lands that had not known the purifying fire of the Reformation. They were horrified by the ever-increasing flow of Irish immigrants into Scotland. The Errolls regarded the Papist religion as a creeping fungus that, if unchecked, would destroy their native land.

Professor Erroll liked to travel, but would not expose his family to the taint of Romanism. Although Miss Erroll had spent many holidays abroad they had all been taken in the Lutheran cities of Germany; and even these had been approached by tortuous sea voyages to avoid any contact with the scarlet cities between Edinburgh and central Europe.

From an early age it was clear that Madeleine had inherited her father's abilities. She was an only child, a plain, shy little girl; as a young woman she had shown no passion except for the binomial theorem and other algebraical mysteries. When Professor Erroll died, her need to live within the strong arms of authority had been met at the Scottish Institute.

The arrival of Mrs Napier had roused great conflicts in Miss Erroll. She acknowledged that she owed the Lady Superintendent obedience, but the woman was an Episcopalian, at least two steps on the way to Rome, in Miss Erroll's opinion. She even admitted pupils of the Catholic faith.

At breakfast that morning Miss Erroll had learned that the Institute was to be 'honoured' – *honoured*! – by a personal visit from the Empress of the French. It was all too clear that Mrs Napier had been planning this event behind everyone's back.

The girls wanted to present a tableau in the salon. They were already discussing how they might persuade Mrs Napier to cancel Monday morning lessons, so that they could rehearse it. Miss Erroll sat at the head of the table in disapproving silence. When the girls asked what she thought of their plans, her comments had been sarcastic and discouraging. The girls had turned away, tittering.

Still consumed by indignation, Miss Erroll toiled uphill and felt one of her headaches come on in the biting wind.

During the service it grew worse, although her church was quieter than most nowadays. The music was still supplied by a choir grouped around the pulpit. There was none of this modern standing up or getting down every few minutes. Miss Erroll let the waves of devotion wash over her, humbly adding her own requests: 'O Lord, if it be Thy will, let that woman see the error of her ways; let Your peace descend into my heart; may I accept the tribulations You send me.'

This was as far as she would go to articulate the hatred she had stifled for so long. In the early days the Directors had been pleased to give her whatever classes she wished. Some of them had even brought their sons to her for tuition. Mrs Napier had put a stop to the arrangement.

Miss Erroll listened to the sermon with warm approval. The minister reminded them that they had recently celebrated the three hundredth anniversary of the glorious Reformation. Yet now, in the city of John Knox, God-fearing people saw the Scarlet Woman of Rome moving freely among them.

'My friends, how often have I stood outside that temple of idolatry in Broughton Place and witnessed to the truth! Still shall I lift up my voice to the Lord so long as the Woman of Babylon defiles this city with her presence. My brothers and sisters in Christ, wrestle in prayer until this evil thing is removed from our midst.'

By the end of the sermon every word from the pulpit was striking Miss Erroll's tender head like a hammer blow. She was filled with guilt: in one or two days *she* would have stood with those minions of Anti-Christ; *she* would have welcomed the Catholic Empress into the Institute. Not personally, of course; nor indeed did Miss Erroll visualise Eugénie in the lurid terms applied by the minister. But her conscience was deeply troubled at the thought of condoning this visit. She began to feel sick, and lights flashed at the back of her eyes.

After the morning service she usually lingered at the church door to talk to some former neighbours who remembered her as a girl. The stirring of old memories provided a little warmth to help her through the week. This Sunday she hurried out as soon as the benediction had been spoken. She walked down the street as fast as her throbbing nerves allowed, stabbing at the pavement with her clumsy umbrella. She would lie down in her room at the Institute before returning for the afternoon service.

Miss Erroll had been making this double Sunday journey for twenty-five years. It had never occurred either to her or her fellow-worshippers that one of them might have taken her in for the interval between the two services.

Mrs Napier had decided she would begin suppressing the results of Miss Stephens' indiscretion as soon as the four pupils involved had returned from church.

On her return from St John's she went to her apartment to remove her outdoor clothes, then to the library on the same floor. This was where the older boarders gathered while waiting for the light luncheon that was taken between the morning and afternoon services. She heard voices behind the closed door, and walked past with a heavy tread so that when she entered she would not have to chide the girls for breaking the silence rule. Then she turned round and went in.

'May I disturb you, my dears?'

They knew that Mrs Napier was pretending not to have caught them out. The habit had endeared her to all the older girls except Christabel, who had realised that the Lady Superintendent made her subordinates enforce unpopular rules which she herself ignored, while absorbing all authority in the school into her own person.

'I have something important to discuss with you before luncheon.' Mrs Napier signalled that they should draw their chairs around her by the fire.

She had heard that they had made some sketches from life, using Miss Stephens as their model. Did they not realise that such a sitting should never have taken place? Mrs Napier allowed herself to sound a little anxious.

Maria Sinclair was prompt on cue. Was there something wrong in so doing? Mrs Napier stroked the girl's head. She

48

hated physical contact of any kind, but the gesture seemed called for. She gave a sad little laugh.

'Your intentions were perfectly innocent, dear Maria. Alas, there are other considerations.'

Christabel's eyes glinted. 'Ah, *les convenances*.'

'Precisely,' said Mrs Napier, annoyed at the irony. 'Decorum is also important.'

She softened her tone again and pointed out that Miss Stephens was scarcely older than her pupils; she shared with them the delightful impulsiveness of youth, and its generosity of heart. Now they had had time to reflect, were they not a little grieved to have taken advantage of a kind nature that must now regret its own imprudence?

'Oh, yes, dear Aunt Napier, it was most thoughtless in us!' cried Jane Rintoul, and Maria and Elaine chorused their agreement.

'There, there, do not be too distressed, my dears. I know that you will do your best to make amends.' She waited confidently.

'Poor Miss Stephens!' cried tender-hearted Maria. 'How can we show our repentance?'

'We could buy her some flowers,' suggested Elaine.

'We might write our apology and all sign it,' said Jane, who saw an opportunity to show off her crested notepaper.

'There's my dear Jane, sensible as well as generous!'

Elaine asked solemnly. 'Shall we show you the letter, Aunt Napier?'

Mrs Napier smiled. 'You are grown-up young ladies, and do not need my advice on what to write. Pen it immediately, and seal it. Give it to me to hand to Miss Stephens. Then you will feel free to look forward to the Empress's visit.'

Mrs Napier was certain that the appearance of Eugénie at the Institute would quickly bury any memory of the sketching episode. She rose to leave the room, but Christabel said politely, 'Mrs Napier, I am afraid that I cannot agree to this.'

The other three pupils gaped at her in astonishment.

'Chrissie! We must make amends,' exclaimed Maria.

Christabel persisted, 'Miss Stephens herself offered to pose

49

for us. We were not at fault. Such a letter might embarrass her.'

Fury surged through Mrs Napier; she took Christabel back to her sitting room. The luncheon bell rang as they arrived there, but Mrs Napier felt that dealing with this vexatious girl was more important than a prompt appearance in the dining room. She was breathing quite heavily as she sat down.

'These are not the manners I expect from the niece of Lady Elizabeth MacKenzie.'

Christabel retorted, 'We both know that manners are not at issue. If you don't believe me, ask Elaine or Maria or Jane.' Christabel assumed that Mrs Napier was trying to shield Miss Stephens by throwing the blame on herself and her friends.

Mrs Napier's dislike of Christabel blurred her judgment. She was superb at manipulating a situation, but not so good at summing people up. Her contempt for those less adroit than herself often blinded her to the strength of their feelings. She regarded the point raised by Christabel as a minor quibble, and passed on to something else. She took Christabel's essay from her writing-desk.

'Miss Merchant has shown me the theme you wrote for Dr Graham. I am amazed at your lapse in good taste, Christabel. Surely you understand that it is most improper to write in such terms?'

Christabel frowned. 'You mean the word "breast"? We often meet it in our reading with Dr Graham.'

Mrs Napier's voice rose a little. 'Do not trifle with me, Christabel. You referred to – to "Miss Stephens' breasts". Alone as we are, it is still most improper to mention such matters.'

'Why? We were given no restriction on our theme. And it was my sincere opinion.'

'You are expos – mentioning details of an intimate nature about someone with whom Dr Graham is acquainted.'

'They were only *words*! If they are acceptable in Shakespeare, why not in my essay also?'

'The works of Shakespeare are literature. The impression is not so immediate.'

Christabel frowned again. 'What about nude studies in the Academy exhibition? And architectural decorations? Dr Graham says that visual representation is far more vivid than words.'

Mrs Napier began to feel that she was enduring one of those mediaeval punishments where two criminals were tied back to back and thrown into a river: the more desperate the struggle, the smaller the chance of survival for either.

She raised her hand. 'Enough! Your essay will be destroyed, and you will sign the letter of apology with the other young ladies.'

'I refuse to do anything of the kind.'

'Then you must go to the studio and remain there alone until you change your mind. Peggy will keep the fire lit and bring you your meals on a tray.'

'Surely you are not serious, Mrs Napier!'

'Assure yourself that I am. I put you on your honour not to leave the studio until I give permission. Please go there at once.'

Christabel glared, and went away. Mrs Napier felt that she had regained control over the situation. After a few hours of solitude the girl would feel ridiculous, and persuade herself to submit.

'Has Her Majesty decided that she will visit this school tomorrow afternoon?' the Marquis de la Grange asked Madame de Saulcy, as they waited to join the Empress at luncheon.

'Finally, yes,' said the lady-in-waiting.

'But word has not yet been sent to them!' cried the Comtesse de Montebello. 'They must be warned.'

'I shall go there immediately,' said de la Grange. The only opportunity he would have to absent himself was now, before the Empress appeared to take her meal. He asked Mr Slaney, the manager of the hotel, to order two vehicles: a private conveyance for himself and a hired cab for Pepa, who would have to inspect the arrangements made for Eugénie while she was at the Institute. It was beneath the equerry's dignity to travel with a servant, even such an important one as Pepa.

They arrived at the very moment when the older boarders were trooping downstairs to the dining room for luncheon. While Peggy went to announce the visitors the marquis stood in the hall appreciating his good fortune. The staircase was the finest feature of the house; and the girls were well aware how graceful they appeared as they descended. They dawdled down, hoping to learn the identity of this interesting-looking foreigner.

'What delight, eh, Madame Pollet? A hive of beauty! Regard that blonde!' cried de la Grange, with more comments of a kind acceptable at the French court, but which would have made Mrs Napier's hair stand on end.

At this point the Lady Superintendent entered the hall. She eddied across the tiles like a water lily, with her hand outstretched.

Nobody had told the marquis that in Scotland one did not pay social visits on the Sabbath. Even Mrs Napier was unable to conceal a slight air of disapproval, a reaction which Madame Pollet misconstrued.

De la Grange explained why he and Pepa had come to the Institute.

'Her Majesty would not wish you to go to any particular trouble, madame. Please continue with your usual routine.'

Mrs Napier did not know that Eugénie's school visits in Paris were so frequent and informal that this was exactly what happened. She thought the marquis a fool to suppose she would take him at his word.

'That is most kind and thoughtful in Her Majesty, sir. Some of the pupils wish to present a tableau, if the Empress will give her gracious permission.'

Jane Rintoul stood on tiptoe to speak over Mrs Napier's shoulder.

'We are showing la Belle France with Joan of Arc and Marie Antoinette paying homage to the Empress, sir.'

Mrs Napier made a gesture to tell Jane that she should

step back; but the marquis was twirling his moustaches as he asked roguishly,

'And which of you adorable young ladies is to represent Her Majesty?'

Jane blushed prettily. 'We are all competing for the honour, sir. I hope the Empress will not think us impertinent. We have no portrait, else we should use that instead.'

De la Grange was enchanted by such modesty. Remembering that Eugénie had a weakness for pretty faces, he assured them that no offence would be taken.

Maria cried out excitedly, 'Oh, monsieur, there is a favour we should like to ask!' She glanced at Madame Pollet as if to enlist her help.

'Ask, *ma petite*,' said Pepa.

'If only – oh, my audacity! If we might but borrow some small article belonging to the Empress to inspire us!'

Mrs Napier smiled warningly. 'Maria, dear, I fear the Marquis de la Grange will think you very bold.'

The marquis was in ecstasy as this fragrant bouquet of young beauties clustered even closer around him. Elaine put her hand coaxingly on the Lady Suerpintendent's arm.

'Intercede for us, dear Aunt Napier. I am sure the marquis wishes to aid us.' She looked at him through her eyelashes.

In halting English, Pepa said, 'There is something. I shall ask *Sa Majesté* to permit me. I bring it soon.'

Elaine made a charming little speech of thanks, in French, and the marquis kissed her hand, crying,

'Bravo, bravo, mademoiselle!'

This whole scene was witnessed by Miss Erroll who had arrived back from church and was unable to pass across the crowded hall. Mrs Napier's use of the pupils' personal names had always rankled with Miss Erroll. The governesses were under orders to address even the youngest pupils as 'Miss Brown', 'Miss Dalrymple', etc.

Miss Erroll's face contorted with fury as she took in what she saw and heard. It was plain that it was all connected with the Empress's visit. She was in an even greater state of agitation as she finally managed to creep round the edge of the hall and take herself upstairs.

While Pepa was being shown the rooms set aside for Eugénie, de la Grange flirted with the oldest pupils. The girls crowded the top of the steps to wave goodbye to the two visitors, the marquis kissing his fingers to them until the carriage whirled him out of sight.

After the meal Pepa made her mistress ready for her afternoon expedition. She brought the conversation round to the subject of the Scottish Institute and Maria's request.

'A tableau? How delightful! What shall we lend them?'

Pepa pretended to give this some thought but she had already made up her mind. She was fiercely jealous for her mistress's honour, and in her opinion the Empress's representatives had not been welcomed with the degree of respect that was their due. She would shame these barbarians with the munificence of the Empress's generosity!

Pepa confessed that among Eugénie's baggage she had packed the replica of the Grecian diadem.

At first, Eugénie was not pleased. Then she began to be amused at the idea that the paste jewel would be worn by the young girl impersonating her. She told Pepa to take it to the Institute that same afternoon.

*In the afternoon, Her Majesty, attended by a French guide belonging to the hotel, took a walk along Prince's Street and Waterloo Place with the intention of ascending the Calton Hill. The disagreeable state of the weather, however, prevented this intention from being carried out; and the Empress desired the guide to conduct her to Holyrood. Her Majesty looked wistfully up at the weather-worn turrets pointed out as the apartments of Mary Queen of Scots; and then expressed a strong wish to see something of Arthur's Seat. The royal party accordingly proceeded eastwards to the Queen's Drive at the foot of the hill, when the excessive keenness of the wind, and the dull heavy atmosphere, caused Her Majesty, with apparent reluctance, to agree to return to the city.*

Peggy had been very put out when Mrs Rogers announced that luncheon was to be fifteen minutes late. Her free afternoon did not begin until everything used for the meal had been cleared away. She washed dishes, scoured pans and stacked away crockery with lightning speed.

The cook snorted, 'It's well seen that you're not to spend the afternoon at kirk!'

'Is that it, then?' asked Peggy, looking for her shawl.

'You're to take a cold tray to Miss MacKenzie in the studio. It's there on the dresser.'

Peggy cast up her eyes as if to say, 'Whatever next?' and scurried upstairs with the plate of cold meat and potatoes.

On the way up she met Miss Erroll, who was clinging to the stair-rail and making her way painfully downstairs to the kitchen. She had felt too ill to appear in the dining room.

'Peggy, could you please bring me up some tea? I have such a headache.'

Peggy was a kind girl and, seeing the governess's pinched face, she promised to bring some tea as soon as possible.

When she returned to the basement kitchen the cook was putting on her bonnet and gloves.

'I'm away the now, Peggy. Mrs Napier just sent word you're to bide in.'

'Me, bide in? I aye get off Sunday afternoon!'

'There's Miss MacKenzie upby canna be left by herself. You can get off Monday instead. Just the evening.'

Peggy replied suspiciously, 'Here, Mrs Napier never said that. It's you that gives the orders down here.'

Mrs Rogers looked a little uncomfortable. 'Aweel, Mrs Napier didna say Peggy Murdo has to bide in, but she said *somebody*'s to bide in. I canna get to the kirk in the morning.'

Peggy said sulkily, 'Right, then, but it's the morn's nicht off for me, and dinna you forget it!'

When the cook had left she took her feelings out on a dishcloth which she slapped along the whole length of the kitchen table. She'd give it half an hour to be safe, and then slip out. And she'd help herself to a cup of tea while she was waiting. That made her think of Miss Erroll, who had vanished from her mind. Peggy made a pot of tea.

There was no answer to her knock at the governess's door. Peggy peered inside. Miss Erroll was lying down with the shutters closed. The maid trod softly to the bedside and put down the tray.

'There's your tea.' Miss Erroll did not reply.

On the landing Peggy hesitated. Miss Erroll's unexpected presence was a set-back to the plan she had in mind. Putting this off for a moment, she decided to check the studio fire. She'd be for it if that gave out. She descended to the floor below.

Christabel was sitting at a window, chin on hand, gazing out at the garden. She turned round and smiled.

Peggy found Christabel intriguing. She didn't behave or speak to her like the other pupils. Peggy could not put her finger on the difference; and even if she had she would not have understood it: her knowlege in that area was confined to what she had learned by sharing a cab with Mr Cargill.

Christabel liked the under housemaid. At least she told herself that she liked her. The fact that Peggy was sparkling-eyed, round-bosomed, and had a pert manner, had not escaped Christabel's notice; but she was too young to have discovered that requited love makes one more sensitive to other enticements, even if they are virtuously rejected. At this particular moment she was filled with remorseful love for Eleanor, and regretted the disloyal way she had enthused over Miss Stephens' breasts.

The studio fire was glowing comfortably and the coal-scuttle was almost full.

'Will you be all right, Miss Christabel? I'm away out.'

'Right as a trivet . . . Lucky you!'

'What's to hinder you jinking out yourself? They're all at the kirk.'

Christabel smiled ruefully. 'Madam Napier put me on my honour, lovely wench.'

'Pooh! My father says forced honour's nae honour.

56

Mistress Rogers wanted to keep me back, but I dinna fash my thumb about *her*. You'll no tell on me, will you?'

'Aha, I discern a secret. Have you a sweetheart?'

'Aye, but I'm no letting on his name to *you*,' said Peggy archly. 'I'm trysting him the morn's nicht in Rose Street. I'm out to see to it the now.'

Peggy went away with an alluring smile, unaware that on several occasions Christabel had noticed her speaking to Mr Cargill in the garden.

After leaving the studio Peggy returned to the bedroom floor. On the landing were two wicker hampers. The larger was for dirty bed linen, which Mr Murdo carried downstairs to the wash-house at the back of the Institute. Similar arrangements were made for linen from Number Ten. The sheets were hung to dry in the garden.

It was not thought seemly to display more personal garments at the back of the school. Every Monday morning a porter collected two smaller hampers and took them to a washerwoman by the Calton Hill. There the young ladies' petticoats and drawers and night shifts were exposed to the whole of Edinburgh.

Peggy lifted the lid of the smaller basket, wincing at the squeak of wicker hinges. She satisfied herself that Miss Rintoul's fine new nightgown was inside and then took the hamper down to the hall – a task she usually did early on Monday morning. She wanted to make sure that none of the girls opened the hamper again before it was taken away. In the hall, Peggy whipped out the nightgown, rolled it into a bundle and hurried through the building to the garden. She ran down the path to her own house.

About twenty minutes later she came out again. During that time she had washed the nightgown, wrung out the garment and steamed it dry by the kitchen fire. It was now hidden inside a small leather bag belonging to her father. She retraced her steps through the Institute and put the bag beside the small hamper. Then she set out for Rose Street.

Odd parcels were frequently delivered or collected from the hall. No one was likely to look into the bag during the few hours it would stand beside the hamper. It would have been simpler to take the bag with her that afternoon; but Peggy was afraid of being questioned about it if she ran into anyone from the Institute while she was out.

The maid's comings and goings across the garden were watched with great interest by Christabel.

Peggy had the address of a Mrs Watson, who let out rooms for short periods. A kind of hotel, Phemie had told her. Phemie worked for a milliner in South Bridge Street and lived with her employer. Peggy put great trust in her elder sister's knowledge of the world.

Rose Street had been intended as a mews lane for Princes Street; but the buildings had been largely taken over for shops and small businesses. At the eastern end, Mrs Watson ran a discreet house of acommodation. She was the first to complain if any two or four-legged pedestrian fouled the pavement outside her door. She had no qualms about calling a constable off his beat if any unseemly brawling took place in the street.

Previously, Mrs Watson had run a brothel in Clyde Street with half a dozen girls and a quick turnover. Advancing years had made her wish for a quieter life and a domestic helper whose rôle could not be confused with the other services she offered. No one actually lived in her house except herself, two tabby cats and a pageboy called Willie. He was the son of a colleague who ran a whore-house in the Canongate.

At the end of his first week with her Willie had confounded Mrs Watson's judgment by stealing a gold watch from a client. He passed it on to his elder brother, a well-known flashman who was one of McLevy's 'bairns'. Mrs Watson was full of wrath against this viper she had nourished. Then it occurred to her (for the watch was recovered) that she now had a collar round Willie's neck. She kept him on, saying that if there was any more prigging or planking she'd have Mr McLevy down as quick as a ferret. Willie had been a model of honesty ever since.

Mrs Watson limited herself to what she called 'the carriage

'trade' – a metaphor, since all her clients arrived on foot and as inconspicuously as possible. Those she preferred were ladies who wished to have a serious talk with gentlemen not their husbands, and vice versa. She also rented to milliners, governesses and even housemaids, provided they were of good appearance and well-spoken. This was on the strict understanding that they made private assignations only and did not cruise the street. Apart from various errands Willie's main task was to keep an eye out for any breaking of contract.

Mrs Watson's rooms were so well run that no clients ever met each other in her house, although a great many did so unknowingly at each other's dinner tables.

The proprietrix spent the middle hours of the Sabbath either sharing a nap with her cats or reading a sermon. However, she remained flexible and always answered the door. When Peggy rang her bell she asked her in because she never discussed anything on the doorstep except the price of a cod's head for her tabbies.

Mrs Watson soon sized Peggy up. 'Where is your gentleman, dear? Why hasn't he come himself?'

'He doesna ken I'm here, ma'am, no yet. He'll not argue about the price of the room, sure's death he'll no.'

'A wee stolen joy is it, hen?' twinkled Mrs Watson.

'I want to be braw for him. Can I send along a wee bag of clothes?'

Mrs Watson trusted her instinct that the gentleman was either Peggy's master or the grown-up son of the house. The clothes would be 'borrowed' from her mistress. Any potential scandal could be turned back on itself. She agreed to a request she normally would have refused. She said she would reserve a room and wrote out the address for Peggy to give to her 'jo'.

'It's yours from seven o'clock, hen,' said Mrs Watson.

Peggy decided she would keep the original note as a lovers' souvenir, and copy out the details for Mr Cargill.

After seeing Peggy out, Mrs Watson returned to *Sermons for Families* by the Reverend Jabez Burns, D.D.

*

Eleanor was hurt to the quick by her quarrel with Christabel. During the whole of her eighteen and a half years she had met with nothing but reliability and kindness from those she loved. Her temperament had none of the fanciful, restless quality that made Christabel so vexatious to those set in authority over her. Eleanor's outlook was realistic; those who took a shallow view of her warm, good-humoured manner were frequently astounded by what they saw as freakish lapses: she would, for instance, appear to treat someone with uncharacteristic hardness; or to break social conventions which she had shown no sign of questioning before. Both judgments had fallen on her when she left home just as her parents were reaching an age when it was her obvious duty to look after them. So said the Stewarts' friends.

It was when 'Miss MacKenzie' turned into 'Chrissie', and the name began to carry overtones she could not put into her weekly letter home, that Eleanor began to realise her unusual situation. During the summer holiday it had dawned on her that the first laird's four-poster bed in Perthshire had been a private world in more senses than one; that away from such privileged solitude life would become more complicated for herself and Christabel.

Eleanor had returned to the Institute, not loving Christabel less, but with a grain of commonsense added to the inner turbulence with which she met her lover after their long separation. Apart from a quick embrace, they had to suppress their feelings. There was no privacy at the Institute.

Following their quarrel the previous afternoon, when at last she was able to stop crying, Eleanor wondered if Christabel was angry because somehow she had sensed this new ingredient in her feeling towards her.

Eleanor had never been in love before; after Christabel's violent exit she was distraught. The physical effects astounded her. That night she hardly slept. However, by morning she was beginning to feel angry that Christabel had accused her of faithlessness. She too had her pride, Eleanor told herself. She would stamp out her grief and henceforth think of nothing but work. She had been unwise to be drawn into this friendship in the first place. She would not meet Christabel at the afternoon service.

The Stewarts were members of the church next to their house in Claremont Street. Eleanor continued to attend the morning service; but since the beginning of October she had walked up to the West End every Sunday afternoon to the church used by the Institute, so that she could snatch a few minutes' conversation with Christabel as the crocodile was remarshalled for the walk back to Moray Place.

As the afternoon service approached, all kinds of excuses presented themselves. What if Christabel now regretted her words? How unkind not to give her the chance to take them back! Eleanor found that she had already put on her outdoor clothes.

She hurried up to the church early enough to be able to watch the pupils of the Institute enter. Christabel usually walked with Elaine Dewar; but Elaine was with someone else. When the minister was half-way through the first prayer Eleanor had to accept the fact that Christabel would not appear. She despised herself for coming to the church at all. How weak to succumb to the attraction of a young woman who was so thoroughly shallow and selfish!

Then misery overwhelmed her. Their quarrel was final. There would be no return to that enchanted world into which Christabel had drawn her. Years of desolation stretched ahead.

Ten minutes later Eleanor realised that the only way Christabel could avoid attending church would be to feign some illness. Perhaps she was ashamed of herself. Hope stirred, and then sank again. Was Christabel really ill? Her wrathful feelings might have thrown her into a fever. Had she even done herself some violence?

The rest of the service unfolded as slowly as a late spring. Eleanor rushed out of her pew as soon as the benediction was over. When the Institute pupils had trickled out, she approached a knot of the older girls.

'Where is Christabel? Is she ill?'

Jane Rintoul took a second or two to recognise Eleanor.

'I don't know, Miss Stewart. Was she not at the service?'
Eleanor longed to slap the cool, disdainful face.

Elaine Dewar said, 'Someone said she'd been put into isolation. Shall I tell her you were asking for her?'

'Don't be such a goose, Elly!' cried Maria. 'How can you speak to her if she's in isolation? Sorry, Miss Stewart, we know nothing about it. She was not at luncheon.'

The three girls turned their backs. They were interested in only one subject: the tableau for the Empress.

Eleanor made herself walk away with a casual 'Thank you.'

Isolation? Her fear coalesced into certainty. Typhoid, diphtheria, cholera? Perhaps, at that very moment, Christabel was being removed to a fever ward in one of the city hospitals. She would have to wait until Monday to find out. Eleanor forgot that Christabel had begun the quarrel. She returned home telling herself that she was heartless and utterly unworthy to be loved.

The front door of the Institute was never locked until nightfall. The glass-paned inner panel was held to be enough to deter those who had no right to enter, even on Sunday afternoons, when all the occupants were at church, or, in the case of the Catholic pupils, had been taken by Mademoiselle Fleury for religious instruction at the Ursuline convent.

This was the time when Mr Murdo would wander round to mend a broken sash cord, nail down a creaking board, or look for jobs of a similar nature. His wife suspected that this was just an excuse, and to pacify her, he would accompany her to church about one Sabbath in five.

Sunday, 18 November was one of these rare occasions. When Madame Pollet arrived at the Institute with the Grecian diadem, there was no one in the building except Christabel. Pepa managed to make her cabbie understand that he was to wait for her. She rang the front bell three times without arousing any attention. She became even more certain that these Scotch barbarians were unaware of the great honour being done them. Again she wrenched at the bell pull, her eyes

62

smouldering. The peal reverberated throughout the empty building.

Pepa stood impatiently outside the vestibule door, not knowing it was unlocked. She peered through the acanthus scrollings and saw a red-headed young woman descending the staircase, reluctantly. Another impertinence!

Christabel unlatched the inner door. The Empress's maid said who she was, and asked for Mrs Napier.

'I am the only person here,' said Christabel. 'They are all at church. In Scotland we go to church in the afternoon as well. Three times, if there is an evening service.'

Pepa was awestruck at such piety. After Mass, Sunday was just like other days, only better.

'*Santo Dios*, so holy! You give it her, miss. This. I bring the Grecian diadem.' She held out the casket and then snatched it back, unable to resist showing off the contents.

'How beautiful! Is it real?' asked Christabel.

'It is almost real. You give to the señora.'

Christabel smiled. 'I don't think that's a good idea. Come inside and I'll show you a place to leave it.'

On the way upstairs to Mrs Napier's sitting room she learned that the paste diadem was to be lent for the tableau. Inside the room, she pointed to the large writing-desk, but Pepa placed the box on a chair standing behind the desk, and held up the key.

'What to do? I must not leave with the casket.'

'M'm,' said Christabel. 'Let me have it. I'll give it to Mrs Napier when she returns to the Institute.' Christabel took the key and put it in her pocket.

As they walked out of the room Pepa said uneasily, 'You do not lock the door. There are no thieves in your city?'

'Oh, goodness, they would never come here. There's nothing worth stealing.'

The Empress's maid pondered on as much of this as she could understand. A strange people, surely. Uncouth, but honest. And strict in their religious duties, in their misguided Protestant way.

Christabel said that the other girls would want her to

convey their thanks to the Empress. 'Their tableau will be very splendid now, Madame Pollet.'

Pepa gazed at Christabel's chestnut-red hair. 'What is your name?'

The young lady told her. Pepa asked, 'Are you not to be *Sa Majesté*?'

The young lady said no, and laughed. Pepa did not ask her to explain the joke because she found talking in English a great strain. She returned to the cab with her pride a little soothed.

'Yet they are still barbarians,' she mused as she rattled back to the hotel to prepare Eugénie's dinner *ensemble*.

Mrs Napier had been correct in thinking that her punishment would make Christabel feel ridiculous. Nevertheless this feeling did not last long.

The more she went over the interview, the more certain Christabel became that the demand to sign the letter to Miss Stephens was unjust and hypocritical. This was despite her growing awareness that her essay had been written out of annoyance at Eleanor.

On first being banished to the studio, Christabel had spent a long time staring out of the window. The view was bleak: a dull winter sky sagging over the Firth of Forth, and the Fife hills already capped with snow. Christabel became bored. After Peggy's comings and goings there was no movement outside. Pepa's visit was a welcome interruption.

Christabel had not kept Pepa waiting deliberately. It was possible to see the whole hall from any floor by leaning over the banister rail; before coming down she had done that for several minutes, to see if the ringing of the bell indicated only that someone was going to enter by the unlocked inner door to leave a parcel.

Having seen Madame Pollet out, Christabel returned to the studio. She took the brass key out of her pocket and threw it from one hand to the other, relishing the thought of Mrs Napier's displeasure when she discovered how unavoidably her solitude had been broken.

The studio presented few distractions. Christabel began shying pieces of coal into the fire from increasingly distant points in the room; then that, too, bored her. She pulled some sketching paper out of a cupboard and hunted for pen and ink. When Christabel felt her energies frustrated, she frequently launched herself into imaginary adventures.

'Sunday, 18 November 1860,' she wrote, adding some decorative flourishes round the date.

Given at Sindog Castle. The fifth day of the siege and still no help in sight. My men are in good heart and we have enough water for another week. Rosalba came to me today and, with tears in her lovely eyes, she implored me to –

Christabel pondered what Rosalba might ask her to do. She walked over to the mantelpiece and ran a finger over the nymphs and flute girls frozen into their marble dance. Her thoughts went to Eleanor, and once more, she felt ashamed of her angry outburst. She would catch Eleanor in the hall on Monday morning and apologise.

Then she remembered that on Mondays and Wednesdays Eleanor did not arrive at the Institute until eleven o'clock. Something like a tear burned Christabel's eye; but she had not wept since a birthday greeting from her mother had reached her from India two years after her parents died in the Great Mutiny.

As always, the onset of disagreeable emotion drove her into an imaginary world. This side of Christabel's nature had not yet been revealed to Eleanor.

Christabel went back to her writing, abandoning Rosalba.

Every day brings the enemy nearer to breaching our walls. To soothe our apprehensions even the bravest of us has turned to childish pursuits. I saw young Melbury – he, my dear Henry, who so courageously snatched me from the krises of our foes – like a schoolboy playing with his marbles, roll leaden bullets across the Residency floor.

Once more the front door bell rang. This time Christabel went downstairs immediately.

'Ranny! What are you doing here?'

In the vestibule was the youth who had been questioned by McLevy at the railway station.

'I was going to leave a message for you, Chrissie. Why have they let you off the holy shop?'

'I'll tell you in a minute. Come inside. What was your message?'

'Mama's arriving from Paris this week,' said Ranald as they walked up the stairs. 'I suppose she will want to see us.'

'*Suppose*! Of course she will.'

'She's only passing through. Could you give a chap some tea? It's dashed cold out there.'

Christabel craned over the banister to look at the hall clock.

'No, I can't, but you may come and sit by my fire for ten minutes. Then you must scamper, because they'll all be back from church . . . Tea!' she repeated scornfully as they entered the studio. 'I thought men were supposed to prefer ale or brandy. Don't they rag the life out of you, even worse than Harrow?'

'Only till I invite them to a set-to with the buttons off. That stops it pretty quickly.'

Ranald took off his cape, pulled a chair to the fire and sat down with his long legs resting on the coal-scuttle

'Don't settle down like that,' said Christabel. 'Tell me your news and then get out as fast as you can.'

'Mama is coming over for the Hamilton Palace ball. It's on Tuesday. She should be here tomorow night or the next morning.'

Christabel thought of the hours that her aunt used to spend on her toilette before going out of doors in Paris.

'That doesn't give her much time to get there, especially if she wants to rest after the journey.'

'I expect she'll manage,' said Ranald, who had observed his mother's miraculous recoveries from fatigue when she

66

was determined to attend some social function. 'Marie's coming with her.'

'Is she staying at Heriot Row?'

'Yes, she asked me to go along and make sure Mrs Veitch had received her letter . . . Why aren't you at church?'

Christabel said that she had quarrelled with Mrs Napier because she had refused to sign an untruthful letter.

'The vile old doggess! Never mind, only one more year and you'll be free of her.'

'Oh, Ranny, I do hate it so!'

'I thought some of the girls were quite jolly. And there's whatshername. You like her.'

Christabel looked away into the fire. 'Eleanor Stewart. Yes, I do. But it's like a prison here. The governesses are so fussy and *stupid*! Well, it's not their fault, poor things. They're terrified of Madam Napier. The masters think I'm trying to catch them out.'

'You want to know too much for a girl.'

Christabel leaned over and pulled Ranald's ears.

'Ow, it was only a joke, Chrissie!'

'Don't you ever say such a thing to me again if we're to stay friends, Ranald Orsini MacKenzie. You don't know what it's like, not being allowed to run or even chase a ball around. You're such a lazy beast you never run at all.'

'Not since '59, thank heaven,' Ranald said. 'Sorry for the old beak of course, but the best thing that ever happened to me.'

'The old beak' was the Vicar of Doncaster, and while they were staying with Elizabeth in Paris Ranald had told Christabel why the Reverend Charles Vaughan had last year resigned from his post as Head Master of Harrow. Ranald had made his exit at the same time, together with some other pupils. Elizabeth had transferred her son to the Scottish Military College. She thought it might brace him up. She also hoped that such intricate English scandals would not be understood north of the Border.

Christabel said, 'I wish I'd known you were coming. I could have given you Alice's letter for Henry Rintoul.'

'Oh, old Henry is chasing in another direction now.'

'I thought he was quite spoony about Alice.'

'Well, maidens locked up in a tower and that kind of thing. Quite intriguing for a while. But Henry is a downright sort of chap, Chrissie. They all are.'

Christabel knew that the cadets of the Military Academy discussed the other sex in ways that would have shocked the sensibilities of Jane, Maria and Elaine. Ranald had told her so after they had been bathing in a river near the country house of one of Elizabeth's Parisian friends.

'It's just their age,' he had said wisely. 'I expect they will be quite house-tamed in five years' time.'

They were drying themselves off on the sun-baked river bank. Christabel was wondering whether she ought to abandon her sodden underclothes; Ranald had stripped completely to enter the water, and lay back with his hands under his head, unconcerned that his cousin was studying with interest her first full view of the difference between male and female anatomy.

Now she said, 'Have you become a downright sort of chap, Ranny?'

He swung his feet from the coal-scuttle. 'Good Lord, no! Waste of time. Blurs the eye for target practice. Can't understand what they see in it.'

'I think I can,' said Christabel, her unhappiness about the quarrel with Eleanor making her more frank than usual. 'Not in *that* way, of course. Someone you love. Women are so much more beautiful than men. They are soft *and* strong, and they smell so nice, and their hair is – I don't mean to be unkind, Ranny.'

Ranald absorbed this new fact about his cousin.

'Well, your argument seems illogical to me,' he answered. 'They aren't all beautiful, and anyway, if you love them, surely their appearance shouldn't signify?'

At that point they heard voices somewhere down below, and the slamming of doors. Ranald leapt to his feet. 'I'd better scarper.'

Christabel picked up his cape and threw it over his shoulders. 'Yes, get out before they catch you!'

'I'll leave a visiting card, and they'll think that's why I called. They'll never know we've seen each other.'

He ran downstairs through the crowd of chattering girls and was on the front steps before he was noticed by any adult members of the Institute.

When she returned from the service at St John's, Mrs Napier took afternoon tea. For a short time she deliberately put aside the problems and strategies that almost continuously filled her mind. She imagined herself, a year hence, sitting at her writing-desk and looking at the new heading on the school's letter paper. It would be crested with a French eagle; underneath would be inscribed *The Imperial Scottish Institute for the Education of the Daughters of Gentlefolk*. And to one side, *Patroness: Her Imperial Majesty, Eugénie, Empress of the French*.

This was the ambition that had seized Mrs Napier as soon as she had learned that the Empress was travelling to Scotland. She had heard rather sooner than most members of the public through a chance acquaintance she had at the French court.

Her suggestion for a visit to the school was presented to the Empress by the Duke of Hamilton, after a series of manoeuvres which would be tedious to describe.

Mrs Napier had of course made no mention to the duke of the reward which she hoped would result from Eugénie's visit. Her request for *that* must wait until the Empress had returned to the Tuileries.

As Mrs Napier sipped her tea, indulging her fancy about the honour she would bring the Institute – an honour which would be for ever associated with herself – a few disagreeable thoughts rose to mar her contentment.

She must find time to pronounce sentence on Miss Stephens.

She must win the battle with Christabel MacKenzie.

A stranger had left a visiting card on the hall table.

This last being the smallest problem, she dealt with it first. She sent for Miss Merchant.

'Ah, yes,' said the governess briskly, after reading the name. 'This was left by Mr Ranald MacKenzie of the Military College, Miss MacKenzie's cousin. Only by marriage, of course.'

Mrs Napier's face darkened at the reminder of Christabel.

'I know of Mr MacKenzie. Why is he styling himself Count Orsini – and why do you say only by marriage?'

Miss Merchant's eyes gleamed. She dearly loved a lord, and a lady even better. At this opportunity to show off her knowledge she forgot her disapproval of Christabel's essay.

'He is the son of Lady Elizabeth's first husband, a certain Count Orsini, who was exiled when the struggle for the liberation of Italy commenced. What a handsome gentleman! He lost everything when he fled. He taught Italian at the Institute. That was a few years before you joined us, Mrs Napier.'

'Really, Anna, sometimes I think you know the *Almanac de Gotha* and *Burke's Peerage* better than the Bible.'

'I hope not,' replied Miss Merchant, greatly flustered. She decided to hold back her next piece of information – that Elizabeth and the count had eloped from the school.

Mrs Napier said contemptuously, 'It will be one of those continental titles. All the children are little counts and countesses. It is of no significance.'

'If Mr MacKenzie is using the title, they must have finally established the date of his father's death. There was some uncertainty, you know.'

'Oh?'

Miss Merchant plunged into her story. Soon after his wedding the first Count Orsini had returned to the fight. He had been executed in the notorious Lombardy purges in 1848.

'That was what everyone thought, when Lady Elizabeth re-married. Her second husband was Miss MacKenzie's uncle. There was a *leetle* scandal when it was discovered that

70

Count Orsini had languished in prison for a long time after the second marriage. Because it meant – well – '

'Yes, yes, Anna, I take your point.' In Mrs Napier's mind Lady Elizabeth slid down from Aristocracy to Degenerate Aristocracy. 'That still does not explain the card.'

Mrs Merchant was wriggling excitedly in her chair.

'It is obvious! He must have had an urgent message for Miss MacKenzie.'

*And since he did not leave one, he went upstairs to speak to her*, thought Mrs Napier.

Miss Merchant continued, 'I rather fancy he came to tell her that Lady Elizabeth is to attend the Duchess of Hamilton's ball on Tuesday. Oh, yes, I am sure that is what it will be. Lady Elizabeth is almost a personal friend of the Empress. It is only natural that she should receive an invitation.'

Miss Merchant was not clairvoyant; she kept a keen eye on the kind of gossip about high-born personages that is to be found in the daily press.

'Yes,' said Mrs Napier, 'the family maintains a house in Heriot Row, and Lady Elizabeth journeys frequently between Paris and Edinburgh. You may well be right about an invitation, Anna. And so – ' 'Lady Elizabeth will wish to see her niece,' interrupted Miss Merchant. She had the triumphant look of a dog that has retrieved a ball. If she had had a tail, she would have been wagging it.

'Ah.' Mrs Napier let out a long breath. In this limited area Miss Merchant's guesses were often accurate.

'Anna, you remember that distressing matter of Miss Mackenzie's essay . . .'

Mrs Napier explained that she had put Christabel into solitary confinement, although she did not go into details about their argument.

'Oh dear, oh dear,' commented Miss Merchant. 'How unfortunate that it should occur at this particular moment. Lady Elizabeth will wish to see her niece.'

'Quite apart from that, it is imperative that the situation be resolved before the Empress's visit. I am hopeful that a few hours on her own may have brought Miss MacKenzie to her senses. I should like you to go up to the studio now and ask her if she wishes to speak with me.'

Miss Merchant bit her lip. 'I, Mrs Napier? Would it not be better if you spoke to her yourself?'

That was exactly what Mrs Napier had no intention of doing. 'I think she may be less hostile towards you, Anna.'

Miss Merchant took the bait. She returned in a few minutes holding a small brass key.

'At first I had great hopes, but alas, no. Miss MacKenzie gave me this and asked me to tell you that the casket is on the chair beside your writing-desk.'

Mrs Napier then discovered the green leather box stamped with Eugénie's monogram and the French imperial eagle. There was also a letter from the Marquis de la Grange explaining why the diadem had been sent to the Scottish Institute.

The Lady Superintendent was as furious as Christabel had supposed she would be, but tried to make the best of it.

'I shall show the diadem to the girls at supper tonight, to induce them to be perfect in their parts. Still, it should not be worn until the Empress is honouring us with her presence.'

Miss Merchant's eyes were full of moisture. 'May I touch it?' she whispered as her hand hovered over the paste crown.

While she performed her act of adoration, Mrs Napier was searching for a way to tempt Christabel into submission that would not undermine her own dignity, and hit on a satisfactory plan. If the girl still refused to sign Miss Stephens' letter, she would tell her that she was profiting from a 'royal amnesty' and dispatch her to Heriot Row to see her aunt. To Christabel's friends her absence during the Empress's visit would seem the worst of all punishments.

Mrs Napier relaxed. That should take care of everything.

'Anna,' she said, 'I have decided to give that silly girl one more opportunity to come to her senses.'

Miss Merchant said, 'You are so kind, Mrs Napier. Kinder than Miss MacKenzie deserves after such conduct!'

Mrs Napier pushed away the compliment. 'I always try to

think of the major good, Anna. At such a joyful time for the Institute we must be generous.'

As the boarders passed through the hall on their way to the dining room they saw Christabel leaning on her heels against the wall. They went by with inquisitive looks; but they did not speak to her because Miss Merchant was on guard in the opposite corner.

Mrs Napier waited until she thought all the pupils would be in the dining room, and then came downstairs.

'Well, Christabel? Have you changed your mind about apologizing to Miss Stephens?'

Christabel's eyes were fixed on the tiled floor. She was gazing at the smaller laundry basket and a black leather bag that lay beside it near the entrance to the vestibule.

'I'm not going to sign that letter, so it is pointless to go on asking me.'

Mrs Napier gave a patient sigh. 'Then you will have to spend the night in the studio. Peggy will come to you later to make arrangements. Please return there immediately. You will go without supper.'

Christabel walked upstairs with the air of someone going to the scaffold. Miss Merchant was reminded of the ending of Mr Dickens' story which she had followed so eagerly some months before in *All The Year Round*.

But Christabel's air of resolution was a very flimsy sham. Later as she tried to fall asleep, she found herself becoming more and more wakeful. The chaise longue was well-stuffed and tightly buttoned; she was all alone, and everyone else had, so to speak, retreated to higher and safer ground. Christabel would never have admitted that this made her uneasy, but her solitude, combined with anger and the discomfort of her makeshift bed, brought on an almost sleepless night.

Miss Erroll had been too unwell to attend afternoon service, but at about five o'clock her headache began to subside. She remembered that she had to supervise the boarders' supper.

As in all tribal groups, certain traditions were maintained

at the Scottish Institute. There was one in particular which Mrs Napier detested.

Breakfast and luncheon brought all the boarders together; but as the little rats were sent to bed with bread and hot milk, only the fifteen or so older girls assembled for supper, and each governess took it in turn to supervise them at the large refectory table. The other teachers ate separately at the far end of the dining room.

The tradition was that the girls at the large table moved on one place each evening. This was to ensure that each of them should be obliged, several times a term, to practise the skills of social chit-chat with the member of staff on duty.

Mrs Napier did not object to this part of the arrangement; what she disliked was that the girl sitting at the right hand of the duty governess had to meet her at the foot of the hall stairs and escort her into the dining room. Mrs Napier thought this most unwomanly. She had a horror of mannishness in any form, and had banned breeches parts from the school theatricals.

Her efforts to abolish this custom had met solid resistance. She had transformed the ethos of the school; she had reduced the Directors to pliable puppets; but she had not been able to stop the girls from escorting the duty governess to supper. So she had given up the attempt, since the only thing Mrs Napier feared was losing her popularity with the girls and their parents.

On Sunday evening, Miss Erroll forced herself to dress and make her way downstairs, not even wondering who would be her escort. All such duties had become torture. The girl waiting in the hall was Maria Sinclair.

'A rather chilly evening, Miss Erroll, is it not?' said Maria. 'May I take you to the dining room?'

Miss Erroll did not reply, but this did not matter, because the escort – courteously opening doors and closing them behind the governess – was supposed to be preparing suitable topics of conversation for the forthcoming meal. Maria had no difficulty in making her choice. She was obsessed by the tableau for the Empress.

Miss Erroll stood stiffly at the head of the table, and muttered a few words in English. This was her one open defiance of Mrs Napier, who had decreed that grace before meals should be said in Latin. There was some shuffling as the space created by Christabel's absence rippled down to the foot of the table. Peggy served the meal.

The conversation Maria tried to launch became a relentless monologue. Miss Erroll could not bring herself to make a single comment on the Empress's visit. Maria told her that the little rats had now been brought into the tableau, which was to be imagined as taking place in the Forest of Fontainebleau. They would provide the leafy background against which Her Majesty, in pensive mood or perhaps riding her Spanish charger (this point had still to be decided) would encounter the spirits of Joan of Arc and Marie Antoinette.

'The development of our theme depends on what object the Empress is pleased to lend us, for naturally it will be the central feature of the tableau.'

So prattled on Maria. Elaine, who was sitting opposite, added, 'We are *fainting* for Mrs Napier to enter and show it!'

Miss Erroll had been lying down when Mrs Napier passed round this news. She spoke for the first time.

'Mrs Napier is coming down to the dining room?'

Elaine nodded eagerly.

Miss Erroll felt the girls could not be blamed for behaviour that should have been guided by their elders. She waited to see what would happen, twisting her hands nervously under the tablecloth.

The Lady Superintendent entered while they were still eating. She looked along the two rows of expectant faces, smiling, and went to sit in the place left empty by Christabel. She placed the casket tantalisingly in front of her.

Under Mrs Napier's eyes none of them dared gobble or push aside their plate unemptied. When Peggy had cleared the table Mrs Napier unlocked the casket.

'What I am about to show you is a replica of a much more valuable object. It is none the less precious for that, since it comes to us from the Empress herself. I shall keep it upstairs in my sitting room until it is used in the tableau.'

Mrs Napier lifted the lid and tilted the box slightly. The gasps and awestruck murmurs would have been most gratifying to Madame Pollet, had she been there.

'Would you *please* lift it out?' pleaded Maria.

Mrs Napier did so, turning the paste crown from side to side, so that the fire of its false brilliants dazzled their eyes. Then she replaced it on its velvet bed and handed the box to the girl on her right.

'Everyone may hold the casket and pass it to her neighbour. I know you will show proper respect.'

The diadem began to travel anti-clockwise round the table. Miss Erroll watched in mounting revulsion as it approached her. As the young faces bent over the casket she was reminded of something her father had told her about Romish churches: that grotesque relics were kept there of the so-called saints, and were worshipped with blasphemous fervour.

Now the diadem had reached Elaine.

'Do you wish to hold it too, Miss Erroll?'

The senior governess made a violent gesture towards Maria, and the casket passed her by. When it returned to Mrs Napier she took it over to the small table and showed it to the governesses. The girls filed out of the dining room, whispering excitedly. Miss Erroll hurried past them.

She retreated to her bedroom and sat with her head in her hands, suffering agonies of guilt for what she saw as her own cowardice. She should have spoken out to Mrs Napier when the girls left the dining room!

The voice of reason tried to persuade her to be more gentle with herself. Her attitudes to Roman Catholicism were already well-known to Mrs Napier. She had made many disapproving remarks on the subject. If she went farther and made some public protest, she would only bring scandal on the Institute. But Miss Erroll knew that reason – so plausible, so full of plain commonsense – was often the disguised voice of the Devil.

She picked up her bedside Bible, closed her eyes and

prayed. She recalled the way in which her father used to solve perplexities of conscience. Nowadays it was considered old-fashioned, or even superstitious. Miss Erroll opened the book at random and planted her finger on the page. When she looked down she was touching verses 14 and 15 in Chapter 10 of Matthew:

> And whosoever shall not receive you, nor hear your words, when ye depart out of that house or city, shake off the dust of your feet.
> Verily I say unto you, it shall be more tolerable for the land of Sodom and Gomorrha in the day of judgment, than for that city.

Miss Erroll's pallid face became even whiter. The conclusion was as irrefutable as one of her algebraic equations. She must depart before the Empress arrived. She would write a short letter which she would post after she had left the building.

Miss Erroll sighed and began to prepare for bed. She was not happy, but at least she felt more at peace with her conscience.

If she could have left the matter there, she might have had a sound night's sleep. But her logical mind insisted on proceeding to the next stage. Practical difficulties began to elbow their way forward. She was filled with anguish at the thought of leaving the place that had been her home for twenty-five years. Miss Erroll tried to drown the clamour of these voices in sleep, but the panic they had stirred up would not be smothered.

Her dreams were vivid and terrible. Several times she awoke during the night and then fell back into abysses of nightmare. Her father was pursuing her with a flaming crown; she ran away from him along the banks of the River Jordan; but he caught her up and threw her to the ground. He towered over her and his face changed into Mrs Napier's. He forced the crown down on her head; then suddenly vanished. In her dream Miss Erroll stood up shrieking at the pain; she tore off the crown and threw it into the river, where it whirled and hissed in clouds of steam.

These events recurred several times, but in fragmented segments and out of order. Once Miss Erroll thought she was awake and saw the crown surrounded by water; another time it seemed that her door was being broken down with axes. She sat up in bed and screamed. Or was that part of the nightmare as well?

# MONDAY

On weekdays, the Institute door was unlocked each morning at six o'clock. The servants put out ashes and refuse before the boarders and governesses came downstairs for breakfast. From seven o'clock onwards the tradesmen began to deliver groceries and other supplies. On Monday morning the first to appear was the porter who collected the two small hampers of laundry.

This Monday, Peggy followed him out to the street with the leather bag into which she had put Jane Rintoul's nightgown.

'Take this with you, Johnny. Here's the address.'

Johnny advanced with a toothy leer. 'Gie's a kiss then. A favour for a favour.'

With a grimace Peggy complied, and the bag was trundled off beside the hampers. It wasn't as if she was stealing, Peggy told herself. She'd wash the nightgown and put it back with the clean laundry when it was returned on Wednesday.

Breakfast was at half-past seven. A little after eight o'clock the boarders met in the salon for hymns and prayers led by Mrs Napier. Afterwards, they usually waited in their classrooms for the hundred day girls and the boarders who lived out. Lessons began at nine.

When Mary went to wake Mrs Napier she found her mistress already dressed, and busy at her writing-desk.

'Would you please bring up some tea and toast, Mary? I shall not be eating in the dining room.'

Mary went to tidy the bedroom and then returned. The room was very cold.

'Shall I see to the fire, ma'am?'

'Yes, please, after you have brought up my breakfast tray. Then tell Peggy I should like to speak to her.'

Mrs Napier was always careful to conciliate those around her if it did not interfere with her plans. She continued, 'Forgive me for being so mysterious. We are to have a very special visitor today.' The news would shortly be out, she thought. Mary went off to create a stir in the kitchen.

Mr Murdo was disgruntled when his daughter brought him Mrs Napier's letters to deliver round the city. He took Monday morning off in compensation for the odd jobs for the Institute which he generally did on Sunday afternoon.

At the end of hymns and prayers in the salon, Mrs Napier told everyone to remain there. She sent Miss Merchant to summon the day girls as they arrived. From her dais, she smiled down at the sea of restless heads which became more closely packed as the pupils thronged into the salon. When most of them were present, she held up her hand.

'Ladies, the Scottish Institute is about to receive a great honour. This afternoon we shall be visited by Her Imperial Majesty, Eugénie, Empress of the French. Please explain to your papas and mamas that this was confirmed only yesterday. The young ladies in residence have devised a welcome for Her Majesty.'

'What about us?' shouted Amelia, bouncing up and down.

'I am coming to that, Amelia. I invite you to line the staircase during the Empress's visit. Your good manners will ensure that there is no unseemly crowding around the Imperial presence. If you wish to join us, return between three and half-past three of the clock. Now you may go home.'

Pandemonium erupted; the pupils hurled themselves towards the doorway and the room was empty within a few moments.

Mrs Napier remarked to Miss Merchant, 'Their poor mamas will be paraded round every dressmaker in the city.'

She then hurried out to intercept the Directors and tell them why the day's lessons had been cancelled.

Very few showed any regret. They were conscientious men;

but commuting between the several schools at which they taught left them no time to relax between lessons, or even to eat at midday. Most of them carried rolls in their pockets which they munched as they trudged round the city.

The only person genuinely displeased was the singing teacher, Robert Cargill. He had hoped to learn what arrangements Peggy had made for them to spend the night together – or as much of it as he dared stay out for. The whole routine of the school seemed to have been upset. Some workmen were already laying a purple carpet on the treads of the staircase; others were hanging enormous oil paintings on the walls.

Mr Cargill wondered if he dared go upstairs to look for Peggy. She usually made the beds after breakfast. He met no one on the two upper flights, but just as he was nerving himself to look inside the pupils' bedrooms a door opened behind him. Twisting round guiltily, he recognised the strained face of Miss Erroll. She was still in her nightgown. She stared as if she did not know him, and withdrew with the same glassy expression.

*Odd old crow*, thought Robert Cargill. Deciding it would be prudent to retreat, he went down the basement stairs towards the kitchen, where he hovered for a while. He used this exit into the garden as a short cut to one of his other schools; indeed this was how he had first met Peggy, at the beginning of October.

He decided he might as well leave through the coach-house anyway, and was half-way down the path when Peggy emerged into the garden.

'Tonight,' she whispered, smiling at his surprised delight. 'Here it's. We're to be there at half seven.' She intended to arrive a little before him.

Mr Cargill took the piece of paper which Peggy thrust at him and stuffed it into his pocket. He winked at her as they parted, hoping he'd be able to read the address. Peggy was proud that she could write as well as read; he never had the heart to tell her that her mispelt scrawls were almost illegible.

Miss Erroll had awakened late that morning. Her head was brimming with a dull, heavy ache. She felt utterly exhausted. There were cracks of light behind the window shutters; but she was too tired to open them. She struggled against the languor that was pulling her back to sleep, and put her feet on the floor. It was too dark to see the face of her watch. She groped her way to the door, where she pulled her wrapper off its hook, and draped it over her shoulders. She heard foot-steps outside. Her fingers seemed quite nerveless but, after a few tries, she managed to turn the doorknob.

Her confused mind pulled out a memory from Sunday afternoon. That would be Peggy coming up the stair; she would ask her for some tea. Miss Erroll opened the door and looked out. She found herself gazing at a strange man, whom on other days she had known as the music master, Mr Cargill.

Miss Erroll had stared at him blankly. She retreated into her room, stumbled back to the bed and lay down again. In a few moments she had returned to deep sleep.

By eleven o'clock on Monday morning Mrs Napier could walk round her domain with confidence. The requests sent out through Mr Murdo had transformed the Institute.

For almost three hours horse-drawn vans had been deliver-ing paintings, furniture, carpeting, rugs and miscellaneous ornaments to adorn the building for Eugénie's visit. Most of this was borrowed. Mrs Napier had leaned heavily on all her connections in the city. The orders were made up in rather a hurry: this resulted in three St Sebastians and a valuable Van Dyck appearing beside some glum city fathers. Whytock's had sent a mahogany commode upholstered in purple velvet for Eugénie's retiring room. Three florists had yielded up their complete stock of forced blooms; and Fräulein Gitsch toiled all morning to arrange them.

Mrs Napier toured the building for about an hour. She smiled, encouraged, but did not interfere. Whenever she met Miss Stephens, she pursed her lips, to remind her that she would be dealt with later.

She was irritated by Miss Erroll's absence. Mary had been

sent to the senior governess's room, and came back to report that she could not be roused.

'I thought her eyes were open, but the room's that mirk I wasna sure. I just let her be.'

The two women exchanged looks. They had a tacit understanding, but Mary never took advantage of it.

'Oh, very well,' said Mrs Napier. 'We shall have to manage without Miss Erroll. Thank you, Mary.'

Mrs Napier returned to her sitting room to look over the mail delivered by the second post. She scrutinised all letters coming into the building, even those for members of staff. The last, addressed to herself, had been posted in Paris. After reading it, Mrs Napier sat back in her chair and smiled with relief. Surely some Higher Power had guided Anna Merchant to warn her about Lady Elizabeth's arrival.

Mrs Napier had no doubt that the harmonious functioning of the Institute was included in the wishes of that Power and that she best knew how to achieve it. 'The major good' was her own phrase for the welfare of her little community. Crushing Christabel MacKenzie would definitely be for the major good.

Mary entered the sitting room.

'Ma'am, Miss Stewart is asking if you want her to stay and help. She's waiting in the hall.'

On Mondays and Wednesdays, because of the timing of her classes, Eleanor did not turn up until eleven a.m. She had asked permission to use these few hours for her work at the dispensaries. Mrs Napier had been unable to find any reason to deny such a worthy request.

Now she saw Eleanor's message as further proof that she was being guided from above. She sent for her.

As Eleanor mounted the staircase, half a dozen people told her about the Empress's visit. She also found out that Christabel was in good health, although no one was sure where she was. Eleanor was immensely cheered.

As soon as she entered the room, Mrs Napier said, 'Miss Stewart, I wish you to carry out a small task for me, which concerns Miss MacKenzie . . . I am pleased by the good reports I hear of your work. I am hopeful that the Directors may soon offer you a permanent post with us.'

This was unexpected. Eleanor had already decided that at the end of her training she would teach elsewhere. The resolve had been made on the day she had overheard Jane Rintoul and her friends as they dangled over the staircase well between lessons.

'*I* don't think she's a lady,' came down in Jane's ringing tones. 'Her father's only a farmer.'

'She's nice, though,' suggested Maria.

'She's cruel, and she hates animals! She took away the cream I put out for Sir Perceval.' This was Mrs Rogers' scare-mouse, a large white cat with bulging eyes, which waddled round the school snarling from indigestion brought on by the pupils' tit-bits.

Eleanor had smiled to herself, remembering how often she had come off the hill in February tingling from the sleet, with slimy, exhausted lambs dangling over her arms.

Other uncomplimentary remarks followed; but Eleanor turned quickly into her classroom and shut the door. She knew that the arrogance of these pampered young women was rooted in the narrowness of their lives. In a few years' time their eyes might open. But term after term, SINDOG would confront her with girls like Jane Rintoul. And Eleanor could not swallow that.

Now her long silence was misinterpreted by Mrs Napier. 'You must not undervalue yourself, my dear. We all appreciate how hard you work for the Institute.'

Eleanor managed to reply that she was glad to merit such a mark of confidence. What service was Mrs Napier going to demand, to justify such an open bribe?

'I mentioned your future only to show my trust in you. I am appealing to you to help us in a sad dilemma. Miss MacKenzie has behaved very foolishly, and refuses to make amends.'

Eleanor wondered what new clash had occurred. She had tried to help Christabel pick her way through a great many incidents in her first year at the school. But Mrs Napier only said that she would leave Christabel to tell her own story. As her friend, Eleanor might have more influence on her than the other governesses.

'I may not wish to intervene in this dispute, Mrs Napier.'

'Oh, I have great confidence in your good sense, once you have heard the details. I want you to escort her to her aunt's house in Heriot Row.'

Mrs Napier explained that Lady Elizabeth was making a brief visit to Edinburgh and wished to see her niece. Mrs Napier had not yet written her reply. Perhaps Eleanor would take this with her?

Eleanor's impatience was growing. 'Where is Miss MacKenzie?'

'She is in the studio. You may find her in a somewhat agitated state. I have been obliged to separate her from her friends since yesterday morning.'

'*Yesterday*!'

Mrs Napier raised her eyebrows at the tone. Eleanor did not ask permission to leave. She said she would wait downstairs for Mrs Napier's letter, and hurried along the landing to the studio.

Christabel was hunched over a stool by the fire. An untouched breakfast tray lay beside her. When she turned to see who had come in, her face was bleak and hostile. She leapt to her feet and ran across the room.

'Eleanor! I am glad to see you!'

She thrust her head against Eleanor's shoulder, and uttered a sound like a dry sob as she clung to her friend even more fiercely than when they had first met after the summer vacation.

'It's all right, darling. Mrs Napier says I am to take you to Heriot Row. Your aunt is travelling from Paris.'

Although the pavements were empty, they walked along the street in complete silence, occasionally touching hands. Christabel rushed into Number Forty-seven calling out to the housekeeper.

Mrs Veitch was opening up a few rooms for Elizabeth's expected visit. As Ranald boarded with Captain Orr, she was the sole occupant of a large town house, the last in an austere Georgian terrace near Moray Place. None of the servants she hired would live in, as they could not endure the silence of the empty building. Mrs Veitch scolded a little when she heard that another bedroom had to be prepared for Christabel.

Christabel said, 'Could you bring us some luncheon, Bessie? Just a tray in the morning room.'

Mrs Veitch had another grumble at how *thrang* she was, but produced a meal of sorts very quickly. Between emotion at seeing Christabel again, and shyness in these strange and rather grand surroundings, Eleanor found it difficult to eat. Everything she had been going to say died in her mouth. Christabel was cheerful and ravenous. She told Eleanor why she had been confined to the studio, and said how delighted she would be to see her aunt.

They heard the basement door open and close, followed by the patter of footsteps up to the pavement. The area gate banged.

'That's Mrs Veitch going off to give her orders to the tradesmen.'

Eleanor asked, 'When will your aunt arrive?'

'Some time this evening, I suppose.' Christabel pushed away her tray and moved closer. 'Eleanor?'

'Yes?'

'How can you ever forgive me? What a beast I am!'

The barriers broke. Eleanor protested, no, it was she who had been at fault. She should not have thrust Dr Blackwell's letter so hastily on Christabel.

Christabel pulled her over to the fire; there were one or two hours of daylight left, but they closed the curtains, drew even nearer, and the afternoon passed in delicious reconciliation. Eleanor did tell Christabel about the tableau; but it is doubtful whether she gave a single thought to the instructions she had received from Mrs Napier.

It was almost midday when Mr McLevy heaved himself out of his fireside chair and put away the book he had been reading for the past two hours. It was a translation of Vidocq's memoirs. The life of this famous chief of the Paris police was far more interesting to James McLevy than the task set him by Lieutenant McLellan. Besides, he felt a strong reluctance to tramp down to the Scottish Institute. There had been a biting frost on Sunday night.

But duty still held its iron grip; McLevy put on his outdoor clothes and wound a muffler round his neck. He asked his neighbour to take in Jeanie Brash.

The deadness of those terraces and crescents behind Princes Street always struck a chill to his heart. Even the street traders' cries were swallowed into the silence of empty streets.

Today Moray Place was unusually lively. McLevy stopped to knock out his pipe against a boot-scraper and glanced at the upper windows. The servants' heads were bobbing to and fro like a puppet show, peeping down at the activity in the street below. A couple of horse-drawn vans were pulling away from the Institute. There was a double stream of move-ment in and out of the big black door; and an amazing number of passers-by were loitering by the railings. Maybe it'd not be so dreich after all.

McLevy was introduced to Mrs Napier. He said he was in charge of the Empress's safety for this particular visit.

Mrs Napier looked at his woollen muffler and thick boots, and then handed him over to Miss Merchant.

Miss Merchant told him that the Directors and the gover-nesses, and any of the day pupils who wished to be present, would be in the building during the visit, as well as all the boarding pupils.

'How late will all these people be admitted, ma'am?'

'Not much after half-past three of the clock. We think Her Majesty will arrive at four, when she has completed her afternoon visit to the Castle.'

Miss Merchant felt ill at ease with this big, lumbering man and his thick Irish brogue. Surely Superintendent Linton might have sent someone more, well, *gentlemanly*?

They went through the public areas of the upper storeys. Miss Merchant hesitated outside the door of the room which had been fitted up as a boudoir. Whytock's splendid purple-upholstered commode had been installed inside it. She fluttered her hands. 'I do not know whether . . .'

'Away with you,' said McLevy jovially, amused at Miss Merchant's genteel scruples. 'If you only knew the places I've had to push my nose into!' He walked into the room and sniffed the heavy scent of lilies and carnations.

'Very bonny.' He threw up the lower sash of the window, and leaned across the wrought-iron balcony overhanging the garden.

'Please do not let the cold air blow on the flowers!'

McLevy withdrew his head and shut the window. 'I wanted a keek at your back premises. I suppose there's an outside door down there?'

'Yes, by the kitchen. It will be locked during the Empress's visit.' Miss Merchant was pleased that she had anticipated the cause of Mr McLevy's concern. 'Her Majesty will linger longest in the salon. The young ladies are to present a tableau.'

'A – ?' McLevy had not caught the word.

In the tone she used to her class of twelve-year-olds, Miss Merchant explained, 'A tableau is a short dramatic scene, or, so to speak, a sun picture of some significant historical moment. Come this way, please, and I shall show you.'

Fifteen little rats were posing in nymph-like attitudes around the salon. Miss Stephens was walking round to correct the droop of a head here, and there the arch of an upraised arm.

'They devised it all themselves,' whispered Miss Merchant. 'Of course, they needed a little help, and they have not yet assumed the costumes they will wear in the performance.'

McLevy was fascinated by the concentration of the small, wobbling figures.

At the far end of the salon, furniture had been lifted on to the dais to form three different levels, and draped with crimson plush curtains. Four older girls lolled across this structure, and disdained to notice the visitor. Miss Stephens told the nymphs to rest, and went across to the main grouping of the tableau.

'Sit more erect, Jane dear. Try to radiate charm and regal majesty.'

'I haven't been given my spear,' said Elaine.

'Take the window pole instead. Yes, that looks very nice.'

The tallest girl mounted to the summit of the dais and stared in a haughty way at the chandelier.

'Smile, Jane, *smile*,' urged Miss Stephens. 'Her Majesty is renowned for the sweetness of her smile. Joan of Arc, draw near and kneel at the Empress's feet.'

Elaine approached and sank to her knees with her hands clasped round the window pole. Miss Stephens clapped.

'Oh, excellent! Alice, dear, La Belle France does not move at all. Now, Maria, this is your moment. To you is entrusted the climax of the whole tableau.'

McLevy saw the girl spoken to mince towards the dais with her hands held out from her sides.

'Miss Sinclair represents that unhappy queen, Marie Antoinette,' whispered Miss Merchant.

Still holding up her imaginary panniers, Maria mounted the various levels of the dais until she stood in front of Jane, bowed her head, and moved her hands towards the other girl.

McLevy chuckled. 'I know the Queen of France lost her head, but why is she handing it to to the Empress?'

'Please, Mr McLevy, do not mock our humble efforts! Miss Sinclair places the Grecian diadem on the Imperial head. Patriotism and beauty are making their obeisance to Her Majesty. Surely you understand the symbolism?'

McLevy had to keep a twitch from his mouth. He presumed that the diadem referred to was some tinsel imitation of the crown of France.

Miss Merchant was vexed that the detective did not appear impressed by the theme of the tableau. After all, it was that which hallowed their little entertainment.

'Why do you not remain with us for some refreshment,

Mr McLevy? Then you can see the afternoon rehearsal when they are dressed in costume.'

'Very thoughtful of you, ma'am. I'd be pleased to accept.'

At half-past one, he was sitting in Mrs Rogers' own chair, contentedly ruminating over the mince and potatoes with which she had so generously heaped his plate. He was talking to the cook as she piped and filled the delicacies that would be offered to Eugénie during her visit.

Rarely did she have such an opportunity to show off her skills with teabreads, scones, and pastries. Not that the Empress would actually taste them. Mrs Rogers' hopes did not rise as high as that. Enough that they should be offered, and that the Imperial eyes should rest on her creation. Then the young ladies would eat them after supper.

Mrs Rogers herself was much more garrulous than the servant maid, Mary, who was keeping an eye on McLevy, her features curiously similar to Mrs Napier's. Just like dogs beginning to resemble their owners, he thought. Mary had a rather throaty Glasgow accent.

At the half-hour Peggy suddenly appeared at the kitchen door with an urgent message for McLevy. 'Sir! Mrs Napier wants you upby in her sitting room.'

Puffing from his large meal, Mr McLevy hauled himself upstairs after Peggy. He had to make his way through a mass of excited pupils who were jumping up and down the staircase. From the landing window he glimpsed a crowd of carriages already occupying the best view-points for watching the Empress's arrival. Despite the chilliness of the air, most of them were open. Many of the overcoated and mantled occupants were eating out of luncheon baskets.

On first meeting Mrs Napier, McLevy had been struck by her calm but powerful self-confidence. He'd seldom met it to such degree in any man, and never in a woman. Yet in a little over an hour something had changed. A stiffness in the way she stood beside her large desk, perhaps.

'Mr McLevy.' She lifted a green leather box. 'This is the casket in which Madame Pollet brought me a replica of the

Empress's Grecian diadem. The diadem was lent to us by Her Majesty for our tableau. A few moments ago, I was about to send for Miss Rintoul, so that she might try it on, and I opened the box. The diadem has been stolen.'

No mere tinsel crown, then! An awkward situation for the poor lady. McLevy's sympathy did not strike very deep.

'The box was not even locked. I never dreamed that in this establishment . . .' For once, Mrs Napier was unable to finish her sentence.

'Quite. What are you going to do, ma'am?'

'What are *you* going to do, Mr McLevy?'

After questioning her for a few minutes, Mr McLevy said, 'I doubt if it's left the building. Anyone who knew it was here is aware that it's only paste. Maybe one of the lassies has taken it for a prank. Out of a grudge that's she's not to be in the play, or some other ill-will.'

Mrs Napier instantly thought of Christabel.

'I could search the building for you. Let me call a constable off his beat, and give us half an hour. If anyone asks, you can make out that it's a precaution for the Empress's visit. I'll not let on what I'm really after.'

Mrs Napier reluctantly agreed. Peggy was sent out to intercept the officer who patrolled the western end of Heriot Row. In the meantime McLevy searched Mrs Napier's rooms.

There was a short connecting passage between the sitting room and the bedroom, with a door at each end. Someone could easily have removed the diadem while she slept without disturbing her. No doors in her apartment were locked at night, in case she had to be roused for some emergency. Mrs Napier's dining room also opened off the sitting room; but neither this room nor her bedroom had external doors.

Mrs Napier said that she had risen at five that morning to write some letters connected with the Empress's visit. She had been in and out of her sitting room ever since. The diadem must have been taken during the six or so hours when she had been sleeping.

Mr McLevy said he was willing to bet that one of the girls had taken the jewel to frighten the grown-ups and would make sure it was found before the Empress arrived. It was unlikely that the 'thief' had taken it to a bedroom, unless there were several of them in on the prank. She must have hidden it in one of the empty public rooms while everyone was sleeping. As she would want to get back to bed as quickly as possible, it was likely that she had concealed the diadem on one of the upper floors.

'That is, supposing one of your lassies did take the jewel,' concluded Mr McLevy. He said he would begin with the attics.

At this point PC Morrison was brought in by Peggy. On most days the appearance of a police officer in his shiny top hat and belted greatcoat would have thrown the Institute into a ferment; but in today's excitement he walked upstairs almost unnoticed.

'There's an entertainment to be put on for the Empress, and some lassie has lost the trinket she's to wear in it,' McLevy informed him. 'The rub is, it seems the Empress knows she's to wear this geegaw and they think she might ask why it isn't there. Most unlikely, but you and me, Morrison, will just have to raik through the place until we find it.'

The constable grinned. 'I'm no complaining. Yon's a bitter wind outby.'

'Aye, well, let's get on with it.' McLevy explained that they were looking for a kind of imitation crown. He did not describe it as exactly as Mrs Napier had to him.

Mary showed them round the attics. There was no gas piped up here, so she had brought an oil-lamp. McLevy disposed of the attics in five minutes.

'Call that a search?' said Mary afterwards. 'I'd do better myself. It must be an elephant you've lost.'

'You'd be wasting your time, lassie.' He wiped a finger along a trunk and held it up. 'Look at this stour. Nobody's been in here for weeks.'

They went through the pupils' bedrooms with equal speed. One small room McLevy entered was in darkness. He was into it before Mary could stop him.

92

'Sorry to disturb you,' he said, backing out. Miss Erroll did not reply.

On the floor below, McLevy had to retreat from the art studio as cries of dismay greeted his entry. The performers in the tableau were dressing for their final rehearsal. PC Morrison grinned again, this time at the look on McLevy's face.

The library was adjacent to the studio, and also faced over the garden. McLevy asked Morrison to help him sweep the books off the shelves.

'Wha's to put all they back?' asked Mary in horror.

'If we find what we're looking for, your mistress will be happy to replace them herself.'

The bareness of the classrooms on the two floors below speeded up their search in that area. The dining room had no place of concealment except two wall cupboards.

'That's that, then,' said McLevy, after a quick look round the remaining rooms on the ground floor. He had already learned that no one had a key to the partition door between Nine and Ten except Mrs Napier, and that the door was always locked by ten o'clock.

When he reported their lack of success, Mrs Napier listened without reaction. Her only comment was, 'I thank you for your efforts, Mr McLevy. Are you sure you have made a thorough search?'

'Aye, if one of your lassies lifted it, I'd stake my reputation on it, ma'am.'

Mrs Napier took the guard off her tongue for a moment.

'Is that worth as much as the reputation of the Institute?' This shambling, elderly man did not look very efficient.

PC Morrison glowered loyally. 'Mr McLevy's the best thief-taker in the whole country – and that's London as well! He's nabbed thousands of them.'

When the constable had left, McLevy leaned by the cheek of the fireplace and took out his pipe and tobacco. He whipped a spill from his pocket and stooped to light it at the fire. It was a measure of Mrs Napier's anxiety that she did not rebuke this behaviour.

McLevy told Mrs Napier that it would be difficult to extend his search of the building without making folk suspect there was more in play than the Empress's safety. Should they not wait and see if the diadem was replaced before Her Majesty's arrival?

'Is there nothing else you can suggest, Mr McLevy?'

Yes, said the detective, he could question all the people who lived or worked in the Institute; but his examination was unlikely to be concluded, much less produce any results, before four o'clock that day.

Alternatively, it might be worthwhile hiring a cab to make a quick tour round the pawnbrokers known to deal in stolen goods. If the diadem *had* been stolen by someone outwith the school who thought it genuine, the thief would either leave town with it, take it to a jeweller to be broken up, or put it out to the uncles. Mr McLevy added that he could insert a notice into the police list of missing property which was printed off daily for all the Station-Houses.

Mrs Napier replied, 'I could not follow your last suggestion unless I had the Empress's permission.'

She thought a moment. Then she said with no sign of emotion, 'I must thank you for your endeavours, but it seems I have no choice. I must inform Madame Pollet. Nevertheless, I should be grateful if you would search the pawnshops. Any possibility, however slight, is worth attending to.'

McLevy admired such clear-headedness. She did not howl or rave, or try to dodge the consequences.

'I shall have to report back to Superintendent Linton, ma'am. Then I'll look in on the uncles. I should be back here by half-past three. If I have made no progress by then, perhaps you will let me know whether you wish me to question the folk that slept here last night.'

Mrs Napier pulled the bell-rope, and demonstrated her gratitude by having Mary walk up the three flights of stairs so that she could walk down again to show Mr McLevy out.

*The Empress, attended by the Comtesse de Montebello, Madame de Saulcy, and the Marquis de la Grange, left*

94

Douglas's Hotel about half-past eleven, in a carriage and pair, drove to Holyrood, and then proceeded round the Queen's Drive.

On arriving at Dunsappie Loch, the royal party left the carriage, and walked along the Drive for some distance, but the grass being wet and slippery, the Empress did not attempt the ascent. In a few minutes Her Majesty drove back to the Palace. The Empress expressed the greatest possible interest in all the relics and memorials of the hapless Mary of Scotland. On the royal party emerging from the gate, a loud cheer was given, and much curiosity was displayed – in some cases, we fear, in an unwarrantably intrusive fashion – to obtain a sight of the Empress. Her Majesty returned to the hotel by the same route as she had taken leaving it.

Shortly after two o'clock, the Empress and suite again left the hotel and drove to the Castle.

Colonel Favé did not accompany the party. While the Empress was at Holyrood, he was arranging the afternoon tour of the Castle. After luncheon he pointed out to Her Majesty, with the utmost respect, that it might appear provocative if he, an artillery expert, should be seen touring a fortification that bristled with gun batteries. Her Majesty needed no reminder that England was consumed with jealous fear of France. Would it not be tactful to absent himself?

Eugénie gave her equerry a derisive look and suggested another reason for the request. The Empress, reputed to be immune to sexual passion herself, had a very racy tongue.

The colonel had in fact planned only to avoid the boredom of continual sightseeing. He was going to spend the afternoon with a cigar and some newspapers, and then rejoin the Imperial party for the school visit at four o'clock.

A little later, as he relaxed in the fragrant blue haze of his Havana, he felt his arm shaken violently. Madame Pollet was bending over his armchair.

'Colonel Favé, they have lost it!' She thrust at him Mrs Napier's letter, delivered a few minutes before by Mary.

Favé smoked on as he read, irritated at the interruption,

but on reaching the words 'police' and 'news journals', he sprang to his feet, grinding out the cigar.

He beckoned a hotel servant and ordered a cab. He ran upstairs to fetch his coat and hat himself, and put them on as he ran down again. Pepa was waiting for him in the foyer of the hotel with Mary.

Disregarding protocol, the colonel waved the two women into his cab. When they arrived at the Institute Favé leapt up the stairs to Mrs Napier's sitting room so fast that Mary could scarcely keep up to direct him. Madame Pollet was not far behind.

Favé introduced himself, and burst out, 'Madame, what a terrible affair! I tremble for the consequences.'

Mrs Napier stared as the colonel began to pace up and down the carpet tearing at his moustache in a way that would have made his valet weep.

If anyone needed to fear the consequences, surely it was herself? If the diadem was not found, so far from securing the Empress's patronage, Mrs Napier might soon not be superintending the Institute at all.

She said, 'The detective officer who searched the building has not given up hopes of retrieving the diadem before Her Majesty arrives.'

Favé came to a halt in front of her and wiped his face with a blue silk handkerchief.

'Madame, madame! As you English say, goddamn for the diadem. *That* is of no significance. But the police – the newspapers. What folly! It is not to be thought of!'

'Ha,' cried Pepa, 'you dare so to speak of the Grecian diadem?'

Favé brushed her aside and turned once more to Mrs Napier, twisting the damp handkerchief in his hands.

Madame must permit him to explain. Itself, this trumpery morsel of paste, it was nothing. But let the journals breathe one hint that it was lost – what a scandal! The peace of Europe might be shattered.

'Oh, come now, sir!'

The colonel went on to declaim a speech more suitable for

the Chamber of Deputies. Mrs Napier caught 'His Holiness', 'Signor Garibaldi', 'delicate balance' and other impressive phrases, but did not grasp the root of Colonel Favé's anxiety.

'Finally, Madame Napier, should any scandal arise during the Empress's visit to Scotland, reflect what use might be made of it by His Majesty's enemies at court! You will not forget that your country and mine are this very week to sign an important commercial treaty. Should any ill-will be stirred up by some insult to the Empress . . .' The colonel's rhetoric trickled away on this last terrible possibility.

Mrs Napier was not unimpressed by the international dimension that had been added to her own problem.

'Your strictures are well-deserved, sir. Yet what should we do? It is now some minutes after half-past two. What happens if the Empress asks why her diadem does not appear in the tableau?'

Favé looked at Pepa. 'Will you tell Her Majesty, Madame Pollet?'

Pepa's eyes flashed murder at Mrs Napier. She began to rant in a mixture of French and Spanish.

'I have an idea,' said Mrs Napier, when Pepa ran out of breath. 'Is there another replica of the diadem?'

Favé translated this question to make sure that Pepa had understood. Yes, that was possible, said the maid. But it would be in the vaults of the jeweller who made the replicas of the crown jewels.

Mrs Napier said, 'I suggest that you send an electric telegraph to Paris through the French consul in Edinburgh. The jewel could be sent here by special messenger.'

'Madame, all that would take at least twenty-four hours!'

'I am aware of that, colonel. You must persuade the Empress to postpone her visit to us. It is the only way.'

Favé kissed Mrs Napier's hand enthusiastically.

'Ah, madame, had you been with us, we should not have lost that little skirmish at Waterloo! Come, Madame Pollet. There is no time to lose.'

Once she was alone, Mrs Napier allowed herself to give

way to her anxiety. She went to the window and gazed down at the large crowd gathered in Moray Place.

'Thou hast shown me all the kingdoms of the earth,' she murmured.

Mrs Napier did not believe in the Devil; but she had no doubt that wickedness was constantly battering at the citadel of the righteous. Could it be, she asked herself, that what simpler minds termed the Evil One was now luring her into international politics in order to bring disgrace on her school? Was she herself to be the instrument of its ruin?

Mrs Napier sank to her knees beside the empty casket and prayed.

Ten minutes later she had regained her tranquillity. She went down to the salon to watch the final rehearsal of the tableau. No one would have known that anything was amiss.

Jane Rintoul looked round expectantly. Mrs Napier reminded Jane that she would not bring down the diadem until the tableau was about to begin. She reproved her for voicing her disappointment.


Pepa and Colonel Favé jolted along George Street in their hired cab. Suddenly the vehicle took a sharp right-hand turn and began to clatter down to Princes Street.

'Where are you taking me?' cried Pepa. 'I have to prepare the gown Her Majesty will wear for dinner.'

Favé put away the notebook in which he had been writing. 'Evidently. But you must come to the Castle with me, Madame Pollet. If we cannot postpone this visit, the truth must be told. We dare not wait until Her Majesty arrives at that school.'

'I shall not do it!' screamed Pepa. 'That stupid woman must tell the Empress herself.'

'Courage, my little Pepa. If I find some means to keep the Empress away from the school, *you* must take my message to the consul. I cannot leave Her Majesty's side.'

'There may not be another replica of the diadem. Have you thought of that?'

'Of course. In that case, Thélin must send us the original. That is what my message says. It is encoded.'

The cab drove on to the Castle Esplande. Colonel Favé stepped out near the entrance gates. Inside them was drawn up a detachment of the 78th Highlanders in full ceremonial dress. Their commander Colonel Ewart advanced hesitantly to meet the cab. Pepa began to climb out after Favé. As soon as her foot emerged, the pipes and drums burst into *Partant Pour La Syrie*, an anthem composed by the Emperor's mother to replace the republican *Marseillaise*. Although out of uniform, Favé automatically came to the salute.

At the same moment the two colonels realised that something was wrong. Colonel Ewart made a quick gesture at the band, and the music droned to a halt.

'Her Majesty is not with you?' asked the Scottish colonel.

Favé exclaimed, 'Has the Empress not yet arrived?'

In step, they moved out of earshot of the guard of honour.

'We have been expecting Her Majesty for almost an hour,' said Ewart. 'What has happened?'

'I have no idea, *mon colonel*. The Empress left the hotel at two o'clock. It is very strange.'

'Are you wanting me to stay, sir?' called out the cab driver. Favé said yes, and asked Pepa to return inside.

The two colonels continued pacing up and down the Esplanade. The guard was told to stand at ease, and the pipers and drummers let their instruments hang slackly by their sides. The minutes passed. Favé glanced at his watch. *What luck*, he thought. When Colonel Ewart was looking the other way he even crossed himself, thanking *le bon Dieu* who had arranged this delay. Only through divine intervention could a carriage spend an hour driving from St Andrew Square to the Castle. At least another hour would go by in touring the points of interest. The Empress would be fatigued. She would need to rest. He would insist on it. She could not possibly visit that accursed school today.

He went back to Madame Pollet and hissed, as he gave her his note, 'Tell him to take you to the French consul!'

The cab drove Pepa away from the Esplanade.

A few minutes after three, Eugénie arrived. She was in excellent humour, laughing at their mistake. She apologised to Colonel Ewart for her late arrival – 'but figure to yourself, my dear colonel! It was an error, the most extraordinary!'

The hotel interpreter had misunderstood his directions. He had asked the driver to proceed to the *fort* (for this was the word used to him by de la Grange, rather than the correct term, château).

On alighting at their destination, Eugénie had been disappointed by the squat little building, although the guns were indeed *formidable*. She had asked to be shown the crown of Scotland. The astonished artillery officers told her that she had arrived at Leith Fort.

While the Empress was being shown round the castle, James McLevy returned to the Institute. He reported that the diadem had not found its way to any of the pawnshops.

By a quarter-past four, the crowd outside the Institute was getting restless. There was a constant, funeral-like circling of carriages round Moray Place as drivers tried to keep their horses warm. Darkness was falling. Favé appeared out of the dusk with a grave face which kept bursting into a smile. Mrs Napier was standing in the hall with some of the Directors and patrons. Favé said that the Empress was desolated, but she was obliged to postpone her visit until Wednesday.

Mrs Napier thanked him, sent both the colonel and Mr McLevy away, and went upstairs to her sitting room. There she fell on her knees to give heaven a brief word of thanks before she went outside to dismiss the crowd.

That evening, the Institute was enveloped in a sulky silence punctuated by short, fierce outbursts of squabbling. The boarders refused to eat Mrs Rogers' cakes and pastries. Stacking the plates brought down from the dining room after supper, the cook sighed, 'To think it's all to do again! It makes you boak.'

Peggy untied her apron to show she would have no part in the washing up. 'You'll mind I'm to hae the evening off.'

Mrs Rogers kept her promise. 'Away you go, then.' She was surprised to see Peggy slip on a mantle and bonnet, and put on a pair of gloves. As Mary brought in the remains of Mrs Napier's supper, the cook said, 'You'll hae to gie me a hand, Mary. I canna manage all this myself.'

Mary went to unload her tray into the stone sink. She looked up through the barred window to the street and saw the under housemaid pass by. 'Is Peggy no going home?' she asked in surprise.

'Wha kens what Peggy Murdo's up to?' said the cook.

Peggy, meantime, was hurrying towards her assignation, half an hour earlier than Mr Cargill, in order to prepare herself. Her mother had often warned her of what happened to girls who succumbed to the wheedlings of gentlemen without cast-iron promises. Peggy was determined not to give her suitor what he wanted until they had reached an understanding. She hoped that Miss Rintoul's nightgown would inflame Mr Cargill into promising either to elope abroad or set her up as mistress of a lodging-house in Edinburgh.

Robert Cargill would have been delighted to run off to Italy with Peggy, and devote the rest of his life to love and *bel canto*; but not at the price of abandoning his children to poverty. He was much too timid to flaunt a mistress in his home town, and his salary was quite inadequate to renting a lodging-house. He was looking forward to the first of many evenings of amorous delight.

So, with their separate dreams, Peggy and Mr Cargill converged on Rose Street. Peggy was shown into the room.

'Just you make yourself comfortable, hen. I'll bring your gentleman to you when he arrives.' Mrs Watson shut Peggy in softly.

A fire was crackling in the grate, adding its light to a stand of candles on a table, where there was also a tray with two glasses and an opened bottle of wine. A large bed took up most of the room. Its coverlet was turned down invitingly.

Beside the dressing table was the leather bag which Peggy had sent ahead. She took out Jane Rintoul's nightdress, and frowned at a slight dampness. After spreading it over the fireguard, she removed her shoes and ungartered her stockings. As she loosened her bodice, she became aware of an acrid odour coming from somewhere near the fire and realised that it was rising from the nightdress. The sour smell became overpowering.

'Damn that Sammy!' Peggy exclaimed. (This was Sir Perceval's unknightly title on his home ground.) The cat must have fouled inside, though she could swear she'd shut the bag. Tears of disappointment rose to her eyes. She had gone to all that trouble for nothing!

After stuffing the nightdress away, she began to loosen her hair. 'Oh, fegs!' she muttered as another vexation struck her. She had meant to put her hairbrush into the bag. She pushed her fingers through her thick, blond locks, trying ineffectually to pull out the tangles.

Maybe she'd put it in after all, thought Peggy hopefully. She unfastened the bag again, and groped under the nightdress. Her hand met a hard object which she drew out. A pool of cold, shimmering fire seemed to float in the air.

Peggy recognised it at once. She had lingered at the end of the dining room when Mrs Napier was showing the paste jewel to the pupils. She thrust the diadem back into her bag, wondering who had played such a cruel joke on her.

There were voices outside the door, and Mr Cargill entered. He did not have the air of a lover about to grasp the fruits of passion. He came to sit on the bed, whipping his topper off with a thump.

'You silly girl, do you know what this place is? You've brought us to a house of accommodation!'

Robert Cargill had had dealings with such places before; but he did not like finding himself in one with a woman from his place of employment.

'A house of what?' asked Peggy, baffled.

Robert Cargill sighed. 'Peggy, Peggy, what an ignorant lassie you are! This is a hure-house. How on earth did you get hold of the address?'

Peggy's dismay drove all thought of the diadem out of her

102

head. The look on her face set Robert Cargill laughing, and Peggy began to giggle too. She gave him a playful push across the bed. There was a tussle, and a long kiss as he pulled her down beside him. When his hands went down to her bare legs, Peggy struggled free.

'Let me sort myself first. Turn your back, Robbie.'

'All right. As you wish.' Robert Cargill smiled at her seriousness, and lay back on the bed, after taking off his coat and jacket. Peggy blew out the candles and began to slip out of her dress.

'You're no keeking, are you?' she asked anxiously, with her back to him.

'I swear not,' he answered, savouring her curves silhouetted against the firelight.

Having removed everything except her under petticoat, Peggy came over to the bed, and let her hands fall to her sides.

'Am I bonny?' she asked, in a blend of shyness and coquetry.

'You'd be even bonnier without that petticoat. Come here and keep me waiting no longer.'

Mr Cargill tore off his trousers and undergarments – Peggy averting her eyes while he did so – and then seized her and stripped off the petticoat.

Peggy stroked Mr Cargill's chest beneath his open shirt. 'You and me's got to have a talk first.'

'Later, you little tease, later.'

It was not quite what she had expected. After a mixture of violence and tenderness, Mr Cargill became sleepy. Peggy lay beside him, wondering whether she ought to remove his hand from the place where it lay. Suddenly he was wide awake again.

'Let's have some wine,' he said.

He jumped out of bed. One bare foot landed on the side of the leather bag. Mr Cargill gave a comic howl of pain.

'What on earth have you got in there?'

Peggy remembered the diadem. As they drank the wine she told him what she had found inside her bag.

'*I* canna put it back in Mistress Napier's room. They'd say I'd lifted it if they saw me. Would you do it for me, Robbie?. If they asked *you*, you could aye say you found it some place or other.'

God, what had he got himself into, thought Robert Cargill. A tremor went through his stomach. He helped himself to a second glass of wine and sipped slowly, trying to think. Desire had vanished.

'I couldn't replace it until tomorrow, Peggy, and it had better go back tonight. They may have missed it already.'

He began to dress, but slowly, so that he would not alarm Peggy. Him meddle with the damned thing? He'd sooner jig naked along Princes Street! Mr Cargill picked up his watch on its chain, and fitted it into place.

'You must do it yourself, Peggy. You needn't actually return the diadem to Mrs Napier's rooms. Leave it somewhere in the building. They may fuss all they like how it got there.'

'But I couldna jink into the school so late on.'

'If anyone spies you, say that you've missed something you left upstairs or in the kitchen.'

Peggy looked a little relieved. 'Aye, maybe I could. Would you like to see it, Robbie? It's awfy braw.'

'No, no! I don't wish to set eyes on it!'

She asked suspiciously, 'Here, you dinna think I'll get into trouble?'

'Oh, not at all, if you're clever.' Mr Cargill was determined not to be dragged into the business.

Peggy suddenly realised that Mr Cargill was fully clothed and ready to leave. She put her arms coaxingly round his neck.

'Maybe we could bide here a wee while longer.'

'I must get home, my dear. Mrs Cargill will think it strange if I stay out any longer this evening. I told her I was attending a meeting of the Philosophical Institution.'

Peggy looked at her lover reproachfully. They had not yet come to an understanding. But she did not know how to keep him there. Mr Cargill left Peggy to dress while he went off to settle the account with Mrs Watson, and was appalled at the price she charged. Back in the room, he thought that perhaps he ought to give Peggy a kiss.

'We'll come back, will we no, Robbie?' she whispered, clinging to him.

'Of course, of course!' He hurried them both out into the street.

Peggy put her arm through her lover's and shivered. The November night was more raw than ever, and she felt a sadness she could not understand. A sea haar was beginning to muffle the gas-lamps. Mr Cargill was stiff with anxiety.

'Shall I put you into a cab?' Ten to one she'd refuse, but at least he'd have made the gesture.

Peggy's eyes were full of hurt.

'Are you no going to chum me home?'

Mr Cargill knew that he was being a lout and a villain, but he could not help himself.

'It's risky for us to be seen together. Be sensible, Peggy. Let me call you a cab.' He was pleading less with her than with his own conscience.

Peggy drew away from him proudly. 'Dinna fash yourself about me. I have two good legs to walk on. Good night to you, Mr Cargill.'

For a few seconds he watched her walking away along Rose Street. Then he crossed to the shadowier side and hurried eastwards.


Christabel and Eleanor's afternoon by the fire had stretched into early evening; and the evening was now late. There had been another meal sent in by Mrs Veitch. Elizabeth had still not arrived. As the chime of St Stephen's clock sounded up the hill, Eleanor counted the strokes.

'Nine o'clock! I must go home.' She tried to stand up, but found it difficult even to untwine her fingers from Christabel's. Christabel pulled her down again.

'Elizabeth will not arrive now. Stay with me until morning.'

'Chrissie, how can I? My aunt will run distracted.'

'Tell her your poor friend is all alone and begs permission to have your company for the night.'

'Darling, I should like that,' said Eleanor. 'How difficult it is to take myself away from you!'

However, she did leave at last. She walked along Heriot Row through the thickening mist, moving from one pool of hazy gaslight to the next. Half-way down the hill, at the entrance to Jamaica Street, a night constable spoke to her and flashed his lantern in her face.

'I wonder if you heard that woman shouting a wee while back, miss?'

'No, but I have not been long out of doors.' Eleanor was sobered by this reminder that she was out alone at an hour when most young women would have been escorted. She quickened her pace, and began to feel some shame about the anxiety she must be causing her aunt and uncle.

She reached Number Nine, Claremont Street, and mounted the inner stair that led to the four separate dwellings. When she put her key into the lock, it turned, but the door would not open. Eleanor rang the bell. There was a sound of shuffling slippers, followed by the grating of the door chain. Her uncle opened the door.

'Where have you been traipsing, my lady? Your aunt's near out of her head.'

'Mrs Napier asked me to take Miss MacKenzie to Heriot Row. I stayed on for Lady Elizabeth's arrival, but it seems she must be travelling by the overnight mail train.'

Eleanor's aunt appeared in the hall.

'Now, now, dinna scold the lassie, Davie. Come away in, Nelly. I kent you'd no do anything daft.'

The relationship with Christabel had never impinged so directly on her family life before. Eleanor's cheeks flamed as she walked over to her own room, saying, 'Christabel has asked me to keep her company tonight. There's no one there except the housekeeper.'

Mrs Stewart's 'Oh', was very quiet. Her husband's reaction was unseen, because he had gone shuffling back to the sitting-room fire.

Eleanor packed a basket while Mrs Stewart stood by and watched. Eleanor explained that she had already eaten at Heriot Row, and assumed she would also take breakfast there. She would probably go straight on to the Institute the following morning.

The meekness with which her plans were accepted made her a little unhappy, and it showed in her face.

'What's the matter, Nelly? Is Miss MacKenzie no well?'

'Oh, no, nothing like that.'

Mrs Stewart was biting her tongue; but she said only, 'You'd best take Jenny with you up the street. It's gey mirk outside. I'll gie her a lantern.'

'Then Jenny will have to return alone.'

'No matter,' said Mrs Stewart, rather sharply. 'Mind you go up by India Street. That's the shortest road back to Heriot Row.'

Eleanor was sure it was not, but illogically felt that obeying her aunt's request would in some way make up for the barrier she had set between them. On the way they passed one or two hurrying figures that appeared for a moment out of the mist and then vanished.

They crossed the opposite end of Jamaica Street; from somewhere nearby Eleanor heard the harsh stutter of a wooden rattle. She realised that the noise was coming from the depths of a basement on the right-hand side of the road.

There was a diffused glow at pavement level. Eleanor looked over the railings. The same constable was holding his lantern over a slumped figure. The basement gate was open.

Jenny tugged at Eleanor's arm. 'Come away, Miss Nelly.'

Eleanor went down the steps. The constable was standing on the stone platform where the steps turned at a right angle to descend to the basement. He looked up.

'Stand back, miss. It's no fit for you to see.'

He swung his rattle again; Eleanor could now make out that the figure at his feet was a woman, apparently unconscious, who lay awkwardly sprawled on the flagstones of the basement. Her bonnet was skewed to one side.

'Is she intoxicated? Let me help you take her to the Station-House.'

The constable bent down, and passed his hand across the back of the woman's hair.

'It's no just the drink, it's the dunt she's gien her heid. I think she's gone.'

He spread his fingers in front of the lantern, where they glistened with a dark stickiness. Eleanor knelt down and groped for the woman's wrist. She was lying with her arms pinned beneath her.

'No, she's still alive.'

Footsteps pounded along the pavement above, and two more policemen descended the steps. They held their lanterns over the body; one of the constables turned it over with his foot.

'Don't do that!' cried Eleanor.

The policemen bent over, and a stronger light was concentrated on the woman's head. *A fine doctor I'll make*, thought Eleanor, as she began to shiver. It was Peggy.

The constable who had been sounding his rattle said, 'The house is on my list. It's locked up and the family's away. We'd best get a doctor.'

'She's deid, Will,' said the officer who had turned Peggy over. 'We'll hae to send for the Criminal Officer.'

The third remarked, 'Och, the silly bitch's fallen in her drink. A street hure, likely.' He stopped abruptly as he became aware of Eleanor, who said indignantly, 'Her pulse is still beating, but you must get her to the Infirmary at once. She may have fractured her skull. She's a housemaid from the Scottish Institute in Moray Place.'

'If she's no deid that means the Police Surgeon as well,' said the constable who had called Peggy a whore, adding, 'I canna think why a servant lassie was dawdling round the mouth of Jamaica Street this late on.'

One of the others muttered, 'Hold your wheesht, Tam!'

The three of them conferred. One set off for the High Street office to summon the Criminal Officer; another went through his duty book for the address of the surgeon, and

108

the third said he would stay with the body until the others returned. They'd take the lass up to the Infirmary if she was still alive.

'Shall I fetch a cab? I'll come with you.'

'You'd have to wait a fair time, miss, so I think you'd best just get away home. I'll take your name and address in case they need a witness.'

Eleanor knelt by Peggy again. She took off her mantle and spread it over the girl.

'Someone should tell her parents.'

The policeman said nothing to this, and Eleanor stood in perplexity. She knew the address of a doctor who lived in Stockbridge, but he might well refuse to come out to a case that belonged to the Police Surgeon. Her own knowledge was still too rudimentary for her to interfere; besides, she had nothing with her that would have been of any use.

By this time a few house doors had opened and some residents from India Street were inquisitively lining the railings. Jenny called down, 'Are you biding there, Miss Nelly?'

Eleanor came back up the steps and held out her basket.

'Take this to Heriot Row for me, Jenny. The number is forty-seven. Tell Miss MacKenzie that I'll be with her as soon as possible. You had better explain what has happened. When you return home, please try not to alarm Mrs Stewart. I'm going to stay here until they take that poor girl to the Infirmary.'

'Will you be home after?' asked Jenny fearfully.

'Not until tomorrow. Go quickly, please.'

Soon afterwards, the Police Surgeon arrived carrying a case of instruments. The policeman with him called over the railings, 'I'm away to the Station-House for the stretcher.'

The constable named Will said to the Police Surgeon, 'This young lady says the lassie's fractured her skull but she's still alive.'

The surgeon glared up at Eleanor as he brought out his stethoscope. 'What right have you to make such a pronouncement? Hold the lantern nearer, constable.'

As he finished his examination the Criminal Officer arrived. The surgeon nodded at him.

'Bruising and lacerations to the face, and probably a skull fracture. Results of the fall, but she might have been pushed. She's still alive, so you'd better see she goes up to the Infirmary. I'll take another look tomorrow, and send up a report.'

He packed his case. As he went, he said to Eleanor, 'Young woman, medical matters are of no concern to persons of the female gender.'

The Criminal Officer took over. It was several minutes before Eleanor could catch his attention. Finally he did turn to her.

'I hear you're acquaint with the lassie.'

'Yes. She lives with her parents quite near here.'

'Then I'd be obliged if you'd go with the constable and tell them what's happened. It'll come better from someone that kens the family.'

The detective bent over Peggy and lifted up Eleanor's mantle. 'Is this yours?' He pressed it into her hands. 'Here's the lads with the stretcher now, and a blanket. Dinna fash yourself, we'll have a cab here soon. The stretcher's just to lift her to the street.'

One of the policeman came up to Eleanor and asked where they were to go. She said she had an urgent message for someone at the end of Heriot Row; she wanted to deliver this on the way to Peggy's house.

Christabel herself opened the door, her face strained and anxious.

'I thought you were not coming back! Then Jenny called to say you'd stopped at an accident in the street.'

'It's Peggy. She was lying in a basement,' said Eleanor. 'I have to go with this constable to tell her parents.'

'But why was she on her own?' exclaimed Christabel. 'Why wasn't —' She broke off her sentence and said instead, 'I'm coming with you.'

As they walked down Church Lane to the mews behind it,

110

Eleanor explained what had happened, without going into details about Peggy's head injury. By the time she had answered Christabel's questions, they had reached the front door of the Murdos' house. The constable knocked several times without any success, and Christabel threw pebbles at the lighted windows above the coach-house. At last they heard Mr Murdo coming downstairs. He only half opened the door, blinking at the light of the lantern hooked into the constable's belt.

'You tell him, miss,' said the policeman.

Eleanor said that she had some important news. Mr Murdo wanted to hear it there and then; but Eleanor refused, and very unwillingly he admitted them upstairs.

By the lamplight it became clear that Mr Murdo must have been on his way to bed when they caught his attention. He had a flannel nightgown pulled over his boots and trousers. His wife still wore her daytime clothes and looked as if she had been weeping.

Mr Murdo threw himself into his fireside chair with an air of separating himself from the rest of them.

'Is it about Peggy?' asked Mrs Murdo.

Eleanor said, 'I am afraid it is. She had a bad fall in India Street. She has been taken to the Infirmary.'

Mrs Murdo immediately broke into angry reproaches.

'Did I no tell you to gang out and look for her?' She turned to the visitors. 'I telt him! When she wasna here at the back of eight, I cried in at the school. Mrs Rogers said she'd been away long since. I kent something was no richt, but him, he wouldna stir himself. Now see what's happened!'

'Ach, she'll be home the morn,' said Mr Murdo, embarrassed at this public rebuke.

'You will have to to to go to the Infirmary to see her,' said Eleanor. 'Peggy is seriously injured.'

'Aye, that's right,' said the constable, more at ease now the news had been broken. 'It looks as if some chiel gied her a shog just on the corner of Jamaica Street. The Criminal Officer's making out a report.'

'What did you say?' roared Mr Murdo, coming to his feet.

He turned viciously on his wife. 'You hear that? What way was she at the end of Jamaica Street at this hour? Up to nae good, that's what. She's a hure, a clarty wee hure. God kens how long she's been at it. I'm no going up to the Infirmary. I'd be black-affronted to cry her mine!'

Christabel listened in horror while a stream of obscenities spurted out of Mr Murdo. Eleanor and the constable, knowing more of the perverted ways in which grief may surface, did not try to interrupt him, while Mrs Murdo looked on in exhausted sorrow.

When Mr Murdo's need to abuse his daughter was satisfied, he sat down with a grey face.

Eleanor said, 'Please go to the Infirmary, Mr Murdo. Think what your feelings will be if she does not recover.'

Mr Murdo wavered. Then he replied obstinately, 'Na, I'll no gang.'

His wife began to shout at him. The constable rubbed his hands and looked imploringly at Eleanor. Christabel whispered to her friend,'Why don't we go there with her?'

Mrs Murdo put on her shawl and bonnet; she looked with hatred at her husband, who was glowering into the fire.

'Suit yourself!' she muttered as she walked out.

'Shall we take a cab?' asked Christabel. The policeman offered to get one for them.

'Nae sense in that,' said Mrs Murdo. 'We'll use our feet.'

Those were the only words she spoke during the thirty or so minutes it took them to walk up over the Bridges and down Infirmary Street. The policeman said he'd escort them to the hospital before he reported.

Eleanor fell back behind the constable and Mrs Murdo.

'What did you mean by asking why Peggy was alone?'

'Did I say that?' asked Christabel in a dull tone. She had been as silent as Mrs Murdo since leaving Church Lane Square.

'Perhaps you will remember later.' Eleanor put her arm through Christabel's.

'Will she get better, Eleanor?'

'I am not very hopeful.'

They had no more conversation until they arrived at the Infirmary. They went across a badly lit courtyard towards what to Christabel seemed a gigantic maze of buildings.

'Let's try the surgical wards first,' said Eleanor. 'They're in the old High School.'

They went up to the main entrance of a two-storey building, dwarfed by its neighbours, and the constable rang the bell. After a few moments a porter opened the door, but was unable to answer their questions. Eleanor asked to see the surgeon on duty, and the porter went off up the stairs at what seemed a deliberately slow, dragging pace.

The hall was a square room spanned by a heavy-browed arch, beyond which a bare stone and iron-railed stairway rose to the upper storey. Doors opened on either side, apparently straight into the wards, which had been fitted into the line of the old classrooms. They could hear voices in the rooms on either side of the hall.

Eleanor suggested that Mrs Murdo should sit down on a wooden bench. 'You too, Chrissie.'

Christabel felt overwhelmed by the stark and chilly hospital. She was amazed that Eleanor seemed quite unaffected by the atmosphere of the place. She was walking to and from the stairway, and turning her head at every sound to see if the surgeon was coming to them.

'Have you been here before?' asked Christabel.

Eleanor replied, still looking intently at one of the doors, 'Yes, I once had to bring someone here from the Dispensary . . . I shall have to find the surgeon myself.'

An elderly woman with a blanket round her shoulders passed crabwise across the hall, bent down by a bucketful of coals. She glanced at them indifferently before banging her way through the opposite door. Eleanor pursued her. When she returned she said, 'That is one of the night nurses. I think Peggy is in her ward, but I can't get much sense out of her. If only Mrs Porter were still here! She goes off duty at eleven o'clock. There are just these poor old souls to see to everything.'

Miss Nightingale had visited the Infirmary in 1857, but her reforms had not yet been taken up in Edinburgh.

Christabel took Eleanor aside. 'I feel so stupid,' she said miserably. 'I don't know what to do.'

'Keep Mrs Murdo company while I look for the surgeon. And tell the constable that we are grateful for his help. He need not stay with us any longer.'

The constable went away, and Christabel sat with Peggy's mother, feeling the cold of the stone floor strike up through her feet. Mrs Murdo's eyes remained fixed on the door through which Eleanor had disappeared. Fear of what she was going to see, added to the effect of the bare-walled, impersonal institution, had made Mrs Murdo dumb. With an awkward, self-conscious gesture Christabel put her arm round the older woman's shoulders. Mrs Murdo gave her hand a quick, nervous squeeze.

Some patients walked across the hall without speaking. A man ran past with the porter and one of the nurses in pursuit.

At last Eleanor came back accompanied by a young man who told Mrs Murdo that he would take her to see her daughter. Eleanor went with them, but was back in a few moments. She sat down beside Christabel.

'There's a policeman beside her bed. She said something about a crown when they first brought her in, but she hasn't said anything since. The surgeon has dressed her head.'

Eleanor took Christabel's hand.

'That nurse is falling asleep in her chair. I'm going to stay here with Peggy. Go back to Heriot Row, Chrissie. You must be at home when your aunt arrives.'

Christabel's protest was interrupted by the entry of two men in police uniform. One of them asked the porter to take his companion into the ward where Peggy was lying. He then came over to Christabel and Eleanor. He was carrying a small leather bag.

'Ladies, I am Lieutenant McLellan of the Edinburgh Police Force. Which of you is Miss Stewart from the Institute?'

'I am,' said Eleanor. 'This is Miss MacKenzie, who is a pupil there.'

'I've sent my constable to find out what condition Peggy Murdo is in. I want to question her about this bag.'

'She will not be able to help you, Lieutenant McLellan. She is unconscious and very seriously injured.'

A vexed look passed over the lieutenant's face. 'Then perhaps you can enlighten me, Miss Stewart. This bag was found near the girl, and the contents suggest that she had been stealing.'

'Why do you say that?' demanded Christabel indignantly.

From the bag Lieutenant McLellan pulled out a crumpled nightgown trimmed with lace flounces.

Eleanor said, 'I know nothing about that garment. It is surprising that Peggy should possess something so fine, but that does not prove her a thief. Surely it is more important to discover who assaulted her?'

The lieutenant looked suprised. 'We shall do our best, as it is connected with the theft of the diadem. That was apparently in the bag as well.'

Eleanor began to say, 'I did not − ' and instantly felt a poke in her back from Christabel's fingers. She finished, 'I did not think that you had any such evidence.'

'We can settle that in the morning. Will you please tell Mrs Napier that Mr McLevy will be sent down to the Institute early tomorrow? Perhaps you would like to use my cab, Miss Stewart. It is very late.'

Eleanor told the Lieutenant that she intended to spend the night sitting up with Peggy. But would he take Mrs Murdo and Miss MacKenzie home? Lieutenant McLellan said he would certainly do that, after he had spoken to the constable who was keeping watch at Peggy's bedside.

Alone with Christabel once more, Eleanor said, 'Maybe Peggy bought the nightgown in one of those old clothes shops in the Cowgate. There seems to be some strange muddle. I suppose Mr Murdo spoke to Mrs Napier after we left. What do you suppose he meant about the diadem being in Peggy's bag?'

'Peggy has helped herself to Jane's nightgown,' said Christabel. 'So Mrs Napier is blaming her for the other theft as well, if there has been a theft as the lieutenant implied.'

'How can you be certain that was Jane's nightdress?'

'Because of the lace,' said Christabel. 'It's woven with Jane's initials. She took great pains to make us notice them, the first time she wore it.'

'How clever you are, darling,' said Eleanor, still not convinced. 'Here is the lieutenant coming back. Please let him take you to Heriot Row, Christabel.'

Lieutenant McLellan had appeared in the hall again, together with the two policemen. He walked over to the young women.

'There is no point in either of you staying, Miss Stewart. I shall return to Head Office with the two constables, and you can take Mrs Murdo and Miss MacKenzie home in the cab. The lassie died a few minutes ago.'

It was well past midnight; the haar was still creeping up from the Firth of Forth, swallowing up fields and trees and stone terraces. Christabel re-closed the shutters on the greyness outside, pulled the curtains together, and returned to bed. Eleanor gasped at the icy touch of her hands and feet.

Christabel curled around Eleanor more like an animal seeking warmth than a lover, and Eleanor felt tears running over her shoulder. Christabel did not move or utter a sound, but the weeping seemed to go on endlessly. Eleanor felt helpless before this half-blighted expression of grief. She put her arms round Christabel.

'Do you want to talk about it?'

Christabel turned on to her back. 'It is the shock, I expect. If I had been properly brought up I would be having the vapours.'

Eleanor was startled that Christabel could be so brutal with herself. 'Not about Peggy,' she said, 'if you don't want to, darling.'

There was a pause. Then Christabel whispered, 'Poor Mrs Murdo! I hope her husband was kinder when she got home.'

After another period of silence, she spoke again. 'I have been keeping things to myself. I think I ought to tell you now.'

But what she said had nothing to do with the way she felt about Peggy's death, nor anything concerning her friendship with the under housemaid. She could not speak about either of these, even to Eleanor. Christabel wanted to discuss whether Mr Cargill had been involved in the attack on Peggy.

# TUESDAY

When Miss Erroll went into her classroom to take the first lesson of the week she discovered that it was already Tuesday.

She was surprised first of all to find the room full of little girls sitting with their books open, eager to begin. This was strange: Miss Erroll's pupils usually straggled in with improbable excuses.

She went to the wall behind the teaching desk, hung up her arithmetical tables and picked up a wooden pointer. The little girls stood up and chorused,

'Bon jour, mademoiselle.'

Miss Erroll frowned and rapped the top of the desk.

'Sit down, please. We shall go through the ten times table. Repeat after me. Ten times one -'

The girls were tittering and whispering to each other. One of them called out, 'It's our French lesson now, not arithmetic.'

Crushingly Miss Erroll replied, 'Your French lesson follows mine at ten o'clock. At nine you study arithmetic.'

The class broke into excited jabbering. At that moment Mademoiselle Fleury appeared. She paused at the door with an enquiring smile, holding an armful of exercise books.

'Oh! Miss Erroll. Is anything wrong?'

A surge of panic plucked at the senior governess. The girls' faces began to waver and recede. She refocused, to see everyone staring at her.

Mademoiselle Fleury said with a slight emphasis, 'On

Tuesday at nine of the clock I teach Rachel and Lily and their friends.'

Miss Erroll drew a gulping breath. She unhooked the tables from the wall.

'Yes, of course. How forgetful of me.' She left the room swiftly, while Mademoiselle Fleury tried to commence her lesson against a rising babble of voices. Miss Erroll walked across the landing to clutch the banisters; she turned her back on the well of the staircase, feeling giddy. Tuesday? How could it be Tuesday? On Sunday night she had retired early with a painful headache. Surely she had not slept through the whole of Monday?

*Control yourself, Madeleine*, she thought. There must be some simple explanation. The girls had short memories. All she had to do was to go to her first lesson as quickly as possible.

But what was her first lesson on Tuesday? Miss Erroll's mouth trembled. She could not remember.

In one of the nearby rooms she heard what could only be described as uproar. She threw open the door prepared to quell the noise. Twelve girls, older than those she had left, instantly fell silent and rose to their feet.

'Good morning, Miss Erroll,' they said meekly.

The senior governess drew another deep breath. She walked to the teaching table and leaned on the chair behind it. The correct text books were lying on the pupils' desks. The comfort of familiar routine lapped round her. She decided to say nothing about the hubbub going on before she entered, and started to go through the exercises.

Miss Erroll's mind began to clear. If this was Tuesday, then the Empress of the French had made her visit yesterday. The lesson passed in quiet routine.

As the next group of girls filed in, Miss Erroll was almost genial in her greeting. She spoke to the one member of the class whom she considered to have a glimmer of mathematical ability.

'Well, Miss Melville, have you recovered from the excitements of yesterday?'

119

'Oh, yes, Miss Erroll. Mama and Papa were out of town yesterday and would not have seen the Empress. Now she is coming on Wednesday I shall sit with them in the carriage.'

Miss Erroll gripped the edge of the table.

'The Empress is to visit us tomorrow?'

The older girls were quite used to hearing news from Mrs Napier which she had not yet disclosed to her staff; so Sally Melville did not find this question odd.

'Yes, in the afternoon.'

Miss Erroll forced herself to begin teaching the class. Half-way through the lesson, she fainted.

James McLevy was still eating his breakfast roll when a constable summoned him to Head Office. There he was told to go to Superintendent Linton's room. Lieutenant McLellan was already present.

The Superintendent said, 'McLevy, only the three of us are to hear about this.' He tapped a scuffed leather bag in front of him.

McLevy nodded. He took out his pipe – an indulgence he allowed himself now he was no longer in the Force.

He was told that a servant girl from the Institute had been assaulted in India Street the previous night, and had since died in the Infirmary. The bag had been found not far from where the girl was attacked.

'I brought in Lieutenant McLellan because I needed to send someone to the Infirmary at once.'

'Very considerate of you not to disturb me, sir,' said McLevy drily.

'It was a wasted errand,' put in the lieutenant. 'She died without saying anything. But we found something last night which connects the girl with the theft of the diadem. We were able to make certain this morning. I've already been to see Mrs Napier.'

The Superintendent pushed the bag towards McLevy.

'See if you can find out for yourself.'

*A couple of weans*, thought McLevy to himself. *Do they think I'm a dog in a circus?* He unbuckled the straps.

'Canny now,' warned McLellan. James McLevy gave him a scornful look, and pulled out a lace-edged nightdress.

'Very nobby for a servant lass.' His nostrils wrinkled. The slightly sour odour was much less strong now, but McLevy had an acute sense of smell. He laughed at the look on the two officers' faces.

'Missed that, did you? What do you think it is? Cats?'

'That's your business to find out,' said McLellan, rather crestfallen. 'Look better in.'

McLevy groped inside. His fingers met a small twist of paper. He brought it out and unscrewed it.

'Ah! Now I take your meaning.' He held up a small crumb of flashing light. 'Well done, the both of you.' His tone was ironical. 'You needn't have wrapped it up. I'd have found it anyway. How can you be sure it's off the diadem?'

The Superintendent said, 'We had it down to a jeweller in Princes Street long before you rose, Jamie. It's paste. He told us if the rest was as good, it's the bonniest fake ever made. And now it's up to you; you began the work, so you can finish it.'

The lieutenant took McLevy away to discuss practical details. McLevy asked, 'Has the report on India Street arrived yet?'

'The Station-House Keeper sent it up this morning.'

'I should like to have a copy.'

McLellan gave this order to a constable and went on, 'The Police Surgeon has sent in a preliminary report. He says it's unlikely she just cowped over. Someone gave her a push down the stairs. The full post-mortem's coming later.'

'Let me have a copy of that too, please.'

McLellan remarked that he hadn't questioned the young ladies from the Institute. They wouldn't have known anything because Peggy was unconscious when she was brought in.

'Young ladies?'

'A Miss Stewart and a Miss MacKenzie. They went up with Mrs Murdo. I presume Mrs Napier asked them to go with her.'

121

'Did Mrs Napier tell you that herself?'

'Well, no . . . What I don't understand is why Peggy Murdo should let herself be chased down the street and killed for a paste jewel. It doesn't make sense.'

McLevy ignored this for the moment. 'Was she leaving the Institute or returning to it?'

'I don't know,' said McLellan, reddening a little.

'I'll go down to the Institute as soon as I have the reports. Mrs Napier will be like a hen on a hot girdle, wanting to keep this out of the papers.'

'It'll not get into the papers,' replied Lieutenant McLellan firmly. 'Not until after the Empress's visit. The Super-intendent has seen to that.'

Ten minutes later, McLevy was walking down the Mound with the loose brilliant again screwed into a piece of paper and tucked into his breast pocket. When he reached Princes Street, he propped himself against a wall and read through the two reports. He nodded to himself. Hmph! A right fankle the lieutenant had got himself into!

When he arrived at the Institute McLevy rang the bell and waited in the vestibule. It was some time before anyone came to ask him in. More than ever, the place had the look of a museum of art, for it had not seemed worthwhile to put away the decorations for one day.

This time Mrs Napier spoke to him in a small downstairs room near the dining hall.

'This is a terrible business, Mr McLevy. That unfortunate girl! Her mother is distraught. Have you been able to discover any more about her death?'

'Her skull was fractured, ma'am, according to the Police Surgeon.'

Mrs Napier's face took on a serious expression but to McLevy this did not seem to be prompted by sympathy for the dead girl. He asked how she had heard the news about Peggy.

'A little before ten Mr Murdo came here to say that Peggy had been found injured in a basement in India Street, and had been taken to the Infirmary. I told Mary to take him down to the kitchen and give him whatever might alleviate his distress.'

Mr McLevy got the impression that Mrs Napier felt the news might well have waited until the morning. No, nothing else had occurred that night, she replied to his second question. So McLellan had been wrong about how the two young ladies had come to be at the Infirmary.

'When did you hear that the lassie was dead?'

'Lieutenant McLellan told me this morning. He said there was strong evidence that the diadem had been in Peggy Murdo's bag. He did not tell me what it was.'

'It was a loose stone from the diadem, ma'am. There was also a nightdress of a very superior quality. I think you should check to see if any such has gone missing.'

Mrs Napier had been standing until now. She sat down at her writing-desk and was quite visibly relieved.

'Peggy was our laundry maid, so of course it would be easy for her to take the garment. How foolish of her! She has paid dearly for both thefts.'

McLevy twisted the hat he was holding in front of him.

'We do not yet know that she stole either.'

Mrs Napier frowned. 'Come, Mr McLevy. Who else would have taken the diadem? I must give some explanation to Colonel Favé and Madame Pollet. They already know it is missing. I shall tell the people here only that Peggy is lying in the Infirmary after a bad fall.'

'But the lassie's parents ken that she's dead.'

'I have persuaded the Murdos to keep the death to themselves for the time being. Naturally, I shall pay for the poor girl's funeral expenses, and put up a headstone.'

McLevy made an inarticulate noise. *Good God*, he thought. *Devil take it that the poor lassie's been as good as murdered. And how will her parents feel when she's accused of theft as well?*

'Do not look so shocked, Mr McLevy. It is for the good of all that there should be no scandal surrounding Her Majesty's visit. Superintendent Linton agrees with me that the death

123

must not be made public until the Empress has left Edinburgh.'

Suddenly, McLevy understood what had happened. He was to be the cat's paw to pull the chestnuts out of the fire for Linton and McLellan. They didn't want to be associated with the irregularity of suppressing the girl's death. His previous annoyance turned into anger. But he kept that to himself. Instead, he enquired, 'I take it you wish me to continue looking for the diadem? I need to find out what time Peggy usually finished her duties, and whether she returned to the building on Sunday night.'

'Need you be so particular in your questions?'

'Yes, ma'am, I must. It is up to you to give an explanation to your staff and pupils. I want to speak to everyone who slept in this building on Sunday night.'

'Very well. I rely on your discretion. Perhaps you would like to go down to the kitchen and speak to Cook and Mary while I assemble the boarding pupils in the salon. I hope you will not have to question the day girls. I do not wish any of this to spread to their parents.'

'Thank you, ma'am.' McLevy went down to the basement.

Mrs Rogers asked immediately if there was any word of Peggy from the Infirmary. With an unusual sense of discomfort, McLevy said he did not know.

He learned that on Monday night Peggy had gone off duty just before seven o'clock, as usual. That left two to three hours to account for before the policeman found her in India Street.

'Do you know if she went home after she left you?'

It was Mary who replied, 'I doubt she did that. I had a keek out the window and saw her gang up the street.'

'Did Peggy leave the building at any time before that?'

'Just outby with the ashes,' said Mrs Rogers. 'That was in the forenoon.'

Mary said, 'There's Saturday afternoon. She aye took Miss MacKenzie doun tae Stockbridge for her lesson.'

'The man's no speiring about Saturday, Mary,' said Mrs Rogers.

*Miss MacKenzie*, thought McLevy. *The same girl who had been up at the Infirmary with Mrs Murdo?*

McLevy also found out that neither the cook nor Mary remembered Peggy having a leather bag with her when she left on Monday evening; and that the back door was locked every night by Mrs Rogers at nine o'clock and the key hung on a hook beside it. There was no duplicate key.

Mrs Rogers asked what all the steer was about.

McLevy had been expecting this and had his answer ready. 'Well, ladies, I'm feared you'll laugh at me. You'll mind that frost we had. The constable warned off two laddies that were sliding on the pavement in India Street, Monday forenoon. Yon's where Peggy Murdo fell. He's been to see their father who's swearing it wasn't his bairns that did it. There's a right carfuffle about it all.'

At this the cook remarked it was awfy how thoughtless bairns could be; and Mr McLevy should see the salt they wasted every winter to save folk going tapsalteerie outside the Institute. Mary stared at him disbelievingly.

Mr McLevy had often been in situations where both sides understood that manipulating the truth was only a move in the game. Now he felt ashamed to be lying to two women who in a few days would wonder why he had misled him.

'Just one last question, ladies. Is everyone who slept here on Sunday night still in the building?'

Mary said, 'You can be sure of that, Mr McLevy. They're never let out their lane. Worse than the jyle, it is!'

McLevy said he'd have a word with Peggy's mother, and he went up to the salon, where Mrs Napier and Miss Merchant had gathered the boarding pupils. To explain the detective's presence, Mrs Napier had told her assistant that a stolen nightdress had been found in a bag Peggy had with her when she fell. She did not of course mention the theft of the diadem. McLevy looked round the girls.

'Now, young ladies, perhaps you may help me solve a small problem. Please see if you recollect whether anything unusual happened in this building on Sunday night.'

By a faint smile Mrs Napier showed she approved of his words. There were shuffles and glances between the pupils.

'Did anyone rise from bed on Sunday night?'

Faces went bright pink. One girl sidled up to Miss Merchant and whispered in her ear.

'Oh, yes, dear.' Miss Merchant beckoned McLevy aside. 'They rose to – ah – answer the calls of nature.'

Something twitched at the back of McLevy's memory.

'Do they have to leave their bedrooms?'

Miss Merchant's face became pink with indignation.

'Really, sir, is it needful to bring up such matters?'

Mrs Napier now descended from the dais. Miss Merchant met her half-way for a consultation. Mrs Napier waved her away and came up to Mr McLevy. She said in a quiet but crisp tone, 'There is a screen in each bedroom and the necessary receptacles are behind it.'

'What arrangements are made about the receptacles?'

Mrs Napier's face took on the glassy look of someone determined not to be embarrassed. 'The under maid empties them each morning while the pupils are at breakfast.'

'Thank you, ma'am. I am trying to establish how the diadem may have left the building.'

Mrs Napier walked out of the salon with Mr McLevy. He told her that he wished to see Mrs Murdo, and saw a quickly suppressed look of concern spring to her eyes.

'I only wish to confirm the times when Peggy came in and out of the building.'

Mrs Napier took him down to the garden herself and pointed out the way through the coach-house. She said, 'I presume that you need not return to the Institute, when the Murdos let you out again into Church Lane Square.'

'I am obliged to question the governessess as well. With your permission, ma'am, I'll do it this afternoon.'

'Very well, if you must.'

McLevy grinned to himself, and then settled his face into a look more appropriate for interviewing the dead girl's parents.

A few minutes later he left the Murdos' house and began

to walk across the cobbled square to the gap in the buildings that led into Church Lane. He was trying to dispel the indignation that was impeding his thought processes. It was no concern of his if Mrs Napier was abusing the Murdos by making them fit in with her plans. He had found out nothing to contradict the most likely explanation: that Peggy had removed the diadem. He had learned more about the two young ladies. Miss Stewart was also mentioned in the report sent up from Stockbridge. How and why Miss MacKenzie had joined her was still a conundrum.

Mr Murdo had told his wife, late on Monday afternoon, that the French Empress was not to visit after all. She was to come on Wednesday. At eight o'clock, fidging to hear more – for her man was as deaf as a fish for the entertaining bits, Mrs Murdo said – she'd gone to have a crack with Mrs Rogers. She'd been dumbfounded to hear that Peggy was away out more than an hour ago. It had given her a real turn: she'd thought Peggy always came straight home after her work.

McLevy then heard that for the past six weeks Peggy had been turning up at eight or nine o'clock, saying that she'd been held back at the Institute. He did not tell Mrs Murdo the truth. If she didn't suspect it now, she would certainly do so after her next conversation with Mrs Rogers.

The lassie must have had a lover, McLevy told himself. Could *he* be mixed up with her death or with the theft of the diadem?

As McLevy reached the entrance to Church Lane, he heard his name called out. Turning round, he saw Mary emerging through the wicket in the coach-house doors. Again he was struck by the faint likeness to her mistress. She ran across the yard to him.

'Sir! You mind asking if anybody was out on Sunday night? I minded just the now, sir, one of the young ladies, Miss MacKenzie, she's away at her auntie's. That's the first house you come to in Heriot Row.'

'Is she the same Miss MacKenzie whom Peggy took out on Saturday afternoon?'

'Aye, sir. There's only the one Miss MacKenzie that bides at the Institute.'

*And the same girl who was at the Infirmary.* McLevy decided that he would call on Miss MacKenzie at once.

Very early that morning, Christabel had wakened her friend with the words, 'Eleanor, when you go to the Institute, you must find out if the diadem really has been stolen. We can't allow Mrs Napier to put the blame on Peggy.'

'Darling, you are still shocked by what happened last night. Even Mrs Napier would not do that.'

She put her arms round Christabel, and one thing led to another. They slept again for about an hour, then rose and dressed. Christabel returned to the same subject over breakfast.

'Will you call back here at four o'clock? Something odd happened on Sunday night. I'm not sure if it has anything to do with the diadem. I want to think it over before I tell you.'

Eleanor decided to leave this remark unanswered. 'I had better leave now, or I shall not have time to see Mrs Murdo before my first lesson.'

'Fifteen minutes,' pleaded Christabel. 'You have only to walk a few steps along the road.'

The conversation then became more personal; it was so absorbing that they both started when Mrs Veitch rushed into the room, crying out in agitation, 'Oh, Miss Christabel, Lady Elizabeth is here!'

Christabel's coffee cup cracked as she dropped it into the saucer, and she hastily withdrew her other hand, which was holding Eleanor's under the table.

'Goodness, I did not know that any train from London arrived so early!' Christabel sprang from her chair as Elizabeth entered.

'Not a train, my darling, only a cab from Douglas's Hotel. That is where I slept last night. You look rather pale, Christabel.' She kissed her niece and looked enquiringly at Eleanor, whom Christabel introduced, not quite centring her eyes on her aunt's face.

Elizabeth untied her bonnet, and handed this and her mantle to Mrs Veitch. She sat down at the table; a scent wafted towards Eleanor which was neither rose water nor lavender but something much more exotic.

'Please forgive me for breaking in on you so impetuously, Miss Stewart. I was eager to see Christabel. And pray do not interrupt your breakfast. I shall join them, Mrs Veitch. I did not take breakfast at the hotel. There is so much to do today.'

Let us admire Elizabeth as she describes her journey from Paris, smiling at Eleanor to include her in the conversation. Her hair is black and glossy, and she has the finest blue eyes imaginable. Her words and gestures are so vivacious that she must be a heartless flirt. You are mistaken: Elizabeth is overflowing with kindness. It is not her fault that as soon as they meet her so many women and every man between twenty and sixty is struck to the heart. She is beautifully formed, neither too plump nor too thin. Perhaps her hands are on the small side. She dresses exquisitely. She is always good-humoured, and to catch Elizabeth's eye is like drinking champagne for breakfast.

If you are an earl's daughter and can be at your ease in any city from London to St Petersburg you are not likely to be fretted by the shackles that drudge the sparkle out of the rest of us. Yet surely even Elizabeth must have felt the loneliness of grief? Her first love was torn from her a few months after their wedding; the only memento, a son who reminds her in no way of his father, and a few vineyards in Lombardy which she has never seen. Her second husband was killed by a fall from a shying horse in the Bois de Boulogne, a few yards from the Empress's carriage.

Elizabeth prefers the company of men, although her few women friends know that she is generous and loyal. Their intrigues and their sorrows are entrusted to her sympathetic ear, but she never matches their confidences with her own. She often talks about life with her two husbands; she never mentions their deaths. Those who meet her at balls and musical evenings ruminate about her secrets. Tall, whiskered gentlemen who take her down to dinner find that these thoughts and Elizabeth's smile make a deadly elixir. She is going to create havoc at the Hamilton Palace Ball.

At this moment, she is pushing her cup aside and saying, 'Christabel, you must come with me to my dressmaker this morning. I wish her to arrange something for you, if there is time. Marie will help you dress.'

Christabel looks dismayed. '*I* am not going to the Hamilton ball, Elizabeth. And I won't wear those awful stays! Please do not try to persuade me again.'

'You silly goose, of course you are not going to the ball. There is another reason, which we shall talk about later.'

Eleanor feels it is time she went to the Institute. Christabel's aunt is overwhelming.

'Will you please excuse me, Lady Elizabeth?'

Elizabeth rises too and holds out her hand.

'I am pleased that we have met at last, Miss Stewart. Christabel has mentioned your name so often.'

Eleanor goes to the hall; there is a painful tension round her heart. She is humiliated when she realises it is jealousy. Christabel is to spend the day with this much-too-fascinating aunt. An aunt, moreover, who permits herself to be called by her Christian name.

Christabel runs after Eleanor and drapes her mantle over her shoulders. An urgent whisper.

'You will come back at four o'clock?'

'Will you not have returned to the Institute by then?'

'I don't know. Perhaps she'll tell me when she's read Madam Napier's letter . . . And speak to Mrs Murdo for me.'

Eleanor is soothed by that *she*. They hug and kiss. Eleanor is further soothed when Christabel stands in the doorway, freezing, to watch her walk away.

Christabel returns slowly to the morning room, where Elizabeth is reading the letters which Mrs Veitch has brought her. Without looking up, she says, 'Darling, I like your little Miss Stewart.'

'She is not *little*. I agree that she is not tall.'

'Then may I say I like your *chère amie*? You must be very

happy at the Institute if all your teachers are as agreeable as Miss Stewart.'

Christabel looks suspiciously at her aunt, but decides not to pick up the gauntlet.

'Why did you go to Douglas's Hotel? Did you know the Empress was staying there?'

'I arrived so late last night that I decided it would be more convenient to go to an hotel. I had no idea that the Empress was still in Edinburgh. The Paris papers said that she was to make a journey north. The Marquis de la Grange took me into the Empress's drawing room. Such a surprise to encounter him here!'

Christabel says, 'Elizabeth, there is something I want us to talk about, and I'd also like to know what's in Madam Napier's letter.'

Her aunt pushes away the pile of correspondence.

'My darling, I am going to retire for two hours. Then we shall see to all these tiresome matters. We are going out before luncheon. I have asked Mrs Veitch to send for a brougham.'

'Why do you want to take me to your dressmaker?'

Elizabeth turns back in the doorway. Her eyes are wide and innocent.

'That is *my* surprise for *you*, darling.'

*Shortly after eleven o'clock, Her Majesty left Douglas's Hotel in a carriage and pair, and proceeded direct to the North British Railway Station, where the royal party purchased tickets at the same window as other passengers. Her Majesty was loudly cheered as she entered the centre compartment of a first-class carriage in the 11.25 a.m. ordinary train for Melrose, and she graciously acknowledged the attention paid to her. The royal party arrived at Melrose a few minutes before one o'clock. After spending about half an hour in the Abbey, the Empress and her suite proceeded to the George Hotel, Melrose, where carriages had been provided to convey them to Abbotsford. On arriving the Empress was conducted over the house by the people left in charge, and exhibited the greatest interest in the memorials of the* genius loci *which were shown to her. On leaving, Her Majesty and suite re-entered their carriages, and drove a little way up the banks of the Tweed. The Royal party left Melrose a few minutes before four o'clock, and at nearly all the stations on the journey homewards – particularly at Galashiels – the Empress was received by enthusiastic cheering.*

When Elizabeth had left the room, Christabel looked at the letters which her aunt had not yet read and saw that Elizabeth had broken the seals of some of them, but had evidently decided it would be too fatiguing to look at the contents. Among these was the letter from Mrs Napier.

Christabel stared at the envelope, trying to divine what was inside. There was no question of her taking out the letter: on matters like this her grandfather had instilled into her a rigid code of honour.

She went to sit by the fire in deep thought. When Mrs Veitch entered to clear the table she snatched Eleanor's unfinished roll from the plate and consumed it, more for sentimental reasons than out of hunger. She had wanted to ask Elizabeth's advice about how she could protect Peggy's good name; but Elizabeth was plainly not in an advising mood.

What she must do, decided Christabel, was to challenge Mr Cargill. She would confront him with her suspicions that he might have been involved in the attack on Peggy. If he was innocent, he would be as eager as herself to produce some facts in Peggy's favour. But if he was not, she might have to report her discovery to the police authorities.

Christabel had observed that on Tuesday mornings, usually at half-past ten, Mr Cargill passed through the coach-house on his way to another school. She settled down to watch the clock. It did not occur to her that to have his *amours* known to a pupil, rather than to the police, would strike Mr Cargill as a choice between drowning and hanging.

When James McLevy left the Institute garden after deciding

to interview Miss MacKenzie, it took him only a few moments to arrive at the end of Heriot Row. He rang the bell of the first house as directed. The door was opened by a foreign-looking woman.

Giving his name, he said, 'I should like to see Miss MacKenzie, if I may,' and followed the woman into the hall.

She disappeared into one of the rooms and, as he waited, from the other end of the hall McLevy heard a woman's voice, pitched half-way between laughter and scolding.

'*Two* dozen shirts, and a *year*'s subscription to have your hair dressed!'

Elizabeth was discussing with Ranald some accounts submitted by tradesmen in Princes Street. Her two hours' rest had been interrupted by her son's arrival.

The foreign-looking woman returned to the hall, smiled at Mr McLevy, and went upstairs. Behind her came out a younger, red-haired girl.

'I am Christabel MacKenzie. Marie said you wanted to speak to me.'

She took him into a room where most of the furniture was covered by dust sheets. When they had sat down she asked, 'Have you come to ask about the diadem?'

McLevy's lips moved a little – the only sign of his great surprise.

'You know about that, do you?'

'Yes, your Lieutenant McLellan told us.'

So! The lieutenant's misunderstanding extended even farther than he had supposed.

'A Miss Stewart was with you at the Infirmary. Did Mrs Napier ask you both to go there with Mrs Murdo?'

The girl looked amazed. 'Oh, no! We went because we didn't want Mrs Murdo to go up on her own. We brought her home when – when –' She did not finish the sentence, and became very pale.

McLevy said, 'I've heard you knew Peggy quite well, Miss MacKenzie. But you'd not be real chums, would you? Her being a servant, I suppose the young ladies of the Institute didn't have much truck with her.'

The girl burst out in passionate indignation, 'It's wicked of them to throw the theft on to Peggy! I know she took the nightdress, but I'm certain she wouldn't steal that diadem.'

*Well, well*, thought McLevy. This was very odd. He went on, 'If you want to help Peggy, you must tell me what happened in the Institute on Sunday. Anything that seemed to you strange or out of the ordinary.'

'I was on my own in the studio,' she said but did not explain why. 'Peggy came in to see to the fire and take away my luncheon tray at about two o'clock. She said she was going to meet someone on Monday night.'

'Someone? A sweetheart?'

Christabel gazed at the floor. 'I suppose so. She didn't mention his name.'

The way she said this was enough for McLevy.

'But *you* know his name, don't you, Miss MacKenzie?'

'Please, please don't ask me to tell you!'

He couldn't help smiling at this naïve appeal, which told him even more. The man must be someone connected with the Institute. He'd learned from Mrs Rogers that apart from Peggy's father the only men who got inside these convent-like walls were the teaching masters. He wondered how he could win the girl's confidence.

McLevy put his hands on his knees.

'I can't help Peggy if you hold anything back from me.'

'But if I give you names I might bring trouble on people who don't know anything about the theft.'

'Well, you tell me what you've noticed, and I'll tell you if it's important. You needn't give me names otherwise.'

He was amused at her look of relief.

'That is the first condition. There is another – that your Peggy really did not steal the diadem.'

The girl looked at him nervously. McLevy decided to try something else.

'How did you know about the nightdress?'

'The lieutenant showed it to us at the Infirmary. I recognised it. He took it out of Peggy's bag.'

'You mean he took it out of the bag he had with him.'

'Well, I suppose it might belong to Mr Murdo or someone else at the Institute. But it was the same as the one I saw on Sunday night.'

This really made McLevy sit up. He asked to hear more.

'I'd been told to meet Mrs Napier in the hall before supper. I noticed this bag beside the laundry basket while I was waiting for her. I thought it a bit odd at the time.'

'Why was it odd, Miss MacKenzie?'

'Because Peggy brings down that basket on Monday morning. And I wondered why the bag was beside it.'

A small pulse of excitement went through McLevy. 'Can you remember anything else?'

Christabel shook her head.

'Well, let's go over it together. The diadem could not have been in the bag when you saw it in the hall on Sunday. Mrs Napier showed it to the pupils after the meal that evening. Then she took the diadem up to her sitting room and went to bed about half-past ten. She rose at five, and was in and out of the room until she noticed the theft.'

'Then it must have been taken during the night.'

Christabel's face had lost its wary, nervous look. 'The doors are locked quite early, and Peggy always sleeps above the coach-house. That proves she didn't steal it!'

'Someone else could have helped her steal it. She didn't take the bag when she went off duty on Monday night, but she had it later. The diadem was inside it.'

'Perhaps the porter who collects the laundry took the bag away with the basket. It wasn't in the hall on Monday morning, when I left the Institute with Miss Stewart.'

'I was just about there myself, Miss MacKenzie,' said the detective with a smile. 'Who hands over the laundry to the porter?'

'Peggy,' replied Christabel in a low voice.

'Now you'll see why I need the name of Peggy's friend. Do you know where they were going to meet?'

After a few moments of hesitation, Christabel said, 'It was in Rose Street. She didn't mention where.'

McLevy's expression did not alter. 'That may help me.'

A fine lace nightdress. An assignation in Rose Street. And a man connected with the Institute whom Miss MacKenzie was reluctant to identify. He could cipher that sum pretty quickly. He might not have to press Miss MacKenzie about the man's name after all. He went on, 'I should like to speak to your friend Miss Stewart, and if possible, not at the Institute.'

'She is calling here at four o'clock.'

'Good!' said McLevy. 'I'll call back then.'

There was only one more point it might be useful to check. He asked, 'Does your school keep any pet animals?'

'There's a cat that belongs to Mrs Rogers, the cook.'

'Does it ever come up from the basement?'

Christabel said, 'It roams round the building all the time, just as it pleases. Why do you ask?'

McLevy felt sure that the red-headed girl was concealing more than the name of Peggy Murdo's lover. He would try out something to see her reaction.

'Because there was a strong odour inside the bag and on the nightdress, as if some animal had fouled both of them.'

The girl was staring at him aghast. He wondered if he had shocked her, but she didn't look like a delicate damsel.

'Come on, Miss Christabel,' he said sternly, 'this really will not do. What else do you know?'

'I *can't* tell you!' she cried. McLevy asked again, but Christabel flushed and refused to speak. She looked so miserable that Mr McLevy felt sorry for her.

'See here,' he said, 'you've been more help than you realise. If I find what I need in Rose Street, I'll maybe not need to get that name from you. But I make no promises. I'll be back at four, anyway.'

He rose and went to call on Mrs Watson.


After the detective had left, without troubling to put on her outdoor clothes, Christabel hurried out to intercept Mr Cargill in the mews behind Moray Place. She waited where the square opened on to Church Lane, too intent on her plan to feel the bitter coldness of the air.

The singing master appeared within a few minutes. His anxious state of mind made him walk right up to Christabel before he noticed her.

The housemaid Mary had accosted him as soon as he entered the Institute that morning and told him – as she had told everyone she saw – that Peggy had been taken to the Infirmary. Mr Cargill's conscience still nibbled him about letting Peggy go home alone from Mrs Watson's; and he now felt even more guilty. But he was much more concerned about why Mary should think that the news of Peggy's fall would interest *him*.

His feelings for Peggy had always been spread-eagled between lust and fear. When Christabel came up to him and spoke her name, Mr Cargill nearly jumped out of his skin. He blustered, and tried to deny that he had been with Peggy on Monday evening.

'Lies,' he stormed, 'malicious lies!' Then, with a backwash of prudence, 'You must have been misinformed, Miss MacKenzie.'

Christabel said that a detective had asked her to name the man whom Peggy had arranged to meet in Rose Street.

Mr Cargill nearly lost his head.

'You gave my name to a police officer?'

'Of course I didn't. But he's coming back. You must help me prove that Peggy didn't steal the diadem. Otherwise I shall suspect that it was you yourself who attacked her.'

Mr Cargill hissed, 'Are you mad? We parted in Rose Street. Peggy went home alone.'

'So you *were* with her last night.'

Mr Cargill squirmed like a skewered frog. He wondered if he could appease the girl by telling her that Peggy had found the diadem in her bag. But she might blab it to the police.

'I must think this over, Miss McKenzie. Give me until tomorrow morning.'

'Very well,' said Christabel impatiently. 'No later.'

'If you're so concerned with the truth,' added the singing master, 'why do you not go to the Infirmary and ask Peggy what happened?'

Before she had grasped their misunderstanding, Christabel had blurted out, 'Peggy didn't recover consciousness, Mr Cargill. She died in the Infirmary last night.'

Robert Cargill moved back convulsively, his thoughts scattered by the news. He hurried off down Church Lane, leaving Christabel calling after him.

Oh, God, there would be a police inquiry. Everyone was going to hear about his connection with Peggy. He would lose his position at the Institute; his reputation in the city. What would happen to his wife and children? And Peggy was dead.

Grief pierced through his panic at last. In an empty corner of a back street, Rober Cargill leaned against a wall and wept.

When his feelings became less violent, he decided to precipitate events himself. Like a man who cannot bear to think about drowning, he found it easier to jump off the sinking ship. For the rest of the day he hugged to himself the small hope of saving something from the catastrophe.

Mr McLevy knew two or three houses of accommodation in Rose Street. It was instinct that made him plump first for Mrs Watson's. If the diadem had got into Peggy's bag without her knowledge, someone must have planted it there.

Mrs Watson was known to abhor planting. But against this discouragement to his theory, McLevy set the discreet nature of her custom. She ran the type of place that someone connected with the Institute was likely to choose. Thus he got it right for the wrong reason.

Mrs Watson frequently did not go to her bed until dawn, and when Mr McLevy rang her bell just before eleven o'clock, she was still slumbering. She opened the door in curl-papers and wrapper, ready to be annoyed. Then her expression turned to one of delight.

'Jamie McLevy, you're a sicht for sair een! What brings *you* chapping at my door? Come away in, laddie.'

Beaming with true pleasure Mrs Watson preceded McLevy on her fat little legs to the kitchen.

'Where's Willie?' asked the detective.

'Och, he's out for the messages. He aye gangs out after his breakfast. You'll take a fly cup, will you no, Jamie?' She settled down behind the teapot.

'Thank you, I will, but I've not cried in for a blether.'

'No?' remarked Mrs Watson cautiously. 'Well, I'll be blyth to help you gin it's no against my reputation.'

'Bella, a young woman was here on Monday night, and a gentleman with her. She had a small black leather bag with straps and buckles.'

Mrs Watson was instantly on her guard. 'Dinna be daft, man. Naebody's ever planked in this house.'

'All I want to know is if the lassie brought the bag in with her. I know she took it away.'

Mrs Watson said grudgingly. 'Well, if you maun ken, it came here by Johnny Halkett the porter, him that has his stand up by Heriot Row. Monday forenoon, that was.'

'What was in the bag?'

'Mr McLevy!' Mrs Watson expanded with wounded virtue. 'I dinna pree other folk's kail.'

'For the sake of what was in that bag, the lassie's got a dunt on the head that's killed her.'

'Oh, mercy sakes! It didna happen here. They were douce as mice, the pair of them. When they left, the bag went with them.' Mrs Watson looked hopefully at McLevy, expecting that he would now rise and go.

'Who took the bag in on Monday morning?'

'Willie. I telt him to lift it into the room the lassie had booked.'

'Are you sure you didn't look into her bag?'

Mrs Watson sighed heavily. 'You're aye howk-howking, McLevy. Aye, then, I did hae a keek. I saw a braw nichtgoun, that's all.'

'Tell me what Willie did during the rest of the day.'

Mrs Watson said that her pageboy had gone out as usual on his morning errands; he returned a little before eleven to clear out the rooms and reset the fires. Between noon and one she always turned him out of the house with twopence

139

in his hand 'to buy a pie for his dinner'. He had to be back by four to light the fires. The evenings were spent in various ways, depending on the needs of her clients. On Monday night Willie had sat with her in the parlour, taking a hand at cards.

'There he's now. I hear him at the door.'

McLevy stood up and put his hat on.

'I'll take the lad away with me. I'll not keep him for long.'

Mrs Watson looked vexed. 'I'll gie him red lugs if he's been prigging again.'

McLevy laughed. 'Rest easy, Bella. I think he's been a gabmouth, but that's all.'

Mrs Watson's resigned look convinced McLevy that she had a clear conscience. He went out to the hall to meet the pageboy and stood over him with a mock glower. Willie had the height of a ten-year-old, although he was already sixteen.

'Willie, your kind mistress says I may take you for a daunder in the East Gardens.'

The boy gulped, 'I've no done nothing, Mr McLevy, sir, help me I've no.'

'Just a few questions, that's all. The sooner you answer me, the sooner I'll let you go.'

Half an hour later, Mr McLevy was walking up the Mound, thinking over the names he had tormented out of Willie. The pageboy had admitted poking about in the leather bag. Aye, maybe he had blethered about what he found there. But only to a few chums in the High Street tavern where he ate his pie.

Names?

The list was long.

McLevy decided that instead of interviewing Mrs Napier's governesses that afternoon, he would track down Willie's cronies. Most of them were local flashmen. But first he'd have a bite to eat and put his feet up at home for a while. He trudged up towards the Lawnmarket.

Outside Old Fishmarket Close, some nagging instinct told him to continue walking. He paused on his aching feet. He

140

couldn't think of anything on Castle Hill that could be connected with the death of Peggy Murdo. Most of the villains he wanted to interview lived much farther down the Royal Mile.

Then it came to him. Several jewellers' shops were located on Castle Hill, some of them mere booths squeezed into the sides of the tenements. One or two were suspected of combining genuine business with the breaking up of stolen jewellery. That is, those that hadn't already been caught and shut down. Behind Peggy's death still lay the puzzle about the diadem.

McLevy hesitated again, and then decided to postpone his dinner. Half-way up the Hill, he saw a crowd of idlers clustered round a jeweller's shop. He crossed the street and went to look.

The little window contained the usual trays of brooches and finger rings, with a few items of plate. The jeweller was also taking advantage of the Empress's visit. One shelf bore a gaudily lettered placard: THE CROWNS OF EUROPE. Round it were pinned engravings of some current royalties. On the shelf were laid out fanciful imitations of coronets, crowns and diadems, most of them rather obviously constructed from whatever trinkets had been in stock.

McLevy laughed. He must have walked past and noticed the display without taking it in. He stood there for a few seconds, wondering if his memory was beginning to fail him.

Then he bent forward and looked more intently at one of the items. His hand went to his breast pocket, and touched the screwed-up twist of paper. The shop bell jangled as he ducked his head in the low doorway and went in.

'Well, Harry,' he said to the jeweller, 'I'll trouble you to let me have a look at something in your window.'

After she had spoken to Ranald about his extravagance, Elizabeth went upstairs again and lay down for an hour. When she returned to the morning room, Christabel was waiting to ask her advice on the best way to prove Peggy's innocence. The encounter with Mr Cargill was not mentioned.

At the end of the story, Elizabeth said, 'I am not sure I approve of your being drawn into such grown-up pranks, Christabel. Unless you know that someone else took the Empress's paste diadem, I think you should leave everything to be investigated by the police officers.'

Christabel's face was charged with unspoken thoughts; but she was as unwilling to reveal them to Elizabeth as she had been to Mr McLevy.

'I still haven't heard what Madam Napier says in her letter.'

'She wishes to see me before I return to Paris. I shall tell you the rest on our way to the dressmaker.'

At this point, Ranald came into the room, and his mother said, 'Ranny is going to take us to luncheon at the Restaurant . . . oh, don't be tiresome, Ranny. If you make objection, we shall go on our own.'

It was still unusual in Edinburgh for ladies to take refreshment in public, except as travellers in the dining room of the better-class hotels.

'After that,' said Elizabeth, as if talking to herself, 'Mrs Gordon shall pin and sew you while I return here to rest. The carriage will bring you back at about half-past five. Then on to the surprise I promised you!'

Christabel protested, 'Eleanor is to call here at four o'clock!'

'My darling, you shall not be parted from your friend for long. While Marie prepares me to go out, why do not you confide in Ranald whatever you wish to say to Miss Stewart?'

That was how Ranald came to hear about the theft of the diadem and the death of Peggy Murdo.

At half-past three that afternoon, Mrs Napier was sitting at her writing-desk with a blank sheet of the Institute's letter paper in front of her. She dipped her pen in the inkwell and wrote 'May it please your Imperial Majesty–' then the pen was laid down again. Completing the letter would be to admit that there was no hope of reprieve. Yet how long would it be prudent to hold it back? Far, far worse to be forced to admit tomorrow afternoon in front of the Empress that she had lost the diadem. The letter must be despatched today.

Mrs Napier dipped her pen again; she begged her Imperial Majesty's pardon for the inexcusable behaviour of an ungrateful servant, who had repaid the kindness of her employers with malice and ingratitude . . .

As the Lady Superintendent sealed this letter, Mary appeared at the door.

'Ma'am, that policeman's here again to see you.'

'Very well, Mary, I shall speak to Mr McLevy downstairs. Would you ask him to wait for me in the hall?'

Mrs Napier gave Mary time to pass on her message; then she rose and walked to the staircase. Coming down the last half-flight she saw the expression on Mr McLevy's face. She hurried to meet him.

Mr McLevy said with a smile, 'I have good news, ma'am. The diadem has been recovered. It was brought to a city jeweller by someone who was not aware that the diadem was only paste. I am almost certain he's the man who attacked your servant lass. The jeweller should be able to identify him.'

'Did you tell this tradesman that the diadem belongs to the Empress of France?' asked Mrs Napier sharply.

'No, ma'am. Lieutenant McLellan told me to take it back to Douglas's Hotel,' he added.

Mrs Napier hid her annoyance. 'Mr McLevy, is the Empress aware that the diadem was lost?'

'I have no idea ma'am. Madame Pollet did not tell me.'

Mrs Napier thanked Mr McLevy, and returned upstairs. She picked up the letter she had written to the Empress and locked it into the small davenport where she kept her private correspondence. It might be prudent to hold this face-saving excuse in reserve.

Now that the main crisis was past, Mrs Napier felt she should turn her mind back to the school's internal affairs.

She intended to have as many complaints as possible when she spoke to Christabel's aunt. She sent for Miss Stephens.

The young callisthenics teacher had died a thousand deaths since Sunday morning, wondering what Mrs Napier might do to her for posing semi-nude in the art studio. She entered the Lady Superintendent's sitting room apprehensively, and was amazed to receive a warm smile.

'My dear Barbara,' said Mrs Napier, 'I am most contrite. Please forgive me for coming upon you rather suddenly at our last meeting. Even when I have moments of rashness.'

Miss Stephens did not dare to agree; but her hopes rose.

'Perhaps some further details have occurred to you about that unfortunate episode in the art studio?'

Miss Stephens' hopes sank again, for she had already told all there was to tell about her life-sitting for the four senior pupils. She indicated perplexity with her eyebrows. Mrs Napier smiled benignly.

'I see you do not understand me. Some hearts are so naturally innocent and generous that they do not perceive the wiles of others. Such is yours, I fear.'

Barbara Stephens was now thoroughly confused. A show of docility seemed to be the best course. 'I shall do whatever you think best, Mrs Napier.'

'Ah, no, you must not act against your conscience. I ask only that you consult your memory a little more strictly. Are you sure that there was no hint given earlier which might have prompted you to make your unwise offer? By Miss MacKenzie, for instance?'

Miss Stephens was not as perceptive as Eleanor, but it did dawn on her that she was being nudged in a certain direction. Apparently Mrs Napier was ready to forgive her if the blame could be placed on Christabel. She flushed in awkward discomfort. 'I shall examine the events again, Mrs Napier, but I cannot be sure that I shall find any difference.'

'Well, if you have nothing to say at present, perhaps you can reflect at leisure and come back to me later.' There was a perceptible cooling in Mrs Napier's manner.

It may be taken for granted that Barbara Stephens was

both truthful and honourable in her dealings with pupils and colleagues. She would never have slandered one of them out of spite. But between the extremes of martyrdom and malice weaker spirits may find memory blurring to their own advantage.

Miss Stephens' fears that she would be sent back to Harrogate revived. She began to recall certain ambiguous words used by Christabel as she stripped off her Turkish smock after their last lesson; their suggestiveness had been reinforced by a glimpse of the girl's supple nudity – for it will be remembered that Christabel never wore stays. The whole *mise en scène* had clearly been designed to trap her into that fatal offer. Miss Stephens grieved aloud that Elaine, Jane and Maria had made no effort to quash Christabel's suggestion. She was deeply wounded at their treachery!

The Lady Superintendent murmured sympathetically and urged her to be magnanimous towards the inexperience of youth. The three young ladies had been most anxious to make amends, she said. Here Mrs Napier handed over their letter to Miss Stephens, and asked her to read it.

'I see that Miss MacKenzie has not joined in the apology,' commented Miss Stephens, now firmly convinced of Christabel's guilt.

'She is obstinate as well as sly,' said Mrs Napier sorrowfully. 'I have had to send her away from the school until she acknowledges her fault . . . My dear Barbara, how thoughtless of me to hold you back from your rehearsing of the tableau! Let us now forget this horrid incident.'

She sent the governess away, well-satisfied with the ammunition her remarks had provided. She decided that on the whole it might still be wise to rid herself of Miss Stephens as soon as she could devise a plausible excuse.

Eleanor rang the bell at Number Forty-Seven, Heriot Row, a little after four o'clock. Mrs Veitch said that Miss Christabel was out at the dressmaker's, and would not be home until half-past five.

Ranald put his head round the door of the morning room.

145

'Do come in, Miss Stewart. Bessie's giving us tea.'

With the tea Mrs Veitch brought in two platefuls of rich pastries. 'Her ladyship sent out for them, but she's no joining you.'

Ranald took charge of the teapot. Eleanor had never seen anyone of the sterner sex pouring tea before.

'Fagging,' he explained at her unspoken amazement, but Eleanor was none the wiser. He told her about Mr McLevy's conversation with Christabel, and Christabel's waylaying of the singing teacher.

'Oh, dear,' Eleanor commented on this second item.

Ranald said that Mr McLevy was going to call in to ask her some questions. Then he held out a plateful of pastries.

'Try one of these angelica things, Miss Stewart. They're ecstasy.'

Eleanor refused, and watched Ranald eat three. She could not think of anything to say to him. He was so unlike the young men she had grown up with.

Ranald licked his fingers with the delicacy of a slender monkey, and remarked, 'Chrissie told me you help at the dispensaries. I'd so like to hear about that. At the Military they lecture us a bit on sabre and gunshot wounds, but it's pretty unreal. They don't explain enough.'

Eleanor began to speak of veins and arteries and tourniquets; she forgot her shyness. They were so deep in conversation that they did not hear Mr McLevy enter the room. The detective stood on the threshold and saw the boy who had called himself 'Count Orsini' deep in conversation with a young woman who was saying, 'In those circumstances you would bleed to death in a few minutes.'

Mr McLevy coughed, and Ranald sprang up.

'Oh, Mr McLevy! Here is Miss Stewart, but I am afraid my cousin is not at home. She will not be back until half-past five.'

Mr McLevy nodded, wondering how he could arrange to question Miss Stewart alone.

The boy asked, 'Has the diadem turned up yet?'

'Yes,' said Mr McLevy. 'It was found about midday.'

'And what about the man who attacked Peggy Murdo?' asked Eleanor.

'No luck, I'm afraid. There's still one person to see, but I haven't run him to earth yet.'

Mr McLevy had taken the diadem back to Douglas's Hotel at midday, after the jeweller had replaced the loose brilliant. Apart from the visit to Mrs Napier, he had spent his time since then interviewing Willie's tavern cronies. At half-past three Superintendent Linton had told him that now the diadem was recovered, it would be best to close the case.

'The lassie's dead, Jamie. Keep your eyes and ears open, but don't stir up any more trouble.' McLevy had walked down to Heriot Row only because he never broke an appointment.

Ranald demanded in an accusing voice, 'You're not going to let them get away with it, are you?'

McLevy twisted his hat. 'Them?'

'Yes, all the people that want to hush it up, and put the blame on Peggy Murdo.'

Mr McLevy was about to make a humorous remark about the young lad's lack of logic. How could 'they' blame Peggy Murdo and 'hush it up' at the same time?

Instead, something extraordinary happened. The two young faces were stamped with the same expression. It reminded him of the look he'd get from his dog if he spoke to her roughly, or went to the door and then changed his mind because he felt too tired to take her out. Her eyes would fill with a kind of anxious grief, and beneath it was disappointment that he'd let her down. The second bit could only be fancy. Beasts didn't think like human beings.

Now the same look was being directed at him by this lad and the young woman. It said that he'd failed them.

The forces of mutiny rose inside Mr McLevy. He sat down, and said, 'No, Mr Orsini, I am not going to let them get away with it.' His tongue refused to call the young shaver 'count', but he had decided he wouldn't ask him to leave the room. He described how the diadem had been recovered.

Then he asked whether Eleanor had noticed anyone in the

street before she stopped at the basement where Peggy had fallen.

'Not until my second journey. The first time I saw only the night constable.'

'You were out twice that evening, Miss Stewart?'

'Yes, I spent the afternoon at Heriot Row with Miss Mac-Kenzie, and I left to go down to Stockbridge shortly after nine o'clock. I returned to Heriot Row about twenty minutes later. Jenny, my aunt's servant, was with me then. We passed two men on their own. I mean each one separately.'

'Were they coming from India Street?'

'I cannot be sure about that. They were both in a great hurry.'

'Did you notice whether they were clean-shaven?'

Eleanor laughed. 'Mr McLevy!'

'Yes, I know it is improbable that you would notice in those circumstances. But it is important. The fellow I have not caught up with – a certain Donald Campbell – has the finest set of whiskers in Edinburgh. He wears them to hide a large mole on his right cheek.'

'Then I cannot strike him off the list for you,' said Eleanor. 'I did not observe him closely enough.'

'So we've drawn a blank,' said Ranald glumly.

'That depends on whether Miss Stewart can remember anything else. Did either strike your notice in any way?'

They sat in silence while Eleanor tried to recall the few seconds in which the figures had loomed out of the mist and then disappeared.

'The second man had his hand up at his face. I think he was holding a handkerchief or piece of cloth to it.'

'He did not merely blow his nose?'

'No,' said Eleanor decisively. 'I am quite sure of that. His head was at an angle, as if he were pressing quite hard against the cloth. He was holding it over his right cheek and eye.'

Mr McLevy sat back and hit his knee.

'That's the man I have to find! Even if he's not Donald Campbell, he's the one who attacked Peggy Murdo.'

'How do you know that?' asked Ranald.

'The post-mortem report said that Peggy Murdo had hair and blood under her fingernails.'

When Mr McLevy had gone, Eleanor rose, and said she must return home. She did not want to cause her aunt any more anxiety.

'Perhaps you would like to see Chrissie later, Miss Stewart? I could walk down to Stockbridge and escort you back here. Safer, I fancy.'

Eleanor suppressed a smile at the formality of Ranald's offer. She said she would be pleased if he would call for her at half-past seven.

'Right you are, Miss Stewart. And I'll tell Chrissie that the diadem's turned up!'

'I think you should call me Eleanor,' said Eleanor.

When he was alone, Ranald reached for the remaining pastries and ate them all. He went out to the hall and wandered up to his mother's dressing room. Lady Elizabeth was about to rise and be dressed for the ball, Marie told him.

'I'm going out,' said Ranald, 'but I'll be back before my mother leaves for Hamilton.'

He thrust his Smith and Wesson into his pocket, put on his cape and walked up to the High Street. There he prowled up and down the grimy closes, looking for a man with luxuriant whiskers and a mole on his right cheek. No one would have been more surprised than Ranald if he had found Donald Campbell, but it gave an aim to his wanderings. He enjoyed walking round cities at night.

He enjoyed himself so much that at seven o'clock he was still exploring the Canongate. It was only his feeling of hunger that made him become aware of the time. He began to run back to Heriot Row.

Mrs Veitch said, 'Your meal's waiting on you in the oven, Mr Ranald.'

'Keep it a little longer, Bessie. I have to go down to Stockbridge. But I'll have a word with my cousin first.'

'Miss Christabel's no here,' said Mrs Veitch with dour relish. 'You'd best take your dinner.'

'Not back yet? She must be!'

149

'She's back frae the dressmaker and away again.'

Ranald looked at the hall clock. 'My mother's train left ages ago. Why isn't Chrissie home yet? Surely *she* hasn't gone with Mama to Hamilton?'

'I dinna ken where she's off to. She had her bag with her, and Lady Elizabeth said neither of them's coming back the night.'

*The grand ball of the Duke and Duchess of Hamilton took place on Tuesday evening in Hamilton Palace. The palace is situated in one of the most picturesque nooks of Clydesdale.*

*The walls were everywhere draped and studded with orange trees and exotics and festooned with evergreens, and the saloons were illuminated with the utmost brilliance.*

*The guests began to arrive about nine o'clock until midnight. A continuous stream of carriages flowed into the avenue. Before ten o'clock the ballroom displayed a scene of beauteous magnificence. The dress of the Duchess of Hamilton was remarked by all. The youthful Marquis of Douglas and Clydesdale, the rooftree of the noble house, and his brother Lord Charles Hamilton Douglas, wore the Highland garb, as did various other guests.*

*The dancing was kept up with delight and enthusiasm to the music of Mr Howard of Edinburgh and a band of 16 performers, the old national reels being evidently the favourite. The company altogether numbered about 400. The dancing was kept up with unflagging zeal until a quarter past four.*

*Some regret was expressed that Her Imperial Majesty owing to her late bereavement and her state of health was not able to witness this scene of princely festivity.*

On the night of the Hamilton Palace ball Mrs Napier went to Dr Graham's house in Moray Place for one of the many entertainments held to honour the Empress of the French, who attended none of them. Eugénie's absence from the great ball made it possible to imagine that in spirit she was present at all these lesser celebrations. She was atomised, so to speak, into almost as many epiphanies as the brilliants in her Grecian diadem, and her phantom enlivened them all with unusual splendour and wit.

Dr Graham's guests were served a meal so prolonged and formal that Mrs Napier feared she might have to withdraw before the tea-table appeared. She herself had instigated the dinner; but on the actual night she wondered whether she ought to send her excuses, in case her attendance might be criticised later when Peggy's death became public. Finally she decided on a compromise. The dinner began at six o'clock; she ordered a carriage for half-past nine. This was to take her to a meeting of the Ladies' Committee of an association set up for the abolition of slavery. She had walked to Dr Graham's house, for they were almost neighbours.

Dr Graham had come running downstairs to seize Mrs Napier's hands as she entered his hall.

'Ah, my dear Mrs Napier, your secret is out! Now we know why you were so insistent for the twentieth of November!'

The maid took Mrs Napier's wrap, as the Lady Superintendent said with a smile, 'I hope you are not going to scold me for my discretion about Her Majesty's visit.'

They went upstairs to the drawing room, regretting that the dates did not coincide exactly. Mrs Graham was standing in the doorway to greet her; Mrs Napier saw that her hostess was wearing a new silk gown and had fresh flowers in her hair.

She knew all the guests. They were the Directors of the Institute and their wives, with parents medical, legal, and literary. Two pupils who boarded with the Grahams came skipping up to Mrs Napier.

'These are the frocks we are to wear tomorrow for the Empress. Do you like them? Mrs Graham said we might stay up to show you.'

Mrs Napier made herself kiss them on the cheek.

'How pretty you look, my dears!'

The two little girls curtsied and ran out of the room. After a few minutes of conversation the guests went downstairs.

There was great fuss made in the pairing off of the guests. Dr Graham took down Mrs Napier.

Four hired footmen in livery waited on them. The table was laid with an elaboration of silver and crystal, and the flowers and fruit had been arranged that morning by a firm of caterers. Mrs Napier sat down with a gratified smile.

She greatly enjoyed being invited out to dinner. At the Institute she was isolated because no one was her equal; in gatherings like this she was among her peers. Tonight's festivity was particularly agreeable, for she was the centre of attention. Everyone's thoughts hummed round the Empress's visit on Wednesday afternoon. The disappointment of Monday melted away.

Mrs Napier set out to be witty and charming, a talent which she had no opportunity to display at the Institute. She described the arrival of the pictures and statuary; the agitation in the kitchen and among the governesses as they scurried around for the second time that week. She soon had the table tinkling with laughter. Those who were to be presented to Eugénie listened with happy smiles; the parents, most of whom would have to wait outside the Institute, basked in reflected glory.

For Mrs Napier the crystal twinkled tonight with a special lustre; the candles seemed to glow with the same joy that lit up her heart.

Before she told Mary to escort her the few yards along Moray Place to Dr Graham's house, Mrs Napier had given thanks for the happy outcome of her troubles. On her knees she humbly begged forgiveness for lack of faith in her own judgment. Heaven approved of her invitation to the Empress. The extraordinary chance by which Mr McLevy had recovered the diadem was certain proof.

The other guests rose to Mrs Napier's mood. The only discordant note was the strange behaviour of Mr Cargill. His eyes remained fixed on her, tormented and pleading. Only the other diners' concentration on herself prevented their noticing as well.

Through the hare soup, the oyster patties, and the other

services of meat and game, his unhappy stare pursued Mrs Napier. When the finger glasses appeared and the cloth was removed he appeared to grow desperate. He did not taste the benedictine ices.

After dessert, the ladies rose with much more alacrity than usual. They would have Mrs Napier to themselves for an hour; there were many intimate details about the Empress's forthcoming visit which must have been withheld from the general company.

But there was only a short interlude of segregated conversation. The tea-table appeared and with it, almost immediately, the gentlemen. They had to suffer much banter about the celerity with which they had consumed their wine before everyone settled once more into the topic that had engrossed them at table.

At a quarter-past nine Mrs Graham suggested that Mr Cargill should play for them.

'Gladly, if Mrs Napier will turn the music.'

Mr Cargill was often invited to dinner for reasons not strictly social. It was understood that he would play for his supper; and this suited him, because it meant he could dine out without his wife. As he went over to the pianoforte he gave Mrs Napier another look of despair.

The Lady Superintendent had been on the point of making her excuses, intending to leave as the audience settled down; but now she decided to find out why Mr Cargill could not play a piece from memory. She agreed to turn over for him.

As he arranged the score of a Chopin étude, Mr Cargill whispered, 'I must speak privately to you at once!'

Mrs Napier bent forward to inspect the final bars of the first page.

'Surely that can be postponed until the morning?'

Mr Cargill began to play. Under an improvised run of trills and glissandos that would have astonished the composer, he hissed, 'No, no, too late! The honour of the Institute is involved!'

Mrs Napier wondered if the singing teacher's mind had become unhinged under the excitement of preparing for the

Empress's visit: she had noticed great variations of mood in him recently. If he had nothing sensible to say she would leave after his first piece.

Mr Cargill's hands were now reproducing the notes in front of him, and he half sang, in time to the melody, 'The – police – are concerned – in this – I – must – see – you – at – once.'

Mrs Napier turned over the page.

'Please control yourself.'

Mr Cargill's hands played on but his eyes did not leave Mrs Napier's face. She was thankful that the angle of the pianoforte and her own stance prevented this from being noticed by the audience.

After he had repeated his message twice the complications of the piece became unfavourable to Mr Cargill, and he was not able to articulate his words into sentences. His agitation increased: he was now breathing in gasps. To the final chords he managed to fit, 'Christabel MacKenzie! Peggy Murdo! The diadem!'

Mrs Napier stepped back from the keyboard and joined in the applause.

'Stand up and bow,' she ordered curtly. She smiled, and as if giving her thanks, said in a low voice, 'I am leaving now. If you wish you may accompany my carriage.'

After saying her farewells Mrs Napier was taken to the room where the maid had put the ladies' wraps. She lingered as long as possible, to give Mr Cargill time to make whatever excuse he could for his own departure. When she could delay no longer she asked the maid to show her downstairs and went out to the carriage she had ordered. There was a hunched figure shivering beside the railings.

Mrs Napier had been startled into taking Mr Cargill seriously; but she would not commit the impropriety of inviting him to share her carriage, especially as his abrupt exit must have raised some speculation among the other guests. Mr Cargill had to walk beside the moving carriage, clutching the window frame as he thrust his head inside, and hopping to avoid the wheels. Their exchange was very disjointed.

'What is this about, Mr Cargill?'

'Miss MacKenzie intercepted me when I left the Institute this morning. She told me that Peggy Murdo is dead!'

Mrs Napier peered in cold astonishment. She had not been mistaken: Mr Cargill's bobbing face streamed with tears.

'Is it true? She said that Peggy had been attacked in the street. Is she really dead? How did it happen?'

Mrs Napier ignored the questions. 'I wish to hear about your meeting with Miss MacKenzie. You are sure it was she?' Her doubts about Mr Cargill's stability returned.

'Yes, Christabel MacKenzie. She wants me to help her prove that Peggy did not take the diadem. She says that if I do not help her, I will be accused of the attack. The police have been to question her, and are coming again.'

Mrs Napier's reactions were hidden as she sat back in the darkness of her carriage. For several seconds she listened to the clopping of the hooves and clatter of wheels on the frosty road. Then she leaned out of the open window.

'Ask the driver to stop so that you may join me. Tell him to drive to your own residence.'

The carriage took them along Heriot Row, up to Princes Street, and along to Mr Cargill's house in Regent Terrace. He was too caught up in his own turmoil to question Mrs Napier's orders. Out of the confusion of that morning his only clear impression was that Christabel MacKenzie was blackmailing him, and he had decided to reach Mrs Napier's ear before she did.

Sitting beside Mr Cargill in silence, Mrs Napier thrust all emotion out of her mind. She examined the stark facts.

Christabel MacKenzie knew that the diadem had been stolen. She must be made dumb, or the consequences to the Institute and Mrs Napier herself would be terrible.

The Lady Superintendent made no excuses to Mrs Cargill for her late visit. The Cargills, she suspected, would soon be too involved in their own domestic drama to spare any thoughts for her. She accepted the tea that was put in front of her and told Mrs Cargill that she wished to speak to her husband alone.

She asked the singing teacher for an explanation.

Mr Cargill stumbled through the details of his association with Peggy. Once he began, he poured it all out, not omitting even the events of Monday night. Mrs Napier listened with contemptuous disgust.

*Fool*, she thought, *corrupt, lecherous fool.*

At the end she commented, 'It would have been possible to tell me in a more rational manner tomorrow morning.'

'I dared not wait! Heaven knows what that girl may have done by then!'

Mrs Napier chose her next words very carefully.

'Miss MacKenzie speaks from an over-luxuriant imagination.'

'Shall I be questioned about the murder, if murder it be?'

'In view of Her Majesty's visit, it is unlikely that inquiries will be pursued as far as that. It would be most injudicious.'

'Thank you, thank you, Mrs Napier!'

Mrs Napier drew back the hand which Robert Cargill was attempting to seize, and put on her gloves. Distastefully, she said, 'Do not *thank* me, Mr Cargill. What you have done puts you beyond consideration. Only the wider interest saves you from open disgrace, not my generosity, I assure you. You cannot continue to hold your position at the Institute. You are fortunate that the matter is so peculiarly delicate. It allows me to offer you the undeserved leniency of resignation, rather than having your position taken from you.'

Mr Cargill bowed his head.

'I shall inform the Directors in writing.'

'That would be in everyone's interests. Please to reflect also, whether you ought to withdraw from any duties which bring you into contact with female pupils at other establishments in the city.'

A protest bubbled up to Mr Cargill's lips. For a moment Mrs Napier thought she had pushed him too far. Then she saw that he would do anything to avoid exposure. That was good. She wanted to forestall the reproaches of other employers should this sordid intrigue ever come to their notice.

Mrs Napier stood up. 'I am glad that we understand each other. If Miss MacKenzie attempts to speak to you again, say nothing and send her to me.'

'Miss MacKenzie shall have no opportunity to speak to me. I shall resign my position at the Institute tomorrow.'

'Not quite so soon, Mr Cargill. Nothing must be allowed to detract from Her Majesty's visit. Please let that go by before you write to the other Directors.'

Robert Cargill was too crushed to see this chink in Mrs Napier's armour. And if he had, would he have had the courage to thrust at it?

The Lady Superintendent was not usually vindictive. If ever she was cruel, it was always in the course of duty and 'for the major good'. On this occasion she was so disgusted by Mr Cargill's debauching of Peggy that she said, as she rose, 'You have been most foolish, Mr Cargill. Had you remained calm, this unhappy scene need not have taken place. The diadem was recovered by the police this afternoon.'

She did not wait for his reaction, but walked straight towards the front door.

It was half an hour before midnight when she arrived at the Institute. Mary opened the front door as Mrs Napier's hand touched the bell-knob.

'I've been waiting in the hall, ma'am. Miss Merchant would like a word before you retire. She says it's urgent.'

Mrs Napier repressed an impatient reply and said she would see Miss Merchant in her sitting room.

'I've kept the fire in, ma'am. There's a letter come for you just a wee while after you went out. I put it on your desk.'

The Lady Superintendent had meant to pass judgment on Miss Stephens when she returned home; but it was much too late to summon the young governess from the house next door. She felt equally disinclined to see Miss Merchant, but it might be unwise to delay hearing what she had to say.

Mrs Napier was not much above two and forty; yet an elderly weariness crept over her as she thought about all the problems that had beset her since Saturday evening.

As she reached her own apartments she heard whoops of laughter from the floor above.

The letter on her desk was from Lady Elizabeth Mac-Kenzie, who said she would call on Mrs Napier as requested, but that her attendance at the Hamilton Palace ball would prevent her from doing this before Thursday, at half-past two in the afternoon.

Miss Merchant's footsteps were pattering along the landing as Mrs Napier read the final paragraph of the letter.

My niece informs me that the Empress of the French is to visit the Institute on Wednesday afternoon. I regret that I cannot be present at such a memorable occasion, which Her Majesty herself has mentioned to me. However, I am sure you will be pleased to hear that one of your pupils has already had the honour of being presented to Her Majesty. It would be most unkind in me to spoil Christabel's enjoyment in telling you the story herself. For that reason, I have brought her back to the Institute before travelling on to Hamilton Palace.

Mrs Napier turned in fury on Miss Merchant as she entered. The plump little governess was quivering with excitement.

'Whatever are you thinking of, Anna? Why has that hilarity been permitted in the bedrooms?'

'Dear Mrs Napier, wait until you hear what has happened! I could not be so heartless – I had to let them express their joy!'

Miss MacKenzie had been brought to the Institute a little before seven o'clock in the carriage that was taking her aunt to the station. The carriage was to be loaded on to the train, said Miss Merchant, as Lady Elizabeth's party would be driving in it to Hamilton Palace after their railway journey. The party consisted of Lady Elizabeth herself, another lady, and two officers from the Castle and Piershill Barracks.

'The officers were in a very good humour!' Miss Merchant could not conceal her scandalised delight. 'Even the husband of the other lady!'

Lady Elizabeth had brought her niece into the Institute, followed by the officers, just as the boarders were coming out from their evening meal. Their uniforms, and Miss Mac-Kenzie's gown, had caused a sensation. The two men had shown off dreadfully, leaping up and down the staircase. They carried Miss MacKenzie on their shoulders to the second landing.

'I must admit she encouraged them. What a wild manner she has sometimes!' Miss Merchant tried to sound disapproving. 'She really looked most elegant, almost pretty. At first I hardly knew her . . . Of course, when I spoke to Miss Mac-Kenzie on her own, it all became clear to me. Lady Elizabeth is a frequent guest at Compiègne and Fontainebleau. Would you believe it, dear Christabel was most reluctant to tell me what the Empress had said to her? I had to exert my utmost efforts to draw it out of her.'

'What did you discover?' The words trailed over Mrs Napier's tongue as sour as gall.

The Empress had expressed a wish to meet Lady Elizabeth's niece when she had heard that she was a pupil at the Institute. Miss Merchant said that this was no doubt a delicate attention to indicate Her Majesty's regret that she had been prevented from visiting the school on Monday. Dear Christabel had recited to the Empress the description of Edinburgh from *Marmion*.

'Thank you, Anna,' said Mrs Napier venemously, as Miss Merchant began to quote. 'There is no need to repeat the performance. I am well-acquainted with Sir Walter's famous lines.'

Miss Merchant blinked, and lowered herself from some inner peak. She looked timidly at the Lady Superintendent.

'Miss MacKenzie is sometimes thoughtless. Yet consider how *ill* it will look if we continue to punish her, someone honoured by the personal notice of Her Imperial Majesty, the Empress of the French!'

She was halted by Mrs Napier's harsh, braying laugh, but pressed nervously on.

'Mrs Napier, I beg you to listen to me. Her Majesty wishes

that Christabel be presented to her formally at the Tuileries. When she leaves us, the reputation of our little community may be in Miss MacKenzie's hands, may it not? So I think – I think–'

Miss Merchant's voice faltered. She was quite overcome by her own audacity and the magnitude of the honour she had mentioned.

Mrs Napier gave a terrible smile and pushed Miss Merchant out of the room.

'The Tuileries, indeed! Even Christabel MacKenzie must be flattered by such an invitation. We must make sure that she does not have to wait for her eighteenth birthday to accept it. I fancy they are not so particular about such matters in France.'

# WEDNESDAY

Pepa had received the diadem from Mr McLevy on Tuesday afternoon. He entered through the back door of the hotel, and there had been a lot of cloak-and-dagger stuff to get the paste jewel to the Empress's head maid without this being noticed by her assistants. On Tuesday night, Pepa had slept with the diadem under her bed.

McLevy had not mentioned that the crown had spent several hours in an Edinburgh brothel. He told Madame Pollet that it had been stolen out of the Institute; but at present, the circumstances were still obscure. He would present a full report when his investigations were concluded.

'I do not care a rotten fig for that,' Papa had said. 'Enough that it is back. I take it to that imbecile woman tomorrow. She must not lose it again.'

She was anxious that no whisper about the diadem's adventures should reach the Empress. However, she wished very much to be revenged on Mrs Napier.

On Wednesday morning Pepa did not go to the Institute until after ten, hoping that Mrs Napier would suffer agonies of suspense. She was bilked, of course. In games of that kind, Mrs Napier had nerves of steel.

But Pepa had another card up her sleeve.

She entered the Institute cradling her parcel with ostentatious care. Upstairs, the Lady Superintendent invited her to be seated, saying how infinitely grateful she was that once more the jewel was to be entrusted to her.

Mrs Napier brought out the green leather case and invited

Pepa to replace the diadem in it. This was done with many frowns and grimaces from Madame Pollet. After reinstating the diadem in its casket, Pepa placed it on Mrs Napier's desk and sat back with a ferocious glare. Mrs Napier smiled.

'Madame Pollet, I shall return the diadem to your keeping immediately after Her Majesty has watched our little tableau.'

Pepa's efforts to miss none of Mrs Napier's meaning gave her a brooding look, which the Lady Superintendent took for offended pride. She had heard that Spaniards never forgave an insult.

'I do not see this tableau, señora,' said Pepa. 'Early I come tomorrow for the diadem.'

'As you wish, Madame Pollet.' Mrs Napier paused for a second. She was anxious to find out whether the Empress knew about the loss of the diadem. 'A letter will be sent to Her Majesty expressing our deepest regret for what has occurred.' She waited to see the effect.

'It was stealed, no?' asked Pepa with a scowl. 'You give the letter to me, please.'

It now occurred to Mrs Napier that if the Empress did *not* know about the diadem's disappearance, the maid had only to breathe a few words in her mistress's ear and the imperial favour would vanish. It would be most unwise to annoy her. So Mrs Napier took out the letter she had already written and handed it to Pepa. Pepa tucked it away, intending to tell Colonel Favé how she had avenged her mistress's honour on these barbarians. But she would certainly not give the letter to the Empress: *santo Dios*, did the señora imagine she was as great a fool as herself?

For her own satisfaction Pepa had also decided to interfere in the tableau. To that end she had spent an hour poring over a Spanish-English dictionary.

Pepa said, 'She must have the hair of *Sa Majesté*.'

'Who, Madame Pollet?'

'She who is the Empress. In the tableau.'

Mrs Napier smiled condescendingly. 'We could have sent for a hair-piece from a perruquier, but we wished our little entertainment to remain simple. Spontaneity is the charm of youth.'

'She with the red hair must be *Sa Majesté*, señora. The Empress told me. Last night when she saw the young lady.'

Mrs Napier's face died into winter. She said slowly, 'Am I to understand that the Empress wishes Miss MacKenzie to represent her in the tableau? Christabel MacKenzie?'

'Yes. She with the red hair. Mac-Ken-zie.'

Pepa's struggle with the northern syllables eliminated any clue to the truth of her statement. Mrs Napier remained frozen while she wondered whether she dared challenge this pronouncement. But the risk of offending the Empress was too great. She must submit.

'Naturally, we shall be delighted to comply with Her Majesty's request.'

Pepa did not grasp the magnitude of the effect she had produced, but she sensed there was something. She went away well pleased with her morning's work.

After Madame Pollet's departure Mrs Napier wrote a note to Dr Graham. That Wednesday morning he was the only Director holding his usual ten o'clock class. The day pupils had been sent home to prepare for the Empress's visit.

Dr Graham was returning the essays on True Beauty. He received the note more than half-way through his lesson.

'Ah,' he said, after reading it, 'Mrs Napier wishes to see you immediately, Miss Rintoul. Miss MacKenzie, you also are to see the Lady Superintendent, but when we dismiss.'

Jane left the room; she returned a little later with an air of stifled grief. Her face was pale and her eyes bore traces of tears. She shook her head violently when begged by Elaine to communicate her distress. Dr Graham pretended not to notice and continued talking about the essays. The note had also warned him that a difficulty might present itself over Christabel's. He finished his comments and picked up a book from the desk. Christabel held up her hand.

'Dr Graham, you have not returned my theme.'

'Ah, no, Miss MacKenzie. Mrs Napier has held it back, but I do not know the reason. You must ask her yourself.'

Dr Graham passed immediately to Edmund Burke's *Reflections on the Revolution in France*, saying that the paragraphs about Marie Antoinette were peculiarly appropriate to that day, and there was just time to read them.

Christabel had remained unusually silent during the lesson, speculating on what Mrs Napier was going to say to her. She wondered if it might be anything to do with Mr Cargill. She was feeling remorseful about the shock she now realised she had given him. She also hoped that Mrs Napier would not keep her for long: Eleanor came into the Institute at eleven o'clock, and she had a great deal to tell her.

Dr Graham dismissed his class, and Christabel went upstairs to Mrs Napier's sitting room. She knocked twice before she was told to enter.

'Christabel,' said Mrs Napier. 'Please sit down.'

She made a heroic effort to crush her loathing for the girl.

Mrs Napier had decided that Christabel must be silenced by being removed from the Institute. Precisely what she would say to Lady Elizabeth to ensure this, she had not yet decided; but she was sure that her own astuteness would carry her through. However, she must deal first with the question of the tableau.

'I have some news for you, Christabel. Madame Pollet has told me that Her Majesty wishes you to represent her in the tableau.'

Christabel clearly remembered that in her brief interview with the Empress, Eugénie had not said anything of the kind. In fact, Christabel herself had mentioned that a Miss Rintoul had been cast in the leading role.

'I have no wish to play the part, Mrs Napier. Besides, Jane would be terribly disappointed if you took her out of the tableau.'

Mrs Napier barely stopped herself from saying that she too would much prefer Jane to play the part.

'You have no choice. Madame Pollet said that it is Her Majesty's particular wish.'

Christabel was sure that there was some mistake. She remained in perplexed silence, and Mrs Napier became aware that since their last interview something had happened to the girl. There was some added layer of experience that had not been there before.

'I hope you do not intend to refuse,' said Mrs Napier, hoping that Christabel would, and so give her another reason for asking Lady Elizabeth to remove her from the school.

'It doesn't matter to me if I play the part or not,' said Christabel, 'but I see that it matters a great deal to you. I'll do it, if you will assure me that you do not intend to accuse Peggy of stealing the diadem.'

Mrs Napier kept her expression bland.

'I am not sure I know what you mean. However, I promise that anything you wish to say will receive my full attention after the Empress's visit. Now, may we please have a truce until that is over?'

'Very well,' said Christabel, 'I'll do what you ask, on the understanding that you will let me speak to you about Peggy Murdo afterwards.'

Mrs Napier deliberately made no comment on this remark. Instead, she said, 'Jane has accepted the change bravely, so please do not tease her with apologies that will only make *you* feel more at ease.'

Christabel agreed to that also and turned to go.

'Oh,' said Mrs Napier, as if the point had just occurred to her, 'we had better make sure that the diadem fits you.' She smiled at Christabel's startled look and lifted the paste jewel out of its casket.

'There,' she said, setting it briefly on the girl's dark auburn hair, 'it is a perfect fit . . . Now you had better go down to the salon to rehearse your part in the tableau.'

Christabel went downstairs, puzzled and dismayed. She realised that Mrs Napier was trying to intimidate her. A feeling of despondency overwhelmed her. Would anyone now want to discover what had really happened to the diadem? The man who had caused Peggy's death might never be tracked down.

As she passed the door where Eleanor usually taught her eleven o'clock lesson, Christabel looked inside, hoping that

165

her friend might be waiting for her there. The room was empty. The little rats had of course been sent to rehearse the tableau, but there was no sign of Eleanor either.

Feeling every bit as dejected as Mrs Napier would have wished her to be, Christabel walked into the salon. Miss Stephens was rehearsing with the little rats. Alice, Maria and Elaine were in the library consoling Jane; their part of the tableau was not to receive its final rehearsal until half-past eleven.

Christabel went up to Miss Stephens, trying to conceal her misery with deliberate rudeness. 'I'm to take the part of the Empress.' She was pleased to see the governess's look of dismay.

'Has Jane asked to do this?'

'No,' said Christabel. 'It was Mrs Napier. She told me a few moments ago.'

Miss Stephens was convinced that the sudden change resulted from something which Christabel had said about her to Mrs Napier. It would be the Lady Superintendent's way of indicating displeasure. She could not conceal her alarm, and this gratified Christabel even more.

'Very well,' the young governess faltered. 'You should go to the studio and put on the Empress's costume. I shall rehearse your part of the tableau very soon.'

Miss Stephens' agitated breathing gave even greater enhancement to her noble contours, and Christabel had caught from her grandfather a most undemocratic gallantry towards beauty in distress. She repented of being so boorish, and made herself as agreeable as possible during the rehearsal.

When Eleanor walked up Church Lane early on Wednesday morning, she saw Ranald hovering at the top of the road. She had not recognised him at first, because he had laid aside his uniform for a top hat and morning coat, and from a distance looked much older than the youth she had met the day before.

'Most frightfully sorry,' he said, as he raised his hat, 'but

166

Chrissie didn't return to us last night. Mama took her to meet the Empress, and then back to SINDOG.'

Eleanor replied, 'I thought that something of that kind must have happened when you did not call on me.' She began to walk up towards Queen Street.

'Aren't you going to SINDOG?' asked Ranald in surprise, following her.

'Yes, but not until eleven. I go to the Eye and Ear Dispensary first.'

He walked with Eleanor all the way to Waverley Bridge, where she stopped and faced him.

'Ranald, there is no need for you to accompany me any farther. I'm sure I shall come to no harm between here and Cockburn Street.'

His face fell. 'Oh, I hoped you'd let me come in with you. I'd like to see what you do there, Eleanor.'

This was awkward. Inside the Dispensary, Eleanor watched and listened, and kept herself as inconspicuous as possible. The medical students tried to flirt with her while they waited for their cases, and most of them assumed that she was preparing herself to take up a place on one of the new nursing courses that Miss Nightingale was organising for the English hospitals.

To enter the clinic with Ranald would rouse the attention she wanted to avoid. As she hesitated, trying to put this in a way that would not hurt his feelings, Ranald said, 'You'd rather I didn't? I'll go away. But you will let me know what happens, won't you?'

Eleanor assured him that she would; and went into the hall of the Dispensary.

It had been set up to deal only with the matters suggested by its title; but as it was situated much nearer to the Royal Mile than the general clinics or city hospitals, there was always a throng of patients hoping to be cured of their septic cuts, their coughs, aches and bruises, or even taking the chance to sit down indoors for an hour or so. Treatment was given if possible. The students would take the worst cases up to the Infirmary.

167

Eleanor laid aside her mantle, bonnet and gloves, and went to the stove to attend to the pans of water which the porter had already set there to heat. The patients waiting outside were allowed in, and spread themselves around the room on the benches and chairs, while the students clustered round the tables and waited for the physicians on duty.

Nothing unusual happened until a young woman supported an elderly man towards the bench nearest Eleanor.

'Would you speak to him, hen?' said the girl to Eleanor. 'I was right by when it happened, but I canna bide on. The mistress'll kill me if I dinna get back to my work.'

Eleanor went over to the bench. The old man had slipped on the icy cobbles outside, and was garrulous with fright.

Eleanor heard his story through twice, while she tried to attract the attention of one of the medical students. Eventually one came over.

'I don't think he's broken any—' Eleanor bit the sentence off. The student gave her a sharp look, and she returned to the table where she had been rolling bandages. All through her conversation with the old man she had sensed that someone was watching her; now she turned to face the hall again and saw Ranald sitting on a chair a few yards to her right.

Eleanor was furious. In that setting Ranald's clothes and confident, inquisitive air made him as conspicuous as a parakeet in a crowd of sparrows. Worse than that, he was trying to catch her eye. She stared at him angrily for a moment, before bending over the table. A moment later, she looked up again. He was still there, and still trying to convey some message. His head tilted back twice towards a bench some way behind and to the left of him.

Sitting there was a youngish man with thick black hair. He was hunched forward, with his head cupped in one hand. The elbow behind it was pressed against the wall. It was such an awkward, strange posture that Eleanor looked harder at him. His other hand held a large white handkerchief clasped over his cheek and eye. There was a large black mole on his right cheek, although he had no side whiskers.

Forgetting all her caution, Eleanor walked over to Ranald and said, 'Go to the Police Office and ask where you may find Mr McLevy. I'll follow that man out. Then I'll come back here for you both.'

Ranald nodded, then rushed out of the hall.

The students seemed to work their way through the waiting patients more slowly than usual. Glancing at the large clock on the wall, Eleanor saw that her time at the Dispensary was nearly over. She had to allow herself half an hour to walk to the Institute.

The patients were sitting haphazardly wherever they had been able to find a bench or chair, but came up in order for their treatment. Eleanor had no idea when the man's turn would come. If she did not leave within the next few moments she would be late for her lesson.

Ten minutes later, Eleanor was still there. She decided to postpone the question of whether her conscience could bear the weight of making a false excuse to Mrs Napier. The man was looking towards the students. He rose, and went forward as the previous patient was sent away.

Eleanor told the student who had lent her the medical plates that she was leaving. She put on her bonnet and mantle, went out of the hall, and stood outside in Cockburn Street putting on her gloves. A few minutes later the man came out of the Dispensary. He had a dressing on his eye and cheek; the bandage holding it in place prevented him from putting on his hat, and he walked bareheaded up towards the High Street.

Following him a few yards behind Eleanor hoped that he would go straight home, and not into a tavern or his place of work. At the top of Cockburn Street he turned left and began to go down the High Street towards the Canongate. Eleanor scanned the crowds walking past St Giles'. There was still no sign of Ranald and Mr McLevy.

Eleanor ordered herself not to panic. Anyone who came into the Cockburn Street Dispensary probably lived nearby. She walked downhill into the Canongate, keepng the bare, bandaged head in sight. The man stopped to go into a tobacco shop, and by the time he emerged Eleanor had drawn to within a few yards of him again.

A moment later he turned off the street into an alley opposite the Canongate Church. Eleanor arrived there just in time to see him disappear through an open gateway in the wall. She hesitated, then walked under the long, tunnel-like arch that roofed the alley to the entrance where the man had disappeared. On the other side of the wall was a small quadrangle surrounded on three sides by a house with crumbling, sculptured pediments over the windows. There was a small but massive doorway with a crest and Latin inscription carved into the blackened lintel. Eleanor went back to the street.

To her enormous relief she saw Mr McLevy and Ranald hurrying towards her, accompanied by a uniformed constable. Ranald reached her first.

'We spotted you when you began to go down the High Street!'

'Mr McLevy, the man has gone into that house in Bakehouse Close with the cock and trumpet over the door.'

'Aye, the Cock and Trumpet,' said the constable emphatically. 'That's Donald Campbell for sure, sir.'

Mr McLevy said, 'Thank you, Miss Stewart. I'll let you know what happens. Come on, Sandy.'

Eleanor put her hand on Ranald's shoulder as the two policemen left them.

'Oh,' he said in disappointment, 'I hoped to go inside with them.'

'Away home with you,' called back the constable. 'Mr McLevy and me'll see to this best ourselves.'

Ranald reluctantly turned back with Eleanor as she began to walk rapidly towards the Institute. By the time they reached Princes Street she was almost running, and her companion protested at such unnecessary effort.

In some exasperation, Eleanor said, 'It is past eleven o'clock, and I shall have to explain my absence.'

'You should not agitate yourself, Eleanor. They will be too

170

fussled about the Empress's visit to notice that you are missing.' Eleanor told him that his optimism was misplaced.

'I wish McLevy had let us go with him,' grumbled Ranald. 'I wonder what that place is like inside? Weren't you longing to know, Eleanor?'

'Not at all,' she replied. 'It's the same as all those filthy old buildings. They charge the tenants five or six shillings a week, the plaster is falling off the wainscoting, and the rooms are crammed with fir beds full of rags. It stinks inside and out.'

'I say,' said Ranald admiringly, 'you have a fine imagination, Eleanor. I can really see the place.'

'I've very little imagination of that kind, as Chrissie could tell you. A medical student took me inside the house. He had a patient there who couldn't walk to the Dispensary.'

She did not tell Ranald that the girl in question had been dying of syphilis.


Mr McLevy and PC Grant walked past the broken door of the Cock and Trumpet and stood listening in the small hall.

'They kind of folk dinna rise till noon,' said the constable.

'There's some of them stirring,' replied McLevy. There were bumps and shouts overhead, and squabbling voices. Then a woman came flouncing down the stairway holding a greasy frying pan over her head.

'I'll no tell ye again, ye thieving limmers! Get your ain pan. The next time it's out of my house for the baith of ye!' She caught sight of the two policemen in the hall, and stopped abruptly with one foot over the next step.

'What are *you* back for, McLevy? He's no here. You searched the place yesterday.'

'Come down, Mistress Dewar, and I'll tell you why we're here,' said McLevy affably. 'Take us inside, please.'

Mrs Dewar shrugged and led the way into a room with a huge open fireplace. On the stone hearth stood a rusty iron stove with a pile of coal and kindling sticks beside it. She knelt and began to rake vigorously through the bars.

171

'Aye? Let's have it, then. I've the house to sort. There's nae time to blether.'

Two girls with tousled hair came into the room giggling. One was in her night shift, and the other was dressed as far as her petticoat and stays. She was whirling a string of sausages round her head.

'Here, mistress, let's be friends. Janet and me's going to treat you your breakfast.'

She, too, came to a sudden halt when she saw the policemen. The girl in the night shift tried to leave the room, but on a signal from McLevy, the constable stepped to the door and barred her way.

'Come away in, lassies,' said Mr McLevy. 'You'll maybe be able to help us.'

'Help you, McLevy?' said the girl called Janet. 'I'll see you in hell first.'

The two girls came forward to the stove and handed their contributions to Mrs Dewar: the sausages, a jug of milk, and a loaf of bread. Mrs Dewar stirred some fat round the pan.

McLevy watched the breakfast preparations in silence. He had often called in at the Cock and Trumpet when he was in the Force, looking for stolen property. The cracked plaster and rafters now grimed with coal smoke had once enclosed a very different kind of company: the house had been built for a Scottish Secretary of State. After hearing that, Mr McLevy had always entered it in a sober mood.

'I'm still waiting,' said Mrs Dewar, giving the policemen a grim look as she forked the sausages.

'Your Willie's sticking to his story,' said McLevy. 'He still says Donald's here.'

She snorted. 'If Willie's a square rap, then I'm the Duchess of Hamilton. He's a lying wee hound. I should ken – I'm his mother.' She continued frying the breakfast.

'That Bella Watson's got him fair ruined,' said Janet, crouching by the stove with her arms round her knees. The other girl leaned across her and pulled a bottle of whisky from behind the coals.

Mrs Dewar nodded towards a cupboard behind her.

'There's some glasses in there. Mind you pay it, Lizzie.'

'Aye, mistress. Is the peelers drinking with us?'

'No, no,' said Mr McLevy. He made a signal to PC Grant, who edged towards the door.

'Och, if you're that proud we'll just take a budge our ain selves,' said Lizzie contemptuously.

'No me,' said Janet. 'I've got in the pin. My head's fair birling after yon stuff Donny gied me last nicht.'

Mrs Dewar shot the girl a warning look.

McLevy said, 'Now, Mistress Dewar, someone saw Donald Campbell enter this house not half an hour ago. Is he in?'

The two girls became still and watchful; Janet froze with the glass of whisky at her lips. Mrs Dewar made great play with setting out the sausages on three cracked plates.

'How should I ken if he's here or no? You raiked the house frae top to bottom on Tuesday, and didna find him. It's an unco thing if a body canna bide quiet in her ain hame without you trauchling the life out of her!'

'That's why I'm asking your help, Mistress Dewar. I don't suppose you or the fancies want to be entangled with a charge of manslaughter.'

The fork clattered out of Mrs Dewar's hand.

'You didna tell me!' She turned to Janet. 'See where you've got us, you glaikit tawpie! I'll gie you your head in your hands for this, Janet Ferguson!'

The girl began to protest. 'Dinna heed him. It's just a dodge to put the cuffs on Donny.'

McLevy said sternly, 'I need no dodge, Janet. We could have mounted the stair and gone straight to your room.'

'Aye, that's right,' said Mrs Dewar hurriedly. 'Dinna make yourself mair of a fool than you are, Janet. Come away, Mr McLevy. I'll take you there myself. He's upby sleeping.'

PC Grant leaned across the door as the two girls tried to follow McLevy and Mrs Dewar. He said, 'You bide here, lassies, and take your breakfast. It'd be a shame to let it spoil.'

Twenty minutes later, Mr McLevy was bending down to

173

speak through the grill of one of the police cells at Head Office. Inside the cell Donald Campbell was sitting on a pallet mattress.

'I just gied her a wee jundie,' he insisted. 'How was I to ken she'd a pate like an eggshell?'

'But you did not stay to assist her, did you, Donald? You must have been aware that she was injured. It's up with you to their lordships this time, Donald. A short drop, maybe.'

Donald's defiance began to waver. 'Mr McLevy, you ken me. I wouldna stamp on a flea.'

'I'll willingly testify to your light fingers, Donald. Your feet I cannot be so sure of. It must have been a hefty kick that sent the lassie down those stairs so roughly.'

Donald gripped the edge of the hard bed with both hands. 'See here, you've got to help me. Tell them I didna mean to cowp her ower.'

McLevy shifted on to the other foot and stretched his cramped neck.

'You must tell me what happened before I may be sure of that. What did Willie tell you he had seen at Mrs Watson's?'

'Ach, he said it was a bonny necklace, or a bracelet, he didna ken what, but it was studded with mair sparklers than one of they jeweller's windows in Princes Street. I thought maybe I'd dawdle about the street till they came out. I was down there at the back of eight. And a gey cold night it was,' added Donald in an aggrieved voice.

'What made you sure it was the lassie who had the jewel?'

'When they split out, she was still gripping fast to the bag. I kent it had to be inside, so I gaed after her and let her fancy-man alone. I just ettled to rax the bag frae her, naething mair. I swear it, Mr McLevy!'

'Go on, Donald.'

'It fell out the damnedest way. She stopped and waited on me, and cried out my name. Weel, no my name. She thocht yon chap had come after her. When I was nearhand she gied an awfy screech and ran across the road. I was fair sweating in case the peelers heard her. I rugged at the bag, and she rugged back, and maybe I did gie her a wee shog. I dinna

174

ken. That's the truth. I wheeched the jewel out and cast away the bag.'

'Where did you conceal the diadem?'

'Snug under my hat, Mr McLevy.' He began to grin, and then with a cry of pain put a hand up to his cheek.

'Yon bitch! That was an awfy scart frae her nails. I was lucky no to lose the sicht of my ee. It was Janet made me go to the Dispensary. She took off my whiskers forbye.'

'What said the fair Janet when you showed her that geegaw out of the lassie's bag?'

Donald looked at his feet and reddened. 'She said if it was real they'd hae all the peelers frae Berwick to John o'Groats on the hunt. She telt me to take it back to the playhouse.'

'But you still showed it to our friend Harry to make sure?' Mr McLevy stood up and stretched. 'Thank you, Donald. Now we have the full story.'

Donald leapt over to the grill and pressed his face against it anxiously.

'Here, you're no leaving, are you, Mr McLevy? You'll speak for me?'

'I'll speak for you in the police court, and whenever you come before the Sheriff. You won't suffer for what you didn't do, Donald. Only for what you did.'

When Eleanor rushed breathlessly up the Institute steps a few minutes before noon, she found the activities of the building clustered into a few rooms. There was such a hubbub of voices that her late entrance went entirely unnoticed. The lesson she should have been bringing to a close had evidently never taken place; the classroom was unoccupied, as were all the adjoining rooms. She went to search for Christabel.

Various Directors and governesses passed her with quick smiles as they hurried up or down the stairs; Mary emerged from the basement to brush the purple carpet that had been laid across the hall; and there was a crescendo of high-pitched squeals as the little rats burst out of the salon and ran up to the studio to take off their tableau costumes.

Wondering whether Christabel had been watching the

rehearsal, Eleanor went to the doorway of the room and looked in. To her bewilderment she saw Elaine, Maria and Alice kneeling before Christabel, who was enthroned on the dais as the Empress of France.

'I think that will be sufficient, ladies,' Miss Stephens was saying. 'Please proceed to the studio, and change into your usual garments.'

Christabel caught sight of Eleanor. She gathered up the folds of plush curtain that represented the imperial train and jumped down from the dais.

'Go and wait for me in your classroom,' she whispered.

She joined her friend a few moments later.

'I've never seen you with your hair up before,' said Eleanor. 'I hardly recognised you . . . Chrissie, please don't! Someone might come in.'

Christabel laughed, removed herself to an adjacent desk, and finished tying back her hair.

'All right, Miss Stewart. Your face was delightful when you entered. I've never seen anyone look so astounded.'

'No wonder! Why are you performing in the tableau? I thought Jane Rintoul was to be the Empress.'

Christabel explained that Mrs Napier had told her it was the Empress's wish that she should play the chief part. 'I don't believe that for a moment. I wish I knew why Madam Napier's doing this.'

'What's the Empress like?' asked Eleanor. Not having been brought up by a Jacobin grandfather she felt some curiosity about the habits of royalty.

'She's very elegant and beautiful, and almost as charming as Elizabeth.'

'Oh,' said Eleanor, trying to sound enthusiastic.

'Elizabeth brought me back here from Douglas's Hotel. She said I couldn't spend the night alone at Heriot Row when she was staying on at Hamilton Palace. She's old-fashioned about things like that. She doesn't mind about Ranald, because he's a man.'

'But Monday night—'

'That's different. There were two of us. And you're grown-up.'

Eleanor was baffled by Elizabeth's social code. She turned to more important matters.

'Chrissie, we've tracked down the man who assaulted Peggy in India Street. I expect they'll have arrested him by now. And Mr McLevy has found the diadem.'

Christabel's elation vanished.

'Eleanor, I have been very foolish. Please advise me what to do.'

'Yes, Ranald told me that you had ambushed Mr Cargill. Don't worry about it, darling. He would have heard about Peggy's death quite soon, anyway.'

Christabel did not look any more cheerful. 'That was silly of me, too, but I meant something else. When Madam Napier asked me to take Jane's part in the tableau, I said I'd agree if she'd assure me she wasn't going to put it about that Peggy had stolen the diadem. She pretended not to understand, and said we'd talk about it after the Empress's visit.'

'Oh, Chrissie!'

'Well, it seemed quite sensible at the time. Then she produced the diadem out of its box! I'd no idea that it had been found, so I was dreadfully startled. What should I do? When I see her after the tableau she may have another horrible surprise up her sleeve.'

Eleanor replied, 'Mrs Napier will be worried that the Empress may hear about the diadem being stolen. If you think about it in that way, it's obvious what you should do. You must go to her and eat your words.'

'Eleanor, I can't!'

'It is not so very dreadful. Just say you want to apologise for speaking on impulse, and making such a rash suggestion. Or could you merely forget that you have asked to see her? . . . No, I suppose not,' said Eleanor, answering her own question. 'Well, go to her with your apology, and Mrs Napier will find some clever way to overlook the fact that you have been extremely impertinent. She will let the whole business die away.'

177

'You really think that's what I ought to do?'

Eleanor said, 'Yes. If you go on annoying Mrs Napier, she may ask your aunt to remove you from the Institute.'

Christabel took Eleanor's hand. 'I wouldn't eat humble-pie even to stay in Edinburgh with you, if I thought she was going to lie about Peggy.'

Downstairs, the bell rang for luncheon. Eleanor laughed, put her arms on Christabel's shoulders, and shook her.

'You are impossible! Far too high-principled for me, and far too inquisitive for your own good. Probably no one will ever know who stole the diadem.'

Christabel gave her an embarrassed look. '*I* know. But it's difficult to tell you.'

At that moment the door opened, and two of the little rats entered. They ran over to Eleanor.

'Miss Stewart, are you going to watch us this afternoon? We're to be ash trees.'

Christabel smiled, and, seeming almost glad to be interrupted, left the room.

*In the middle hours of Wednesday afternoon, Her Majesty proceeded from Douglas's Hotel to the Scottish Institute for the Education of the Daughters of Gentlefolk, in Moray Place, where a large gathering of well-dressed people awaited the arrival of the Empress.*

*The Empress was received by the Patrons and Directors of the establishment, and the Lady Superintendent had the honour of conducting Her Majesty to the main salon, where the young ladies had devised an entertainment for Her Majesty. Several of these fortunate pupils were then presented to the Empress, who expressed great delight at their performance, and questioned them about their studies.*

*Her Majesty spent almost an hour inside the Institute, and then proceeded with her suite to the waiting carriage, round which an even larger crowd had assembled, although darkness was now falling.*

*It is indeed gratifying, that while Eugénie, Empress of the French, visits the land of her ancestors, Her Majesty's*

*condescension should be extended to the youthful inhabitants
of a city which is universally acknowledged as pre-eminent in
the British Isles for the number and quality of its institutions
dedicated to the education of the young; and that she should
favour in particular one devoted to the advancement of her
own sex; and which, having been founded in 1835, this year
celebrates its Silver Jubilee, and once more proudly makes
good its claim to be the first such establishment in the United
Kingdom to undertake that our young ladies shall enjoy the
intellectual privileges which have hitherto been confined to
their brothers.*

The crowd was slowly dispersing from Moray Place;
carriages were driven at walking pace through the thinning
clusters of pedestrians that ebbed away through the four exit
roads.

Inside the Institute, Mary worked her way down from the
upper floors, extinguishing the blaze of wax candles, one by
one, and relighting the gas jets which they had replaced.

Mrs Napier stood on the outside steps, surrounded by the
Directors and their wives. The visit had been a magnificent
success. She had been presented to the Empress by Colonel
Favé as soon as Her Majesty arrived, shortly before four
o'clock. But there had been one item to mar Mrs Napier's
pleasure.

On their way to the salon the colonel had whispered to
her, 'Madame, please forgive the zeal of a devoted servant.
Her Majesty knows nothing of the affair of the diadem.'

He passed to Mrs Napier the letter of apology which she
had given to Madame Pollet that morning. With a shaking
hand, Mrs Napier thrust it deep into the foliage of a huge
majolica pot outside the salon.

She flushed with anger as she realised how the little Spanish
woman had tricked her. The Empress's wish to have Christabel in the tableau was probably fictitious as well. Perhaps
Madame Pollet and Christabel had hatched the scheme
between them. Her hatred of the girl redoubled. Not only

would she rid herself of Christabel MacKenzie, but she would make sure that her exit was a disgraceful one.

These thoughts scourged Mrs Napier as she escorted the Empress into the salon; but she made herself put them aside and kept her face serene, even while she was watching Christabel's performance.

The Empress was enchanted by the tableau: she kept turning her head to smile at her two ladies-in-waiting; she asked for the four main performers to be brought to her after it was over.

When the Empress left the building, Colonel Favé and the Comtesse de Montebello lingered a moment to renew their thanks to the Lady Superintendent.

'All has gone well,' said the colonel, throwing a marked significance into his tone.

The Lady Superintendent suddenly realised that the diadem scandal was still a potential threat to Colonel Favé's standing with the Empress. His own reputation was involved in keeping the secret. And once the coveted honour was granted, it could not be taken away. Into Mrs Napier's mind sprang an audacious plan.

'Sir, I venture to hope that before the close of the year, Her Majesty may graciously allow the Imperial name to be attached to our establishment, to remind us of this happy occasion. How worthy a diadem that would be to crown our Jubilee!'

Colonel Favé thought these words very audacious indeed. Such unsophisticated bluntness was quite at odds with his impression of the Lady Superintendent; and he understood perfectly the hint of blackmail. The colonel had already assumed that some favour might be granted to mark the visit, but not for a year or two. Hiding his displeasure, he bowed over Mrs Napier's hand; he murmured that he would always be at madame's service to present her hopes to the Empress.

The countess was even more amazed at such presumptuous behaviour.

When the royal party had driven away, Dr Graham spoke

180

for the whole group of Patrons and Directors clustered around Mrs Napier.

'What was the meaning of those intriguing words you spoke to Colonel Favé?'

'My dear friends, very soon our beloved Institute shall bear a new and prouder title: *The Imperial Scottish Institute*. And I am bold enough to think that Her Majesty may condescend to be our Patroness.'

There was a spontaneous round of applause. The group encircled Mrs Napier; the clapping became slow and solemn. Mr Dubuc and Dr Graham had tears in their eyes. Dr Graham took her hands, overcome by emotion.

'This is the most memorable day of my life, of all our lives! And it is you, my dear Mrs Napier, who have given it to us. Something must be done – nay, *shall* be done – to show our appreciation.'

There was a fervent murmur. The other Directors and Patrons pressed forward to give their congratulations. Mrs Napier held out her arms in a gesture that enfolded them all. 'This has been my golden secret, dear friends. How happy I am that I can share it with you at last!'

She stood on the front steps as they went away with admiring backward glances. The wave of her right hand was almost regal. She watched until they had disappeared along the street, and then returned to the salon. She mounted the dais.

The pupils had flocked in from other parts of the building. With an air of happy exhaustion they gazed up at Mrs Napier, waiting for some word or sign to seal the end of this wonderful day.

Mrs Napier smiled benevolently at the radiant faces.

'We shall show our appreciation of Her Imperial Majesty's visit by dividing it from our daily tasks. You shall return to *those* refreshed and inspired by the honour so graciously bestowed in this, the year of our Silver Jubilee. First, let us give thanks for our blessings.'

She bowed her head, and offered a prayer long enough to ensure that any adults still on their way out would not be swept off their feet by the effect of her next announcement.

After the amen she said, 'We shall meet again on Friday morning. Thursday is to be a holiday.'

With cheers, whoops and yells the pupils at last released their over-stimulated emotions. The noise did not last long: the salon emptied in a flash as the girls ran to rejoin their parents. Mrs Napier looked on contentedly, thinking how the pupils would spend the next day spreading the news of her triumph around the city. Miss Merchant and Miss Erroll were standing beside her.

Miss Merchant said, 'I never understand it. They shoot away like uncaged birds, but they are always so happy to return. What do you think, Miss Erroll?'

The senior governess did not reply. Miss Merchant said with concern, 'Miss Erroll?'

The senior governess half turned her head. Her look was ghastly, and her eyes were unfocused.

Miss Merchant whispered, 'Are you unwell again, Madeleine? Let me escort you to your room.'

Something between a sigh and a grunt came from Miss Erroll's lips as she left the salon. She had the air of a sleep-walker, thought Miss Merchant. Before she could mention her anxiety to Mrs Napier, the Lady Superintendent turned to her.

'Anna, there is something I wish us to discuss in private.'

They went up to Mrs Napier's sitting room. There the Lady Superintendent told Miss Merchant that Peggy had been assaulted in India Street and had subsequently died in the Infirmary. She did not mention the theft of the diadem.

'Forgive me for not telling you the full story before, Anna. I could not inflict my anxiety on any other until Her Majesty's visit was over.'

'And the purloined nightdress?' asked Miss Merchant, after expressing shock and horror.

'As I told you, it was found in a bag beside her. I do not know if that was the reason for the attack. I am concerned about possible scandal. Before Her Majesty arrived, Mr McLevy handed me a communication from Superintendent Linton. The police have arrested the man who assaulted

Peggy. The case will come before the police court on Thursday or Friday.'

'I do not suppose the girls or their mamas will be greatly interested in Peggy Murdo,' said Miss Merchant complacently. 'What is there to be anxious about?'

'The Superintendent has assured me that our name will not be mentioned. But can we rely on that? I do not trust these people who write for the news journals. If a whisper should reach them about the circumstances of Peggy's death—'

Miss Merchant tried to allay Mrs Napier's fears.

'I have heard that the Empress is to leave Edinburgh tomorrow. So there is no danger in that quarter.'

'But I have not yet told you the worst, Anna. Christabel MacKenzie has somehow come to hear of all this. She may stir up trouble out of sheer malice.'

Mrs Napier looked enigmatically at her assistant. She had not fully decided on the best way to discredit Christabel, and it was difficult to make use of Miss Merchant's alert ear for gossip without telling her more than it was safe for her to know.

Miss Merchant suggested that they should wait to see how the matter was reported in the news journals, and then decide on a course of action.

'How practical you are, Anna!' said Mrs Napier, knowing that loyalty was never undermined by a compliment. 'I am thankful for your commonsense. I am afraid that Miss Erroll is failing.'

Miss Merchant felt a throb of pleasure. No one could have failed to notice how much the Lady Superintendent had come to rely on her in the past few days. Not that she wished Miss Erroll any harm; but it would be agreeable to step into her shoes.

Mrs Napier let Miss Merchant chatter on about poor Miss Erroll's headaches, and how bravely she strove to carry out her duties in spite of them, while she herself pondered on the dangers still lurking in the connection between Peggy's death and the loss of the diadem. This one-sided conversation was interrupted by a loud rap at the door.

Mrs Napier called, 'Come in, please.'

The door opened slowly, and Christabel entered.

Rather to her own surprise, Christabel had enjoyed taking part in the tableau. In so far as such a passive role could be played, she had played it to the Empress and the two ladies-in-waiting, and had been rewarded by their attention. Once the tableau was over, her thoughts went back to the apprehensions that had filled her since that morning.

She did not return to the salon with the other performers after they changed out of their tableau costumes, and when she did come down, it was almost empty. Christabel felt a twitch of anxiety as she looked for Eleanor, and realised that she had already gone home.

Eleanor's commonsense had warned her that it would be unwise to be seen talking privately to Christabel on such an over-charged evening. She had given the best advice she could; she went away in an uneasy state of mind.

The aftermath of Wednesday afternoon produced a relaxation of normal rules. The boarders sat in clusters on the stairs or in corners of rooms usually barred to them in the evening. They whispered over their memories, happy but fatigued.

Christabel passed from group to group, not joining any of them. She decided that she would follow Eleanor's advice. It would be best to get the unpleasant scene over as soon as possible.

The effort to nerve herself for the deed made Christabel give the Lady Superintendent's door a bold and peremptory knock. Then her courage failed her. She pushed the door open slowly and found that Mrs Napier was not alone. Miss Merchant was sitting with her.

'What is it you wish, Christabel?' asked Mrs Napier, not hiding her surprise. It was unheard of for even the senior pupils to approach Mrs Napier's sitting room unbidden.

'I wondered if I might speak to you about that matter I mentioned this morning,' said Christabel, glancing at Miss Merchant pointedly.

'I see.' Mrs Napier was granted a moment to decide what she would do, as Mary entered with the tea tray.

'It's very near the boarders' supper time, ma'am,' said Mary, 'so I'll take it back if you dinna want it.'

With her eyes still on Christabel, Mrs Napier said, 'Leave it, Mary, thank you. And will you please bring two more cups out of my china cabinet. Miss Merchant and Miss MacKenzie will be joining me . . . Sit down, Christabel.'

Coincidence had offered Mrs Napier an unexpected gift. It was in such bold seizures of the initiative that much of her mastery lay.

Miss Merchant was shocked at this pert invasion of the Lady Superintendent's sanctum. Christabel's presentation to the Empress had begun to lose its spell. She wondered at Mrs Napier's magnanimity: sorely tried by that wretched girl, she could still address her with cheerful friendliness!

Christabel was taken aback by the prospect of Miss Merchant staying to watch her eat humble-pie. Mrs Napier usually preferred to conduct her duels without witnesses. She sipped the tea unhappily, trying to make conversation about the Empress's visit.

Mrs Napier set down her cup with only the faintest hint of coming to business.

'Now, Christabel, as you know, Lady Elizabeth is coming to see me tomorrow.' She smiled at Miss Merchant and Christabel in turn. 'Some of our fledglings seem to think us perfect ogres and dread such interviews.'

Christabel smiled back politely, but began to feel in danger.

'You are old enough to take a more sensible view. Do not you think so, Miss Merchant?'

The governess felt she could now safely assert her new position. 'Indeed, yes. Christabel is a most grown-up young lady,' she said, using the forbidden Christian name.

Mrs Napier approached the precipice and beckoned Christabel towards it. 'There have been some disagreements between us lately, and it is best for us to settle them before your aunt and I meet to discuss your progress. What you say now may well influence what I have to tell Lady Elizabeth.'

Christabel hesitated. Mrs Napier gave an encouraging smile. 'You may speak freely before Miss Merchant. She knows all my thoughts on this subject.'

Miss Merchant glowed with pride that she had been chosen to be the confidante of such a woman. Mrs Napier was so wise, so reasonable, so far-sighted! Only a heart of stone could refuse to bow before such generosity.

'You are sure that I may speak out?' Christabel did not wish to put Mrs Napier at a disadvantage. This foolish chivalry had been caught from her grandfather.

'Of course, my dear. You have heard me say so.'

Christabel fell over the edge.

'Mrs Napier, I wish to apologise for speaking so rashly this morning.'

Mrs Napier inclined her head graciously; and had matters been left at that, all would have been well. However, Christabel thought that Miss Merchant already knew about the theft of the paste crown. She was also choking over her humble-pie, and could not resist adding, 'I am sure we are both aware that Peggy did not steal the diadem.'

Mrs Napier's expression did not alter. She caught Miss Merchant's eye.

'Christabel, I fear that your lively imagination is running away with you. We all delight in your brilliant talents, but there is a distinction between real events and the promptings of fancy.'

Christabel persisted, although with a growing feeling of alarm.

'I know Peggy took the nightdress, but that was different. You mustn't blame her for the theft of the diadem as well.'

'Why should I blame that unfortunate girl for something that never happened?' asked Mrs Napier mildly.

Christabel looked from one woman to the other, so shocked that she forgot all Eleanor's good advice. Mrs Napier had actually told a lie! Christabel was very observant, but had not yet grasped that adults oiled the wheels of everyday life with many small acts of deceit. She was completely outflanked.

She stood up and said in an unsteady voice, 'The diadem was stolen on Sunday evening. Mr McLevy found it again in a jeweller's shop in the High Street.'

Mrs Napier's face showed a careful balance of pity and sorrow. 'My dear child, whatever are you saying? You tried on the diadem this morning in front of me, did you not? It has not left this building since Madame Pollet brought it here on Sunday.'

'Miss Merchant—' appealed Christabel.

Miss Merchant was trying hard to remain silent, but she was provoked into saying, 'Oh, Christabel, how can you tell such tales?'

Christabel panicked and lost her temper. She shouted, 'It's a lie - a lie! The diadem was taken out of this room on Sunday night. I saw Miss Erroll steal it.'

Indignation loosed Miss Merchant's tongue. 'You wicked girl! Is there no limit to the falsehoods you will tell? Mrs Napier, you are far too lenient with her. I cannot sit here and listen to such terrible slanders.'

By the time that Miss Merchant turned her wrathful face to Mrs Napier, the Lady Superintendent had managed to hide her astonishment at the one detail in the conversation which she had not foreseen. She said coldly, 'I hope it will not be necessary for Lady Elizabeth to hear about this. I will give you an opportunity to take back your words. You have been very taxed, Christabel, and I do not wish to be cruel. I am willing to forget this scene if you will apologise for your untruth.'

Christabel sat down again, twisting her hands in her lap, quite unable to cope with the situation. Mrs Napier looked at her with sombre compassion. Or so it appeared to Miss Merchant. With an air of resigned sorrow, Mrs Napier continued, 'Go away now, Christabel, and try to compose yourself. Think carefully. There is still time for you to retract your rash words before I speak to Lady Elizabeth tomorrow afternoon.'

When the door had closed on Christabel Miss Merchant

said, 'Oh, Mrs Napier, was that wise? Heaven only knows what she may say to the other girls!'

Mrs Napier smiled. She knew exactly what she was doing.

A little later, Miss Merchant also left the room, longing to confide in someone. Yet to tell the other governesses would cause stupefaction and gossip. Normally, Miss Merchant enjoyed this response; but her new status forbade such pleasures. To hoard the information would bring deeper satisfaction, as Mrs Napier came to rely more and more on her wise counsel. Still, one duty was plain. She must warn Madeleine Erroll of the terrible accusation made against her.

Mrs Napier sat on in her sitting room. Her brows were tightened in a frown of concentration as she tried to work out the reason for Christabel's remark. She decided it must be an attempt to break out of the corner into which she had pinned the girl.

At a quarter to six Eleanor was in the middle of describing the Empress's visit to her aunt and uncle. She had stood at the back of the salon with the pupils and student governesses who were allowed into the room to see the tableau. Eleanor dwelt longest on how Christabel had borne herself, impersonating the Empress of the French.

At the end of Eleanor's account, Mrs Stewart rose to see how Jenny was getting on with supper.

'You'll be fair fidging to see Miss MacKenzie and have her own story.'

As she spoke there was a loud jangling at the bell. Eleanor went to answer it and found Christabel leaning against the doorpost, with no hat, no mantle, her eyes hot and angry.

'May I come in?' She sounded as if she had been running.

'Of course. Come to my room.' She led Christabel to her small bedroom to find out the reason for this sudden visit before she took her through to her aunt and uncle. Christabel sat on the bed hugging herself and shivering.

'You shouldn't have come out without a mantle, Chrissie. You are shaking with the cold!'

'It's because I am so angry. That's why I left the Institute.'

188

She told Eleanor how she had apologised and how Mrs Napier had denied that the diadem had ever gone missing.

'That's my fault,' said Eleanor. 'I advised you to go to her.'

'How can she lie so boldly, and in front of Miss Merchant, too! How can she not be ashamed that I know she lies? Why doesn't it *burn* her?'

Eleanor had met several of Mrs Napier's manipulations of the truth before.

'She cares nothing for the opinions of anyone whom she considers her inferior,' she said. 'It is like –' she searched for a comparison – 'well, as in the ancient days of slavery, when the Roman emperors did not mind to have slaves cut their misshapen toenails, because they did not think of such people as human.'

Christabel began to laugh. 'Eleanor, what silly, wonderful things you say! Toenails!' She went off into paroxysms of hysteria.

After holding her tightly until she had calmed a little, Eleanor said, 'I think you should lie down and stop talking for a while.'

'You're not going to leave me, are you?'

'No, I am going to fetch you something to drink.'

She went back to her aunt and uncle.

'Christabel is overwrought about some happening at the Institute. I'll talk to her for half an hour and then walk back with her. I'm going to make her some tea.'

Mr Stewart followed his niece to the kitchen and insisted on dropping a large tot of brandy into the cup.

Christabel coughed over the fortified tea; she drank it in gulps, with long pauses as she stared at the wall.

'In a little while, you must borrow a mantle from my aunt and we'll walk back to the Institute together,' said Eleanor.

Christabel pounded the bed. 'I'm not going back there tonight.'

'Did anyone see you leave the building?'

'I do not care if they did. She *can't* say I lied. Mr McLevy knows the diadem was stolen. So does Mr Cargill.' She saw the look in Eleanor's eye. 'No, I shan't mention anything

189

about it to him again, I promise. But there you are! That was another lie, about Peggy being in the Infirmary, when she was – was already dead.' Christabel's voice wobbled.

Eleanor spoke gently, 'I'm very glad to see you, but you shouldn't have walked out like that, Chrissie. You have given Mrs Napier something else to use against you.'

'Elizabeth would never believe her if she said that I had lied.'

Eleanor sighed. Sometimes she felt twenty years older than Christabel. 'It'll not happen like that . . . Please let me take you back to the Institute.'

'No, I shall spend the night at Heriot Row. I shall go back with Elizabeth tomorrow afternoon.'

Christabel's face was dark and obstinate. Eleanor said tentatively, 'Mrs Napier must feel very confident that everyone will believe her story. There's obviously far more in this than we suspect, Please, please, let the whole matter drop. After all, Peggy did take the nightgown. There may have been some kind of silly lark about the diadem, and it all went horribly wrong.'

'But she didn't take the diadem! I tried to tell you this morning, and I couldn't. It was Miss Erroll.'

'Miss Erroll!' Eleanor laughed. 'Oh, darling, what an absurd idea!'

'No, listen. You remember, Madam Napier made me sleep in the studio on Sunday night. I kept on waking, and then I heard a noise outside. I opened the door a little, and there was Miss Erroll walking down the stairs. She made a clinking noise with – well, she was holding something. I looked over the banister and watched her cross the hall. She put the diadem into that bag we saw at the Infirmary. It was standing beside the laundry basket. Then she came back up the stairs, moving in the strangest way, as if she were sleep-walking. I think her eyes were shut – but it was too dark to be sure. I stood in the doorway until she passed me.'

'It must have been very dim in the hall as well, even with the gas burning,' said Eleanor doubtfully. 'Did you actually see her put the diadem into the bag?'

'No, but I saw her open the bag, and the clinking had stopped when she came upstairs. When Mr McLevy said it was as if a cat had fouled inside the bag, I realized at once. I saw her empty it into the bag.'

'*Empty*? What was she holding?'

Christabel flushed and did not answer. Eleanor cried in exasperation, 'Tell it out, Christabel, and don't be so missish!'

'Very well. It was a chamber pot.'

Eleanor's expression did not change. She said, 'I do not see how that proves it was she who took the diadem.'

'She carried it downstairs carefully, held out in front of her. There was this clinking noise as well. When she came back up she just let it hang by her side.'

'Well . . .' said Eleanor. 'Perhaps you are right.'

Christabel seized her arm excitedly. 'This is what happened, Miss Erroll used the chamber pot, and carried it down to Mrs Napier's sitting room. She put the diadem in the pot and then walked down to the hall. Perhaps she meant the diadem to go out with the dirty linen, and mistook the bag for the basket . . . Eleanor, can someone plan to do a thing like that when she's still asleep?'

Remembering the state in which Christabel had arrived, Eleanor thought it best to postpone this discussion.

'Let's talk about that later, darling. You'll not speak about this to anyone, will you? Not even for Peggy.'

'Of course I won't!'

'Well, I think you should go to your aunt's house now, Chrissie – unless you will consider letting me take you back to the Institute,' she added, still hoping that Christabel would change her mind.

Christabel said she would go to Heriot Row at once if Eleanor would spend the evening there.

'Elizabeth won't scold me so much for leaving the Institute when she sees you with me,' she joked. Eleanor did not share this opinion, but she agreed to go.

However, when they arrived, Elizabeth was being dressed by Marie. She had been invited to have dinner at Douglas's

Hotel with the Empress and the Duke of Hamilton. She had only a brief conversation with the two young women, but she made a point of seeing Eleanor on her own for a few moments.

All through Eugénie's visit, Miss Erroll had stood or walked one pace behind Mrs Napier. That was her place, her duty. This forced homage had strained her self-control to its limit. When the tour of the building was over, she trailed behind the imperial party into the salon hardly able to walk.

Her revulsion was so strong that she began to think she might be going mad. When she sat down for the tableau, she found herself almost directly behind the Empress, who was placed in the middle of the front row. Miss Erroll leaned to one side so that the hateful figure would not be in her field of view.

She saw Maria, furbelowed as Marie Antoinette, walk stiffly across the room holding up the panniers that supported her satin gown. When she reached the dais, a little rat, blacked and turbaned, fell on one knee and held up a green leather casket. From it Maria took out the Grecian diadem.

A gasp and swiftly hushed whisper went round the salon.

Miss Erroll's head jerked back as the lustre of the brilliants shot into her eyes. Maria mounted the platform and placed the diadem on Christabel's head.

By a curious chance – due to the way the audience sat – it appeared to Miss Erroll that the diadem had alighted on the head of Eugénie. Her sight blurred, and her mind refused to take in what followed. She was aware of nothing more until she dragged herself upstairs to her own room after the Empress's departure.

Miss Erroll stumbled to the bed and sat down, shaking as if she had a fever. The events of the past hour shuttled to and fro, distorted by other memories, like the hallucinations of drunkenness, although Miss Erroll had no experience of that state.

She held her hands to her face and moaned as she rocked backwards and forwards. The room was illuminated only by the flames behind the steel fireguard; but the flickering light hurt her eyes and reminded her of the flashing from the diadem. She opened her bedside cupboard, took out the chamber pot, and vomited.

After she had been sick, the frenzy in her head receded. She lay back on the bed, retching occasionally as waves of nausea flowed back; but they returned with less and less force. Eventually she was able to lie there without feeling queasy. She was depressed and exhausted, but calmer.

She had no idea of the time; in any case, going down to supper was out of the question.

Miss Erroll sat up, made herself go over to the cupboard where she kept her handkerchiefs, and dabbed some lavender water on to a square of cambric. She pressed this to her forehead and temples, shuddering at the sharp odour. A general feeling of discomfort and misery had overtaken all other sensations. She sat in the armchair, leaned her head on her hand, and closed her eyes.

There was a knock at the door, which she ignored. It was repeated. A voice said, 'Miss Erroll, it is I, Anna Merchant. May I come in?'

The senior governess lifted her head and looked at the door. The question was repeated.

'Come in,' she whispered, in a voice much too low to be heard. The door opened nevertheless, and Miss Merchant entered.

'I have been so concerned about you, Madeleine. You did not appear at supper, so I knew that your headache must have returned. I have brought some drops which were most efficacious when my dear mama used to suffer from the same trouble.'

Miss Erroll waved towards a table without speaking. Miss Merchant put there the bottle she had brought, and drew up a small wooden chair beside Miss Erroll. She got up again to light the gas. Miss Erroll blinked, and shielded her eyes. Miss Merchant bent forward to inspect the wan face, and decided that this was no time for pity.

'Madeleine, it is my duty to speak to you about something

193

which concerns the Institute. That dreadful child Christabel MacKenzie has been causing even more trouble. Her aunt comes to see Mrs Napier tomorrow afternoon. I hope that Mrs Napier will be frank with her.'

Miss Erroll shut her eyes again and hardly seemed to be listening.

'We should all support Mrs Napier in a request that the odious girl be removed from the school. Your voice, as senior governess, would carry the most weight.'

Miss Merchant peered at the woman whom she now confidently regarded as her predecessor, irked by her lack of interest.

'Madeleine, are you paying heed to me?'

Miss Erroll opened her eyes. 'I can hear you, Anna.'

'You must do more than *hear*. Christabel MacKenzie has also slandered you with an atrocious fib. She told Mrs Napier and myself that on Sunday night you tried to steal the Empress's diadem.'

Miss Erroll turned her head and Miss Merchant saw a stirring of something in her eyes that frightened her into silence.

'Well?' said Miss Merchant uncertainly, after a few moments. Still Miss Erroll did not answer.

Miss Merchant wanted to run away from that dreadful look. Yet she could not leave matters there: she owed it to the Institute, and to Mrs Napier, who wished to share the burdens of office with her. She must be brave.

'Madeleine,' she said, in a tremulous voice that was trying to be firm, 'I am going to bring Christabel MacKenzie to you. You must tell her to her face she is lying. Then I think you should allow us to consult the school physician in your behalf.'

Without waiting to see the effect of these words, she hurried out of the room to look for Christabel.

Miss Erroll sat in the same position for another ten minutes or so. She remembered her dream about the banks of Jordan; weaving in and out of it were images which became more vivid than the room in which she was sitting.

Miss Merchant had thrown more coal on the fire; its banked-up heat began to draw an unpleasant odour from the bedside cupboard where she had replaced the chamber pot. As her nostrils took this in, the pictures in Miss Erroll's mind became more precise and focused.

She cried aloud, biting her hands so that the pain would drive the images away; but they danced on and on. They were grotesque and filthy; they were delusions – how could they not be? Yet they were insistent; they forced themselves into her mind, wearing the mask of truth. Finally they spiralled into a needle-bright equation.

If she had done *that*, she was degenerate, and not fit to live. If she imagined such things, she was mad.

Miss Erroll lifted her pocket bible from the top of the bedside cupboard. She opened the front cover and leaned towards the fire. On the flyleaf was written, 'To MADELEINE DUNLOP ERROLL, from her loving parents, 5 May 1817, her seventh birthday.'

She shut the book, and still holding it firmly in one hand used the other to put on her mantle and bonnet, although she did not tie the strings of either. Then she went downstairs and walked out of the Institute.

# Thursday

On Thursday morning, not long after breakfast, Mary rang at the Stewarts' door and said that Mrs Napier wanted to speak to Eleanor at the Institute.

'Today, Mary? We have a holiday.'

'This forenoon, she said. As soon as possible.'

Eleanor was almost certain that she knew why the Lady Superintendent wanted to see her. After leaving Christabel the previous evening, she had reflected on the implications of Mrs Napier's lie. If she suspected that Christabel had shared the dangerous secret about the diadem, her attempts to silence Christabel would include Eleanor. The only matter in doubt was how Mrs Napier would set about this.

Eleanor told her aunt that she had to go out. Mrs Stewart was ruffled at the summons. Eleanor was being 'taken a loan of'. When she had her 'papers' – by which Mrs Stewart meant the completion of Eleanor's training – she should not be so easy-going with her employers.

Eleanor was amused at the illusion that being a full-time governess would give her greater status in Mrs Napier's eyes. She walked up Church Lane, and resisted the temptation to ring at Lady Elizabeth's door for a few words with Christabel before she went into the Institute.

The school was deserted. The boarders had been taken out on some expedition, with the promise that they would also watch the departure of the Empress of the French. Mrs Napier came straight to the point.

'Miss Stewart, I wish to find out whether Miss MacKenzie

visited your home yesterday afternoon, after the Empress left us.'

Eleanor admitted that Christabel had come to her.

'Where is she now?'

'She went on to her aunt's house in Heriot Row shortly after six o'clock.'

This seemed to take the wind out of Mrs Napier's sails; but she soon recovered.

'That is no excuse for your not informing us at once. We were all most concerned when we discovered her absence. Your thoughtlessness, if I may give it so charitable a name, has caused us a great deal of anxiety. I shall have to speak about this incident to Lady Elizabeth.'

'She already knows, Mrs Napier. I accompanied Christabel to Heriot Row, and Lady Elizabeth questioned me about what had happened. When I offered to inform you she asked me to leave the matter in her own hands.'

Mrs Napier faltered again, but only for a moment. 'Did you not realise how grossly impertinent it was to call on a lady of such high social standing, when you were unacquainted with her? At such an hour, too! You astonish me, Miss Stewart. I thought we had remedied some of the deficiencies in your breeding.'

So far, the effort to grasp Mrs Napier's intentions had kept Eleanor calm; but this last remark was too much for her. She retorted, 'I *am* acquainted with Lady Elizabeth. I was introduced to her on Tuesday morning when she arrived at Heriot Row.'

Too late, she realised what she had done. Like the shutter of that new-fangled device, the camera, comprehension flashed across Mrs Napier's face.

'When I sent you to Heriot Row with Miss MacKenzie, you actually spent the night in the house?'

'Yes,' said Eleanor, wondering how far Mrs Napier would probe the situation.

'Why? There is a resident housekeeper, I believe.'

'My reasons are private, Mrs Napier. I am not obliged to discuss them with you.'

Mrs Napier said angrily, 'I see you are determined to abet Miss MacKenzie's misconduct. I have thought for some time that your influence over her is most undesirable. You have clearly abused your private meetings with her.'

'Your remarks are very general. In what way is my influence on Miss MacKenzie so undesirable?'

Mrs Napier did not reply at first. For once, her feelings showed on her face. Eleanor saw her look of outrage change into suspicious doubt; but whatever thoughts came into her mind were clearly rejected as incredible.

'You do not answer my question,' said Eleanor.

Mrs Napier brought out in a blustering tone, 'You have encouraged Miss MacKenzie in a number of preposterous falsehoods –'

'About the Empress's diadem, and the death of Peggy Murdo?'

Mrs Napier gave Eleanor a look of pure hatred. Her right hand smoothed the surface of her desk. Eleanor realised that she had been foolish to reveal how much she knew about these matters; but she was too angry to care.

'There is something else,' said the Lady Superintendent, also smoothing all expression out of her voice. 'I see that you have been listening to idle gossip; but I knew that already from Mrs Murdo. She tells me that you may be asked to testify on – on the matters to which you refer.'

'Mr McLevy said that was possible, but only if the case goes up to a higher court.'

'Indeed? Well, I am sorry, Miss Stewart, but I cannot give you permission to testify. The name of the Institute must not be mentioned in any legal proceedings.'

Eleanor felt another surge of anger, but made herself speak quietly.

'Forgive me, Mrs Napier, I do not think the choice lies in your hands. My evidence may be of very little importance; but if I am called as a witness I have to appear.'

'If there is any such prosecution, it can be successfully concluded without your help. You have only to say that you are reluctant to speak in public, and you will be excused.'

Mrs Napier still found it difficult to admit that any such case existed.

'I do not see how anyone can predict the outcome of the trial. I certainly shan't refuse to testify, Mrs Napier.'

The Lady Superintendent leaned across the desk and folded her hands together.

'Very well. I cannot prevent your appearing, of course, but you will not be allowed to do so as a member of the Institute. I shall ask you to resign your place before the case comes up. Would you like to think this over, Miss Stewart?'

'I do not need to. But I shall not resign, Mrs Napier. You will have to dismiss me.'

Eleanor went home by a roundabout route to avoid passing Heriot Row. Telling Christabel before she returned to SINDOG to face Mrs Napier would only make it more likely that the encounter would be disastrous.

Mr Cargill too had left home early that morning, but he was out on the street long before Eleanor. It was still dark when he set out. He went first to Moray Place to leave his letter of resignation at Dr Graham's house, slipping it furtively through the letter box without ringing the bell. Then he strode up the Mound towards the Castle, in the hope that the breezy air of the Esplanade would refresh his brain.

Mr Cargill's footsteps got no farther than a Lawnmarket tavern. There he sat and brooded in a dark corner. He was still grieving for Peggy, but the main focus of his thoughts was a wish to be revenged on Mrs Napier. Would she have been so quick to dismiss the best singing teacher in Edinburgh, if she hadn't been afraid that scandal might blow away the Empress's favour? (Mr Cargill had a good conceit of his own talents.)

Damn it, no! Mr Cargill banged his fourth brandy and soda on the table. He'd dearly love to spoil her triumph. If only he dared to splash the whole story about Peggy across the news journals! That would certainly cooper her plans with the Empress.

Mr Cargill sagged over his glass, feeling sorry for himself, and full of maudlin regrets for Peggy. He had an aching need to talk about her to somebody. Perhaps that policeman, or detective, or whatever he was, could tell him why Peggy died. What was his name?

Another brandy and soda brought it back. McLevy. Mr Cargill went down to the Police Office.

Near the foot of Old Fishmarket Close he found the house he was directed to. He went up the turnpike stair and peered at the doors. He knocked at one, but there was no reply. As he tried the next Mr McLevy came up the stairs behind him with a dog at his side. He took his visitor in with him.

Mr Cargill began by saying how surprised he was that he had not been interviewed over Peggy Murdo's death. Not caring any longer, he told McLevy why.

'Sir, we didn't need to find you,' said McLevy. 'The chap's been nabbed.'

He looked quizzically at this slightly fuddled man, wondering what his motives were. He didn't strike him as a broken-hearted lover.

'I'd like to hear more,' said Robert Cargill. 'Who found her, and about the man who attacked her.'

'I can't do that, sir. My report's to be presented at the police court. Superintendent Linton might be willing to tell you. Or ask Miss Stewart and her chum Miss MacKenzie.'

Robert Cargill flinched at Christabel's name. He turned to go.

'By the way,' said McLevy, 'you can maybe do something for me. I'm on a new case. I'm trying to trace a New Town resident, and I have only a name to go on.'

'I live in Regent Road,' said Mr Cargill.

'Aye, sir, but you're often in the New Town. She was still clutching this book in her hand.'

Mr McLevy opened the flyleaf of Miss Erroll's bible.

'Yes,' said Mr Cargill. 'I do know her.'

McLevy put on his coat again.

'I'm sorry to ask you, sir, but we need someone to identify the body. Would you come up to the Dead House with me? No, Jeanie, you bide by the fire. I'll not be long.'

Fifteen minutes later Mr Cargill emerged from the Police Office, extremely pale. He had been sick. He had never been in a mortuary before.

'Step up with me to the house,' said McLevy. 'I've something inby that'll settle your stomach.'

He took Mr Cargill back home and gave him a large glass of whisky.

Mr Cargill drank and then turned aside, retching again. He would never forget the distortion of Miss Erroll's face – what was left of it. The rest had been mercifully hidden under her woollen gown.

'It usually is the Dean Bridge,' said Mr McLevy, 'though I've heard of one louping off the Scott Monument. It's too easy. They keep asking the Council to raise the parapets. Has she any relations?'

Mr Cargill muttered, 'Mrs Napier would know about that.'

'Will you tell her, sir? There's a paragraph going into the *Courant*, but we didn't give out the name.'

Mr Cargill went downstairs and walked slowly uphill towards the High Street, still feeling shaken by what he had seen in the mortuary. He passed the building that housed the clattering presses of the *Courant*. Mr Cargill halted, as he saw a way to get even with Mrs Napier. No harm done if it didn't work; and by Jove, it was worth a try!

'The journal's no ready to go out yet,' said the first man he accosted. Mr Cargill explained that he feared a relation had met with a fatal accident. He took out his purse and held up a guinea.

'You can have this if you bring me a copy.'

The man disappeared and came back in five minutes holding up the newspaper sheet.

'Here it's. Mind yourself – the print's still wet.'

Mr Cargill handed over his coin, seized the damp piece of paper and rushed off. He went into the same tavern again and ordered another drink. He read the account of Miss Erroll's suicide, nodding to himself. From a leather case he took out a stick of graphite which he used to jot down notes on music scores. With a smile, he circled the paragraph, and wrote a message beside it. Then he walked down to Mrs Watson's house in Rose Street.

Would she oblige him? He wished her pageboy to deliver this newspaper for him. He would make it worth her while. No, he would not give his name, either to her or to the person who was to receive the journal.

Mr Cargill pulled out another guinea from his purse and handed it to Mrs Watson. Willie was told to take the *Courant* to the address the gentleman gave him: Colonel Favé, Douglas's Hotel.

'Now, Christabel,' said Elizabeth, 'you must tell me what you wish me to say to Mrs Napier.'

She was taking a late breakfast at Heriot Row, and had asked her niece to join her. Christabel, who had already eaten, was walking restlessly about the room. Eleanor had agreed to meet her there at nine o'clock, and it was already half-past ten. Elizabeth had come downstairs just in time to prevent Christabel from visiting the Stewarts' house in Claremont Street.

'I am sure that Miss Stewart has some excellent reason for not calling here,' she said. 'If all goes well, I shall suggest to Mrs Napier that you dine with me this evening, and I shall invite Miss Stewart to join us. That will be much better than a hurried conversation in her own home.'

Christabel agreed, and curbed her impatience. Elizabeth returned to their afternoon meeting with Mrs Napier. She would take Christabel to the Lady Superintendent herself, and try to ensure that the first minutes of their encounter were not too unpleasant. After that, Mrs Napier would wish to speak to Elizabeth privately. She put her question again.

'Surely what you say to Mrs Napier depends on what she says to you?' asked Christabel.

'My darling girl, we know what she will say to me. You have told a pack of monstrous fibs, and since you refuse to admit your fault, I must take you away from the Institute.'

'But I haven't, Elizabeth.'

'I did not say that you had, Christabel. I was putting Mrs Napier's point of view. What am I to say to her?'

'Tell her that she lies!'

Elizabeth put down her fork. 'How fortunate that it is Ranald, and not you, who is to go into our Foreign Office. I do not think, somehow, that diplomacy is your *forte*. Have you any suggestions, except my giving a brutish reply to your Lady Superintendent?'

Christabel shook her head.

'Then am I to accept this rebuke on your behalf, and remove you from the Institute? You do not seem very happy there, apart from your friendship with Miss Stewart. We might find some school for you in Paris until the autumn. After these unpleasant events, that might be the best course. Shall we do that? . . . Please answer me, Christabel.'

Christabel did not wish to say outright that the prospect of being removed from Eleanor's company was unbearable.

'Oh, Elizabeth, you are so clever about things like that! If anyone can outwit Mrs Napier, it is you.'

Her aunt laughed. 'Is that a compliment? Well, yes, I do have a plan. I spoke privately to Colonel Favé last night after dinner. We have come to an understanding about *l'affaire du diadème*. Mrs Napier is pressing the colonel for a favour from the Empress. Her Majesty does not like her graciousness to be taken for granted. Colonel Favé is afraid that Mrs Napier will *jostle* the Empress, and he will then be blamed. He became even more fearful when he heard about the death of Peggy Murdo.'

'You told him about that!'

'I had to explain your situation. We agreed that we might serve each other's interests. I am to let Mrs Napier know that she may have her basket of bonbons, provided she does not ask for it before the New Year. Provided also, that she will forget her last conversation with you. You will forget it too, Christabel.'

Elizabeth waited, but there was no response.

'So you do not have confidence in me after all?'

'Yes, I do, but I wish there were a simpler way.'

'There is. You might say that you will expose Miss Erroll if Mrs Napier does not withdraw her charge that you have been lying. I am sure that she will comply at once.'

'What a shocking suggestion, Elizabeth!'

'Here is another. I wrote to Mr McLevy yesterday and placed your dilemma before him. He is prepared to support your story that the diadem was stolen and that he recovered it. Of course, that would also cause difficulties.'

'How so?'

'The police establishment is as anxious as Mrs Napier for this whole business to be suppressed. If Mr McLevy goes against their orders, he will incur some odium.'

'Why do you bring up all these impediments, Elizabeth? I believe you want me to be court-martialled and drummed out of the regiment.'

'Darling, I am only trying to show you that life is never as simple as it seems to be, and the only way to make it so is to be very, very ruthless. Your implied rebuke is deserved, of course. Such a moralising role does not suit me at all.'

Christabel said, 'It's all very well, Elizabeth, smiling like that. It may work wonders with Colonel Favé and Mr McLevy, but it won't do for Mrs Napier. She is a Siberian tiger.'

'Then we must hope that my little basket of bonbons will tempt her. I shall present it very artfully.'

'Providing that nothing goes wrong,' said Christabel pessimistically.


Willie delivered Mr Cargill's newspaper to Douglas's Hotel shortly before noon. Colonel Favé's valet was called downstairs to receive it while he was packing his master's luggage.

The colonel took the news-sheet from his servant and turned it perplexedly from one side to the other. Then he laid it on a table, and found the marked paragraph. After reading this with a frown, he bent closer to make out the pencilled message. Mr Cargill had written, 'This is the senior governess of the Institute, Miss Madeleine Erroll. Her name will be made public tomorrow. Beware of scandal. A Friend.'

'Sacred name of a dog! Is there to be no end to this miserable affair?'

Colonel Favé called out to his valet, 'Bring the messenger to me!'

The valet ran out of the room and found Willie still waiting in the foyer of the hotel. Having seen Mrs Watson receive a whole guinea merely for arranging this delivery, he was hopeful that something might come his own way.

When the valet returned upstairs with the pageboy the colonel's room was strewn with the articles he had so carefully packed, and the colonel himself was on his knees, burrowing into the largest portmanteau like a dog frantically searching for its bone.

'Where is my writing case? Find it at once! I must write a letter.'

The valet walked over to a console table beside the window, and picked up the case.

'There it is, colonel. It has not yet been packed.'

'Why didn't you tell me? Have you found the messenger?'

'Yes, colonel. He is waiting in the corridor.'

Favé wrote the letter at great speed, and sealed it with a wafer as he could not find any matches for the wax. He took it to Willie himself.

'Who gave you that newspaper?'

'I dinna ken, sir.'

'*Who?*'

'He does not know, colonel,' interpreted the valet, who had become acquainted with one of the chambermaids.

Full of misgiving, Favé said loudly and slowly, 'Bring back to me a piece of paper signed by the person to whom I send this letter. Then I shall give you money. Do you understand?'

'Aye, sir. How much?'

'How much do you ask?' replied Favé, uncertain about the appropriate tip.

'Seeing you're a stranger, sir, I'll do it for a guinea.'

*A message was despatched to Mr Stewart, the Superintendent of the Edinburgh and Glasgow Central Terminus, intimating*

*that the Empress intended leaving Edinburgh by the 12.45
train for Perth. Mr Stewart immediately prepared a handsome saloon carriage for Her Majesty. At about half-past-
twelve, the luggage, which was both ponderous and bulky,
was brought down from the hotel. The crowd filled the whole
central portion of the Waverley Bridge. Sharp at the hour –
12.45 – the Empress and suite, in a carriage and pair,
followed by other carriages containing the servants, passed
along the Bridge.*

*On getting down to the Market Street gate, the crowd was
very dense. The Empress's carriage passed inside the gate and
to within some twenty yards of the saloon Her Majesty was
to occupy. The Empress seemed to be in excellent spirits,
and repeatedly smiled and bowed in acknowledgment of the
plaudits which resounded on every side.*

*We understand that Her Majesty will today prosecute a
journey to the north. We are sure our readers will join cordi-
ally in the hope that the weather will be such as to enable
this exalted visitor to the country of her forefathers to
contemplate the scenery of the land of the mountain and the
flood with much personal enjoyment and benefit.*

After her interview with Eleanor Mrs Napier went to look
for Anna Merchant. Miss Erroll had not presented herself
for any duties since the Empress's visit.

'This is becoming intolerable, Anna. I am sorry for the
poor woman, of course, but I must think of the major good.
The Institute cannot lean on a broken reed.'

Hesitantly, Miss Merchant said, 'I took it on myself to
send Mary up to Miss Erroll's room, a few moments ago.
She is not there.'

'Has she gone out? It is a holiday, but she should have
consulted me before leaving the building.'

Miss Merchant gulped. She had an uneasy conscience
about passing on Christabel's accusation to Miss Erroll.

'Mary said that her bed does not appear to have been slept
in.'

206

'Why did Mary not come to me with that news?' Mrs Napier asked with annoyance.

'Well, Mrs Napier, we have not yet replaced Peggy, so Mary's work has doubled, and she did not have the time. And I expect she thought that the information should be conveyed by myself. Mary is always most scrupulous about keeping to her place.'

'Yes,' said Mrs Napier. 'We must find a replacement for Peggy.'

She then returned to her sitting room to open and read her unusually large correspondence. Most of this was from the Directors and Patrons, the parents of her pupils, and other people closely connected with the school.

Letter after letter glowed with congratulation on the success of Eugénie's visit. There could be no doubt that Mrs Napier had indeed brought the Institute a diadem for its Jubilee. Morever, news of the honour that was to be bestowed on the school had already reached far beyond the small group to whom she had spoken on the Institute steps. The Directors and Patrons had informed their friends, including many of the parents. Mrs Napier herself had told the governesses after supper.

Mrs Napier smiled happily when she saw that her 'golden secret' had become an open one. There was a letter from Amelia's mother, hoping that Mrs Napier would not take it amiss if she told her friends in confidence. Dr Graham had enclosed a blank sheet on which he had fancifully inscribed the new crest and title of the Institute. It differed from Mrs Napier's own vision in one way only. Under the words 'Patroness: Her Imperial Majesty, Eugénie, Empress of the French' Dr Graham had written, 'Lady Superintendent: Mrs Margaret Napier'. And lightly pencilled beside it, (*For as long as she wishes!*).

Mrs Napier felt that her cup ran over with joy and honour. For the briefest instant she admitted some memories of her life as it had been before Providence had sent her to rule the Institute.

Like so many Scots, she had risen to eminence from small

beginnings. Heaven had marked her out for favour. If she had not exchanged the Calvinism of her youth for the gentler bosom of the Episcopalian Church, she would have claimed that she was one of the Elect.

Mrs Napier relaxed pleasantly as she re-read the letters and answered those from the most important parents and Patrons. Not for years had she felt so much at ease, her spirits buoyant with an almost youthful happiness. Although November lowered outside, her sitting room seemed full of sparkling summer light. She left her writing-desk and spent the rest of the morning in an arm chair before the fire, meditating on her victory with a satisfied smile.

At about half-past twelve, Mary knocked at her door and handed in two letters. She said apologetically, 'They didna arrive thegither, ma'am, but I was that trauchled in the kitchen I didna bring up Mr Cargill's when he gied it in.'

After leaving the *Courant* at Mrs Watson's, Mr Cargill had gone into yet another tavern, and written a personal message for Mrs Napier, which he had delivered to the school himself.

The Lady Superintendent said with a kindly look, 'That is of no account, Mary. I know how busy you have been. You shall have someone to help you very soon.'

'Thank you, ma'am,' said Mary gratefully. 'Yon other one's just come by a wee pageboy, and he's wanting you to sign for it. It's frae Douglas's Hotel.'

Mrs Napier took a sheet of the school notepaper, smiling as she thought how soon that plain heading would be transmuted by the lustre of Eugénie's patronage. She wrote her name, and a suitable phrase to acknowledge receipt of the letter.

From Douglas's Hotel! That was swift indeed. However, she would look at the singing teacher's message first. It would be almost sacrilegious, after reading the Empress's letter, to pollute her eyes with a reminder of Mr Cargill's debauchery. Mrs Napier opened what she assumed would be a copy of his letter of resignation.

Mr Cargill had been as blunt as possible. He advised Mrs

Napier to scan that day's *Courant*. In it she would find an account of Miss Erroll's suicidal leap off the Dean Bridge, a few hundred yards from the Institute.

'Dear Heaven!' Mrs Napier whispered to herself. For several minutes she remained completely motionless. Her shoulders drooped a little. Then she sat upright again. It was a grievous piece of news. The gossip about it might even reflect on the Institute. But it would eventually die away. She must be thankful that it had come too late to annul the honour she had wrested from the Empress of the French.

Mrs Napier picked up the letter from Douglas's Hotel. The envelope was not of the quality associated with imperial handwriting. It might be, however, that Colonel Favé had only written the address. The Empress herself would surely have penned the message confirming her favour.

Mrs Napier lifted her paper-knife and then put it down, wishing to savour the moment of triumph. But her eagerness would brook no delay. Agitation was an emotion unknown to Mrs Napier, yet something like it was quickening the beat of her heart as she slit the envelope.

The letter inside was written in the same hand. It was short and curt, and in the third person.

Colonel Favé demanded that Madame Napier withdraw the request she had made on Wednesday afternoon. Recent events at the Institute made its promotion impossible. Two violent deaths, on top of the unsolved theft of the diadem! Should madame be so imprudent as to persist, he would lay all the circumstances before Her Majesty.

Dr Graham was a very busy man. Besides teaching at many schools in the city, he was a past President of the Educational Institute of Scotland and still much involved in its business, a popular lecturer and elocutionist, author of several works published by Messrs Chambers, and frequent contributor of poems and essays to various magazines.

Dr Graham had no engagement at other schools on this day, so he had decided to use the rare luxury of the Thursday holiday to polish a set of verses on the music of his native land. The housemaid had tyrannically refused to break her dusting routine, so he had been banished from his study to the chillier environment of the drawing room, where the fire was not lit until early afternoon. He might have joined his wife and children, but Dr Graham knew from experience that his Muse sulked when she had to share his attention with family gossip.

Dr Graham had nearly completed three stanzas before the maid brought up Mr Cargill's letter of resignation. He read the note with great consternation, and decided that he ought to discuss it with Mrs Napier. A woman's gentle touch might persuade Mr Cargill to change his mind.

Dr Graham worked on at his poem and was amazed to discover that the morning had already gone when his wife summoned him (for the third time, she said) to luncheon.

After the meal, he had to read his stanzas to her and hear her comments. So it was well past two o'clock when he finally set out for the Institute.

Naturally he did not ring the bell, but entered the building as his own domain. He knocked twice at Mrs Napier's door, and when he received no reply turned the handle and looked into the room. They were on familiar enough terms for him to be able to do this. Assuming that Mrs Napier would soon return, Dr Graham went to the fire, and stood warming himself for a few moments. Then he looked at the pictures on the walls, some of which were water-colours of Indian scenes, possibly painted by Mrs Napier herself.

Dr Graham already knew them well, but studied them again, scrupulously averting his eyes from a letter which lay face upwards on the davenport. One picture showed the school for Eurasian girls which Mrs Napier had organised in Calcutta after her husband's death. It was because of her success with this, as well as her distinguished connections, that the Directors had offered her her present position soon after she returned from India. Her husband had been related to Sir Charles Napier, the conqueror of Sind. She had once said that she herself came from the west of Scotland.

Dr Graham became a little impatient. He looked at his

watch. He had a lecture to prepare for the Philosophical Institution. Surely Mrs Napier had not left the building? Perhaps he should find out from the servants.

At that moment, Elizabeth and Christabel entered. When Dr Graham had introduced himself to her, Elizabeth said, 'No one came to the door when we rang, so my niece brought me up here. I was to meet Mrs Napier at half-past two.'

Dr Graham remarked that Mrs Napier's absence was strange; he too had hoped to speak to her. Should he pull the bell-rope and ask Mary for an explanation?

His ring was not answered for several minutes. Mary eventually appeared, but wearing her outdoor clothes, and out of breath.

'Aye?' she questioned them abruptly, quite unlike her usual manner.

'Where is your mistress?' asked Dr Graham.

Mary pulled off her bonnet and mantle and hurried through to the bedroom without answering.

'Mary!' cried Dr Graham after her. 'Come back and give us an explanation at once!' The maid reappeared at the door of the passage leading to the bedroom.

'I'm to pack her claes,' she said irritably. 'I've just seen her off on the Glasgow train. She's no coming back.'

Miss Merchant uttered a stifled scream; Elizabeth gave Christabel a glance that repressed whatever she had been going to say.

Dr Graham was speechless; but at last he managed to say, 'Don't talk such nonsense, Mary! Try to recollect. What message did Mrs Napier leave for us?'

'She didna leave any,' replied Mary in a sulky voice. 'I've telt you. She's away, and no so much as back of my hand. You'll no see her again. It was yon letter she got frae the Frenchman. That's the maist she let on to me.'

She walked over to the davenport and picked up Colonel Favé's letter. 'Here,' she said, almost tossing it at Dr Graham, 'take a read of this if you want to ken why.' Then she returned to the bedroom.

Dr Graham and Miss Merchant went down to his classroom. They stayed there for another two hours, talking about the day's events. Reading the colonel's letter, Miss Merchant recalled what Christabel had said to herself and Mrs Napier about the diadem. She suspected that there must be a great deal more behind this than the Lady Superintendent had revealed. She decided to tell Dr Graham only what she knew about Peggy, and claimed to be baffled by the colonel's reference to the theft of the diadem.

'How fortunate that Lady Elizabeth and Miss MacKenzie went away so quickly!' said Dr Graham. 'Miss MacKenzie will have made little of Mary's remarks. We may rely on Lady Elizabeth's discretion not to enlighten her.'

Elizabeth had taken her niece away immediately after Mary had made that startling announcement.

Miss Merchant said in a worried voice, 'I fear that Miss MacKenzie already knows about Peggy's death. Mrs Napier told me so yesterday.'

'But she said nothing about the diadem?'

Miss Merchant was relieved that she could answer this question with a truthful 'No'.

Their discussion was interrupted by the arrival of Mr McLevy. He said he had some distressing information which he felt Mrs Napier should hear before anyone else; and it was some time before either teacher would admit to him that the Lady Superintendent had disappeared. It was Miss Merchant who finally told him. Mr McLevy made no comment, but gave them the news of Miss Erroll's suicide.

Miss Merchant said, 'It was her headaches, of course. My dear mama also was tempted to the brink of self-destruction.' After a seemly interval she asked the detective if he knew anything about the Empress's diadem. Had there really been a theft?

Yes, the diadem had been stolen, said McLevy, and there appeared to be a connection with Peggy's death. The details were not yet clear. Yes, Miss MacKenzie had been most helpful in leading him to the man who had attacked Peggy, but they must excuse him from saying any more at present.

After McLevy left, Dr Graham gave a deep sigh. He

remarked that everything he had told them dwindled when put beside the precipitate departure of Mrs Napier.

'I shall place a paragraph in the news journals,' said Dr Graham. 'Something to the effect that Mrs Napier's – ah – sudden collapse has obliged her to withdraw from her duties at the Institute. We must hope that what she said to us last night about the Empress will be put down to – ah – the stress of mental anguish.'

Miss Merchant nodded gravely. 'What are we to do about Miss MacKenzie? It would be most ill-advised to let her return to the Institute next term.'

'That problem may not arise. When I was escorting Lady Elizabeth to the door, she too seemed to feel that it would be best if her niece completed her education in Paris. She is taking her away with her, and will decide later whether she should return.' Dr Graham paused. 'One point must be settled at once. Whom are the Directors to appoint in Mrs Napier's place, to take charge of the Institute, even as a temporary expedient? She must be someone of discretion.'

Miss Merchant dropped her eyes, hardly daring to breathe.

'Who but yourself, Miss Merchant?' said Dr Graham. When she looked up, he was smiling at her. Daringly, Miss Merchant laid her hand on the Director's large, furry paw.

'I shall bear the burden worthily, dear Dr Graham!'

When he had gone, Miss Merchant decided she would like to inspect her new quarters, although she would not move into them until tomorrow. She went up to the Lady Superintendent's sitting room and approached the large writing-desk.

Normally, Miss Merchant told herself, she would have been incapable of prying into others' private papers. Mrs Napier's hasty flight now made this inevitable. Miss Merchant searched for the keys, and then unlocked the top section of the desk. There she came across the thick black ledger. After discovering what it contained, she read her own entry with profound attention. She then set the book aside, deciding that she would take it to her room and consume the contents at leisure that evening.

213

A voice spoke behind her. 'Why's it you and no Miss Erroll in charge?' Miss Merchant started.

Mary's tone was not exactly impudent, but Miss Merchant thought she detected an assumption of equality which displeased her. It was embarrassing to be found turning over Mrs Napier's belongings, even though she did it out of necessity.

'You will hear about that tomorrow,' she replied. The catalogue of disasters was turning into a Spanish tragedy, and she could not bring herself to tell a servant about Miss Erroll's death before she had informed the governesses.

'Do you know, Mary, I have no idea where any of Mrs Napier's relations live. I am looking for an address to write to.' It was the best excuse she could find.

Mary burst out laughing. 'You'd be wasting your time.'

'How dare you!' Miss Merchant was all the more outraged because she had never heard Mary speak out of turn before. 'You impudent girl! I cannot allow you to remain with us. You will leave our service at once.'

'What, and no warning?' asked Mary, with a look of amazement.

Miss Merchant hastily modified her attitude, fearing the consequences of resentful gossip.

'I shall give you ten pounds instead, and that is a great deal more than you are entitled to.'

'Away with you, Miss Merchant,' replied Mary good-humouredly. 'I'm no going. I'll look after *you* now, like I looked after her, all they years. Dinna fash yourself, I'll no blab. Did I let on about yon letter? I kent a sight sooner than the rest of you. And other things, forbye.'

Miss Merchant was too horrified to speak for several moments.

'What are you talking about?' she demanded, unconvincingly, when she found her tongue. An appalling possibility struck her. Had this girl been blackmailing the Lady Superintendent? 'You had better explain yourself, if you have anything to say,' she went on, tightening her lips in warning.

'But you'll no let on if I tell you?' Behind the hesitation in

Mary's tone there was a clear hint of relish about what she was going to say. Miss Merchant waited apprehensively.

'It was like this, ma'am. My mother and my auntie ran a wee drapery shop in the Gorbals, and one of they traveller chaps cried in with swatches of cotton frae India. He and my mother got blethering away, and he said, her being a widow, why did she no join the fishing fleet?'

'This is very tedious,' said Miss Merchant, relieved that nothing worse was to be disclosed.

'Aye, ma'am, I'm sorry to take your time, but I'll not be long. Yon's the boats that went out ilka year with the lassies for India. They're fair desperate to marry out there, he telt us, and maybe she'd catch herself a captain, and when the fever got him she'd come hame with a braw pension. My mother was sweir to gang, her having the shop, so my auntie said she'd sail out in her place, and she'd do better than a captain. She was nearer ages with me than my mother. She was good at the high English, even then. Yon's all twenty years syne, ma'am.'

'So you have a connection with Mrs Napier through your aunt?' said Miss Merchant, reassured by the return of Mary's deferential manner. 'Well, I commend your loyalty. Old servants must certainly be considered part of the family. But since Mrs Napier will not be coming back to us, Mary, you really would do better to rejoin your mother.'

She must persuade the girl to leave. Even if she did hold her tongue, her presence at the Institute would be a permanent embarrassment.

'My mother's deid lang syne,' said Mary sorrowfully. 'That's how I went to find Mrs Napier when I had word she was back frae India. She didna want me round at first, but I stuck like a burr.' She said, with a return of brisk cheerfulness, 'I'm no losing my place just for kinship.'

Like a quivering wave, the truth hung poised; and then crashed over Miss Merchant's head.

'You mean – you *cannot* mean – '

'Aye, ma'am. Mrs Napier is my auntie.'

Elizabeth held the teapot over Christabel's cup. As she poured, she remarked, 'I think there has been enough talk about that sad topic. Shall we agree not to refer to it again?'

This was accompanied by what Christabel called an 'Elizabeth look'. Christabel had received many of these in their first months together, when her aunt had been trying to impart, more subtly than by direct prescription, some nuance of social behaviour.

It was four o'clock. They were taking tea in the morning room. Neither of them had touched the plate of teabreads which Mrs Veitch had baked that morning. Elizabeth was vain of her fine figure, and Christabel's appetite had been shocked away when she returned alone to the Institute to say goodbye to her friends, and had heard about Miss Erroll's suicide. It had been impossible to keep the news secret.

The doorbell rang. Christabel sprang to her feet.

'That will be Eleanor!'

'No, I think it is Mr McLevy. He wishes to speak to you. After I have greeted him, will you see him alone, Christabel?'

Mr McLevy took a cup of tea, and politely ate a scone.

'One of my most interesting cases,' he commented, after telling Christabel about the day's proceedings at the police court. Carefully looking aside, he added, 'I'd burn a pound of tobacco to know how the diadem got into Peggy Murdo's bag.'

Christabel told him.

'Yon poor woman,' said McLevy. 'She must have been sore trauchled to do a thing like that.' As he rose to leave, his tone changed. 'Maybe we'll work together on another case some day, eh, Miss Christabel?'

'I'm afraid that's not likely, Mr McLevy. I am going to Paris on Monday.'

The detective held out his hand. 'It's goodbye, then.'

'There's a favour I'd like to ask you. Eleanor and I are going to Peggy's funeral service tomorrow. It is in the Murdos' house. I don't know whether Mr Murdo will go to the churchyard. It would be dreadful if no one except the church officer was at the graveside.'

In Scotland, at this time, only male mourners accompanied the coffin to its grave.

'Yes,' said Mr McLevy, 'I'll see the lass home.'

After dinner Elizabeth excused herself to Eleanor and Christabel. She had to spend some time with Marie, she said, to discuss arrangements for the journey back to Paris.

When they were alone, Eleanor explained that she had kept away from Heriot Row in case Christabel might fly into a rage when she heard of her dismissal, and jeopardise herself even further with Mrs Napier.

'Well, you are reprieved now,' said Christabel. 'She will not have had time to tell Miss Merchant.'

'I'm not sure that I want to be reprieved,' said Eleanor. 'I don't know whether you are coming back to the Institute next term.'

'No, I shall not. You must leave too, and study in Paris. That's what I suggested a long time ago.'

'Darling, you know I cannot do that, and you know why. I meant that if you *are* coming back, I can't bear to continue in this fashion. We must see more of each other, or less. I've decided to go to America in the New Year. I shall go down to Liverpool and work my passage over on one of the Atlantic steamers as a stewardess. It means looking after sea-sick women in their cabins . . . Chrissie, please, please, don't look at me like that!'

'Shall we not try to live our lives together?'

Christabel's question was so forlorn, and her voice so lacking its usual vigour that Eleanor was almost defeated. But she knew that her decision was right.

'Darling, we cannot find that out by seeing each other a few minutes each day at the Institute. There has to be another way.'

'We shan't see each other at all! Is studying with Dr Blackwell more important than that?'

'We'll discover what is important when I'm in America.'

'But it is you who are going away, Eleanor!'

'I am the first of us to go away. You will find something

217

that you want to do as well. Surely you will not go on living in idleness in Paris? I don't think I should continue loving you if you did that, Chrissie.'

Elizabeth returned to the room and said with a smile, 'What is Miss Stewart's answer?'

'I haven't asked her yet,' said Christabel, almost in tears.

'And I thought you were merely waiting for me to leave the room, Christabel! Miss Stewart, I am hoping that you will agree to spend some time with Christabel and myself in Paris at the end of your winter term. You would be welcome to stay with us for as long as your duties permit.'

'Eleanor, please say yes,' begged Christabel. 'Only one or two weeks, before you sail from Liverpool!' She was certain that once she had Eleanor with her in Paris, her friend would never leave. 'Even if you refuse me, you cannot refuse Elizabeth!'

Unfairly as that was put, Eleanor found that she could not refuse Elizabeth.

What happened at the trial, how Mr Cargill thereafter made his living, whether Mrs Napier was ever heard of again, and whether Eleanor was persuaded to study in Paris: all these are matters which lie outside the six days covered by the scandal of the false Grecian diadem. Only one question remains.

Let us return to Eugénie's departure from Edinburgh.

*After she had taken her seat in the railway carriage, she several times looked out, smiled and bowed, and something having apparently occurred to amuse the Imperial fancy, Her Majesty leaned forward once or twice seemingly convulsed with laughter, and the train at length moved off amid the hearty bursts of cheering from all who witnessed this departure.*

Why did the Empress laugh?

Madame de Saulcy said, 'Colonel Favé looks pleased to be

leaving Edinburgh. He has found little in this city to excite him.'

The Marquis de la Grange remarked with a smile, 'I would not say that, madame. Colonel, what did I hear you say yesterday to Madame Pollet about theft and violent death? Might that have been at the Scottish Institute?'

Favé glared at the marquis.

'I was repeating some nonsense I overheard in that school.'

A flash of surprise passed over de la Grange's face. 'My little jest seems to have found a target,' he murmured.

The Empress turned from the window, and as she sat down asked, 'My dear Frédéric, whatever do you mean?'

Favé said bluffly, 'Oh, young girls are so romantic! Your Majesty's visit turned their heads.'

'No doubt they were dazzled by the Grecian diadem,' said the marquis, who knew nothing, and was only trying to tweak the colonel's tail. Favé stiffened.

The Comtesse de Montebello sensed that something was wrong. She intervened quickly. 'Your Majesty, I adore little schoolgirls. How they love to frighten themselves and imagine terrible adventures! Did Her Majesty ever do so with the Duchess of Alba?'

She smiled at the Empress, and although Eugénie did not answer the question, she smiled back, for already happier memories of her sister had begun to replace that dark, corrosive torment.

Encouraged by her mistress's response, the countess said slyly, 'Does Her Majesty permit me to mention the time she tried to run away from her school in Bristol? To sail to India, as I recall.'

The Empress laughed and laughed.

# Historical Note

The extracts relating to Eugénie's movements in Edinburgh are taken from the *Scotsman*; the description of the Hamilton Palace ball is from the *Courant*, which also mentions the confusion between Edinburgh Castle and Leith Fort. These two papers have supplied many background details for Edinburgh life in 1860. I have pruned their reports, since Victorian journalism, like the Empress's luggage, was both ponderous and bulky. Otherwise I have quoted without alterations. Passages relating to the Institute are paste, and not the real thing.

James McLevy was a policeman who retired in 1860 and published two collections of his cases a year later. In 1975 a selection of these was brought out by Canongate, Edinburgh.

Apart from Dr Graham and Mr Dubuc, the Institute teachers are entirely fictional, and not intended to bear any resemblance to anyone living or dead. The Institute itself is based on The Scottish Institution for Young Ladies, in Moray Place, which existed from 1834 –1870. I am grateful to Mrs Ann Hope for drawing my attention to this school but I am entirely responsible for the way I have enlarged the meagre known facts. At a time when most girls' schools were at the stage of Miss Pinkerton's academy in *Vanity Fair*, the Institution was remarkable for the breadth of its curriculum, pre-dating Miss Buss and Miss Beale by about twenty years. It certainly has a claim to the honour of being the first school in Britain to offer girls a serious secondary education.

The topography of Edinburgh New Town is accurate, although I have used the 1860 version of street names.

The Cock and Trumpet, described in McLevy's memoirs, now houses the Scottish Craft Centre.